**'You say you know how to use your dagger? Then defend yourself, my lady,' William said, his voice deathly quiet.**

He took a step away from Eleanor and turned his back on her. She opened her mouth to ask what he meant, but with a speed that took her by surprise William twisted the sword about his wrist and spun round.

Before Eleanor could react William had the sword held full at arm's length, pointing at her breast. The tip was barely a hand's breadth from touching her dress. The words died on Eleanor's lips and the only sound that came out of her mouth was a soft whimper. Her head jerked up in shock and she discovered William watching her intently, his face fiercer and more determined than she had ever seen him look.

## Author Note

A widow in the Middle Ages was in a better position than most women. While there *was* pressure—either to remarry or enter a convent—a widow had a degree of independence unavailable to wives and daughters and was able to run her own affairs, often carrying on with the businesses left by her husband and acting as guardian of his estate until any children came of age.

The only real person mentioned in this story is John Fortin, a merchant who traded with Bordeaux in the late 1290s. He might have been generous enough to allow others to invest in his ventures, but whether he did or not the wine trade out of Bristol flourished from this period onwards and was a great opportunity for those with the finances available to make their fortunes.

A few inspirations helped me get into Will and Eleanor's minds. This quote by Giacomo Casanova was one: 'A girl who is pretty and good, and as virtuous as you please, ought not to take it ill that a man, carried away by her charms, should set himself to the task of making their conquest.'

'Thunder Road' by Bruce Springsteen was also playing in the background when I wrote, and on the journey to and from work while I did a lot of my thinking.

For readers wishing to search online for locations, or visit them, Eleanor's house is heavily modelled on St Michael's Mount, but also owes some influence to Lindisfarne Castle on Holy Island. Sir Edgar's fortified house is based on Ightham Mote in Kent and Stokesay Castle in Shropshire.

# A WAGER
# FOR THE WIDOW

Elisabeth Hobbes

First published in Great Britain 2015
by Mills & Boon, an imprint of Harlequin (UK) Limited,
Large Print edition 2015
Harlequin (UK) Limited, Eton House, 18-24 Paradise Road,
Richmond, Surrey TW9 1SR

© 2015 Claire Lackford

ISBN: 978-0-263-25576-8

Harlequin (UK) Limited's policy is to use papers that are natural,
renewable and recyclable products and made from wood grown in
sustainable forests. The logging and manufacturing processes conform
to the legal environmental regulations of the country of origin.

Printed and bound in Great Britain
by CPI Antony Rowe, Chippenham, Wiltshire

**Elisabeth Hobbes** grew up in York, where she spent most of her teenage years wandering around the city looking for a handsome Roman or Viking to sweep her off her feet. Elisabeth's hobbies include skiing, Arabic dance and fencing—none of which has made it into a story yet. When she isn't writing she spends her time reading, and is a pro at cooking while holding a book! Elisabeth lives in Cheshire with her husband, two children, and three cats with ridiculous names.

### Books by Elisabeth Hobbes

### Mills & Boon Historical Romance

*Falling for Her Captor*
*A Wager for the Widow*

Visit the Author Profile page
at millsandboon.co.uk.

To my mum,
who inspired a love of reading and history
and who took me round castles as a child.

# *Chapter One*

Eleanor Peyton was never certain what was worse: the dreams where her husband died, or the ones where he was still alive. The former were always the same: Eleanor would stand and watch as though she was carved from granite, unable to move while Sir Baldwin clawed helplessly at his throat, sliding to the floor of the feasting hall. The screams of their wedding guests would ring in Eleanor's ears and she would wake sobbing and shaking.

Tonight's dream was the latter type. Eleanor could almost feel Baldwin's breath on her face as he drew her close for a kiss, his brown eyes filled with a warmth and hunger that he had never exhibited while he had lived.

Though three years had passed since his death, Eleanor woke with her heart racing, aching for something she could not name. They had never shared this bed, yet she felt his presence surrounding her like a shroud.

Wiping a sleeve across her damp eyes, Eleanor untangled the sheets from around her legs and drew back the bed curtains. Soft grey light was beginning to find its way through the gaps in the heavy curtains covering the windows. Slipping a fur-trimmed surcoat over her linen shift, Eleanor hurried across the chilly stone floor to the window seat. A biting squall was blowing in from the sea, tossing fishing boats around the jetty at the shoreline. Eleanor settled herself on to the thick cushions, curling her bare feet beneath her, and waited for the sun to rise.

She was perfectly placed, therefore, to spot the rider on horseback as he galloped down the road from the nearby village, coming to an abrupt halt at the water's edge. He dismounted and paced back and forth, searching for something. At this time of year the arrival of a message from her father was neither unexpected nor welcome and Eleanor frowned to herself. Soon the tide would go out, revealing the causeway and the messenger would find his way across the narrow path that separated the islet from the mainland. The man lowered his hood, revealing a shock of hair the exact copper shade of Eleanor's own. At the sight her heart leapt and she broke into a smile.

The door opened and Eleanor's maid entered carrying a basket of wood.

'Jennet, come look.' Eleanor beckoned. She indicated to the figure huddling in the rain as the sea slowly receded. 'Go tell Goodwife Bradshawe we have a visitor for breakfast, then help me dress. I need to look my best. I can't have my brother reporting back that I'm fading away in my isolation!'

An hour later Eleanor stood in the doorway, watching with amusement as her brother made his slow ascent up the steep hill. He paused at the gate to hand his horse to a waiting stable boy before climbing the winding pathway of old, granite steps, the sleet making his progress slow. Eleanor grinned to herself at the sight of the heir to the barony of Tawstott red-faced and breathing heavily with exertion.

'Good morning, Edmund. You must have risen early to beat the tide!'

Her brother scowled and pushed his dripping curls from his eyes. 'Why couldn't Baldwin have built a house somewhere flat?' he grumbled good-naturedly.

It was a familiar joke and Eleanor laughed. 'It's

because you're a year older now. You didn't complain when you were twenty-five.' She reached up to bat him on the arm. Edmund caught her hand and drew her in a hug before holding her at arm's length and examining her carefully.

'You're thinner than last year,' he announced, 'Mother won't be pleased.'

Eleanor rolled her eyes. 'I assume I will have a few days' grace to make myself look presentable? I don't have to return today?'

Edmund shook his head. 'No. Now please can I come in? I need some wine to take the chill from my bones!'

Arm in arm, Eleanor led her brother to her favourite room, a cosy chamber overlooking the causeway. Food was waiting on the table before the fireplace and a maid poured goblets of warm wine and ladled steaming oysters into bowls.

Edmund pulled a fold of parchment from his bag and handed it to Eleanor. She examined the wax seal, recognising the crest of Tawstott and the personal arms of Sir Edgar. She dropped the letter unopened on the table and returned her attention to her bowl, scooping up the last of the creamy sauce with a hunk of bread.

'Aren't you going to read it?' Edmund asked.

'Is there any need?' Eleanor stared into her

brother's green eyes, so similar to her own. 'It will say the same thing it has done for the past three years. Our father reminds me that he tolerates my stubbornness in choosing to live in my husband's house, but a spit of land cut off by winter storms is no place for a lone maiden. He commands my attendance in Tawstott over midwinter. Am I right?'

Edmund nodded. 'I believe the term he uses is "wilfulness", but otherwise, yes. He is sending a carriage three days from now to give you time to arrange your affairs.'

Eleanor scowled. 'He's so sure I will obey him. I hate it! Remind Father that I have my own carriage. I'll travel in that.'

Edmund patted her hand, but she whipped it away, ignoring his injured look.

'Eleanor, don't be like this.' Her brother frowned. 'We all worry about you, living here alone.'

'I'm not alone,' Eleanor said lightly. 'I have Jennet and Goodwife Bradshawe to keep me company. I spend my days reading and weaving, or walking on the shore.'

'You used to spend your days dancing and riding! You're only twenty, Eleanor. You should marry again.'

Eleanor pushed her chair back abruptly and

walked to the window, her heart beating rapidly. At Edmund's words the walls seemed to darken and close in.

'I was lucky that father chose me a husband I would have been happy with. I don't intend to risk my luck or my heart again.'

'When have you ever risked your heart, Eleanor?' Edmund snorted. 'You didn't love Baldwin.'

'I might have grown to in time!' Eleanor retorted. 'I was fond of him.' Her eyes fell on the portrait of her late husband. 'Baldwin was a kind and gentle man. Life with him would have been safe and peaceful.'

Her brother looked at her disbelievingly. 'Safe and peaceful? You don't have the faintest idea what love is.'

Eleanor glared at him, hands on her hips, her hands itching to slap him. 'And you do? Tumbling into bed with tavern wenches isn't love, Edmund,' she scolded.

For a moment they could have been children arguing again. Edmund laughed. 'Fair point, though there's a lot to be said for a quick tumble to lift the spirits. You need someone to kiss you properly, Sister. You might find you enjoy it.'

Eleanor blushed, the memory of her dream rising in her mind. She took a deep breath and turned to face her brother. 'We have a day together, let's not quarrel. There are bows in the armoury. Do you think you've improved enough to beat me yet?'

Edmund's archery had improved, but Eleanor had the satisfaction of taking six out of the ten targets and the day passed quickly. Her heart sank when the causeway bells rang out, signalling the dusk tide. They stood together, watching as the water rose higher. In ten minutes more the tide would begin to cover the causeway. Edmund took his sister's hand and kissed it formally. 'Baldwin wouldn't have wanted you to bury yourself away like this, you know.'

Eleanor's heart twisted. 'He wouldn't have wanted any of this! He wanted to grow old, to have children, to live…' Her voice cracked as the unfairness of it struck her. She took a deep breath and fixed a smile on her face.

'I do love it here,' she told him. 'I have so much to do, managing the estate the way Baldwin would have wanted it run. I don't get bored, or lonely.'

Edmund raised an eyebrow. He didn't deny her words, nor did he confirm them.

'One day you'll have to marry again,' Edmund said, 'or find a very good reason why you won't.'

With a nod he mounted his horse and walked it across the granite path. Eleanor watched as the mist swallowed him up before pulling her hood up and striding back to the house, her mind fixing on the tasks that would occupy her for the next few days.

Three days passed in such a whirl of organisation that Eleanor barely had time for sadness. It was only on her final morning as she wandered through the rooms, running her hand over furniture and tapestries, that her eyes began to sting. When she came to the portrait of Sir Baldwin, she stopped and regarded the serious man with the thinning hair and anxious face. She briefly raised a hand and touched the canvas in a gesture of farewell. She looked around her home one final time and began the descent to the waiting carriage.

They travelled fast inland, but it was late afternoon before Eleanor's carriage reached the crossing of the River Taw. The wide river was unusually high for the time of year and moving faster than Eleanor had seen it before. Hers was the only carriage waiting to cross so the driver manoeuvred it into the front of the ferry. The craft, no more than a large, flat platform with low wooden railings at either side, dipped from side to side alarmingly.

Eleanor's stomach heaved as the cramped carriage rocked on the chains suspending it within the wooden frame, adding to her sense of nausea. She peered through the curtain.

'I'm going to get out,' she told Jennet. 'I think I'll feel more nauseous if I stay inside.' Eleanor fastened her cloak around her shoulders and drew up the hood, squeezing her way past the maid's knees. A blast of wind hit her as she climbed down, whipping her cloak up around her. She clutched the edges tightly together with one hand while she gripped the low railing of the ferry to steady herself.

The ferryman braced his back and rammed his pole into the riverbank. The craft creaked alarmingly as it started to move away from the shore, the great chain that spanned the river pulling taut.

The shrill blast of a hunting horn sounded, ripping apart the peace. A commanding voice shouted, 'Ferryman, stop!'

Eleanor peered back at the riverbank. A rider on an imposing chestnut-coloured horse was galloping along the road at the edge of the water. He pulled the horse up short.

'You're too late, my friend, the current has us now,' the ferryman called back.

'Wait, I tell you. I must cross today. I have business to attend to.' The rider's voice was deep and urgent, his face hidden beneath the hood of a voluminous burgundy cloak. The ferryman shrugged his shoulders and dug his pole into the river, pushing further away. Keeping one eye on the drama playing out, Eleanor walked carefully around behind the carriage and made her way to the other side of the deck to get a better view.

What happened next had the texture of a dream. The horseman cursed and wheeled his mount around. He galloped away from the water's edge, then turned back. With a sudden bellow he cracked the reins sharply and sped back towards the river. As the horse reached the edge, the rider spurred it forward. The horse leapt through the air with ease to land on the deck alongside Eleanor. The ferry bucked, the far end almost rising from the water. Hooves clattered on the slippery wood and the animal gave a high-pitched whinny of alarm.

It was not going to stop!

As a cumbersome-looking saddlebag swung towards her, Eleanor threw herself out of its way. The railing caught her behind the knees and she stumbled backwards, her ankle turning beneath her with a sickening crunch. Crying out, she flailed her arms helplessly, unable to regain her balance as the river came up to meet her.

She saw the horseman lunge towards her, felt his fingers close about her wrist. She gave a sharp cry as her shoulder jolted painfully and her feet slid on the deck. Cold spray splashed over her face as her head fell back, her free fingers brushing the surface of the water.

'Take hold of me quickly. I can't stay like this for ever,' the rider ordered, tightening his grip on her wrist.

Eleanor raised her head to find herself staring up into a pair of blue eyes half-hidden in the depths of the voluminous hood. The rider was leaning along the length of his horse's neck, body twisted towards Eleanor at what seemed an impossible angle. She fumbled her free hand to clutch on to his arm and he hauled her back to her feet. As she stood upright a spear of pain shot through Eleanor's ankle. She gave an involuntary gasp and her knees buckled.

With the same speed as his initial rescue, the rider threw his leg across the saddle and dismounted with a thud. His arms found their way round Eleanor's waist, catching her tight and clasping her to him before she slipped to the ground.

'I've got you. Don't wriggle!'

The man's hood fell back and Eleanor saw him clearly for the first time. He was younger than his voice had suggested. A long scar ran from the outside corner of his eye and across his cheek, disappearing beneath a shaggy growth of beard at his jaw. A second ran parallel from below his eye to his top lip. His corn-coloured hair fell in loose tangles to his shoulder. Close up his eyes were startlingly blue.

Footsteps thundered on the deck as Eleanor's coachman appeared. It struck Eleanor suddenly that the man was still holding her close, much closer than was necessary, in fact. She became conscious of the rise and fall of his chest, moving rhythmically against her own. Her heart was thumping so heavily she was sure he would be able to feel it through her clothing. As to why it was beating so rapidly she refused to think about.

'You can let go of me now,' she muttered.

The horseman's eyes crinkled. 'I could,' he said, 'though I just saved your life. There must be some benefits to rescuing a beautiful maiden in distress and holding her until she stops shaking is one of them. I suppose a kiss of gratitude is out of the question?'

'You didn't save my life. I *can* swim,' Eleanor cried indignantly. It was true she was trembling, but now it was from anger. 'I am most certainly not kissing you!'

The man's forehead crinkled in disbelief. 'Even though I saved you from a cold bath?'

Eleanor's cheeks flamed. 'It was your fault in the first instance, you reckless fool. You could have capsized us all. Your horse might have missed completely.'

The horseman laughed. 'Nonsense, it was perfectly safe. Tobias could have cleared twice that distance. If you had stood still none of this would have happened. You panicked.'

With an irritated snort Eleanor pushed herself from the man's grip, contriving to elbow him sharply in the stomach as she did so. She heard a satisfying grunt as she turned her back. She headed to the carriage, but her ankle gave a sharp stab of pain. She stopped, balling her fists in irritation. The horseman leaned round beside her. 'Allow me,' he said and before Eleanor could object he had lifted her into his arms and strode the three paces to the carriage. With one hand on the door handle he cocked his head. 'Still no kiss? Ah, well, it's a cruel day!'

'There are no circumstances under which I

would kiss you!' Eleanor said haughtily, sweeping her gaze up and down him.

His face darkened and Eleanor took the opportunity to wriggle from his arms. Biting her lip to distract herself from the throbbing in her ankle, she swung the door open herself and climbed inside, slamming it loudly behind her.

Surreptitiously she peered through the gap in the curtains while Jennet fussed around exclaiming with horror at Eleanor's brush with death. The horseman was facing the river, deep in conversation with Eleanor's driver.

'Who do you think he could be?' Jennet asked curiously.

The heat rose to Eleanor's face at the memory of the man's arms about her waist. Baldwin had never held her so tightly or so close.

'I have no idea,' she replied icily. 'Nor do I care. How dare he blame me for what happened and to hold me in such a manner! If my father was here he would have the wretch horsewhipped for daring to lay a finger on me!'

She flung herself back against the seat and shut the curtains firmly, not opening them until the ferry had come to a halt and she heard the clatter of hooves as the rider left the craft.

*At least he had the sense not to jump off as well,*

she thought, breathing a sigh of relief that she would not have to encounter the stranger again.

The stars were out by the time they reached the long road that lead to Tawstott Mote, Sir Edgar's manor that lay beyond the market town bearing the same name. Eleanor could not suppress a smile. Every year she resisted returning, yet there was something in the sight of lamps glowing in the windows of the long, stone building that brought a lump to her throat whenever she saw them. As they crossed over the moat and into the courtyard she leaned forward, anxious to catch a first glimpse of the heavy oak door standing invitingly open.

Her mother was waiting in the Outer Hall. Lady Fitzallan gave sharp orders for a bath to be prepared and would hear no protestations from Eleanor.

'Your father is in his library at the moment. His business should be finished with by the time you're presentable,' she told her daughter as she ushered her up the broad staircase.

Half an hour later, clean and warm, Eleanor knocked softly on the north-wing door to Sir Edgar's library and walked in.

Two men were sitting together at either side of the fire. Sir Edgar's face broke into a wide beam at the sight of his daughter. Eleanor's eyes passed from her father to the face of his guest and her skin prickled with a sudden chill. His gaudy cloak had vanished and his hair was combed smooth, but even so Eleanor would have recognised the horseman anywhere.

# Chapter Two

'Ah, Eleanor, it's good to see you again, my dear,' Sir Edgar Fitzallan cried. The Baron of Tawstott strode across the room and kissed Eleanor warmly on both cheeks. Eleanor dropped into a formal curtsy before embracing her father tightly. All resentment at being summoned home melted away as he enveloped her in a hug.

The rider had jumped to his feet upon Eleanor's arrival, his eyes widening the slightest fraction as he looked at her. Could he be as surprised as she herself was at coming face-to-face again? He swept a low, elegant bow as Eleanor stared at him over her father's shoulder. His head was down now, hiding his face from view, but she could all too clearly remember the way his eyes had glinted when he'd held her in his arms.

With difficulty Eleanor tore her eyes away from the stranger, her mind whirling as she tried to fathom why he was in her father's house. He had mentioned having business to conduct before he jumped his horse on to the ferry, but at the time it had not occurred to Eleanor to wonder where he was travelling. If he had dealings with the baron, she hoped it would be concluded quickly and he would be gone before long.

'Forgive me for intruding, Father,' she said quickly. 'I did not realise you had a guest. I will leave you in peace and come back after he has left.'

Eleanor made to leave the room, but Sir Edgar tugged her back.

'There's someone I want you to meet,' Sir Edgar said. He tucked her arm under his and led her unwillingly towards the fire. Eleanor took a deep breath. She would greet him politely and leave. It would be done with in a matter of minutes.

Sir Edgar pushed Eleanor gently forward until she was standing opposite the man.

'Let me introduce Master William Rudhale, my new steward. Master Rudhale, this is my daughter, Lady Peyton.'

Eleanor stared wordlessly at the man for what felt like minutes as her father's words sunk in. *His steward!* Surprise fought with dismay in her heart that the man was not simply a visitor. They would be living under the same roof until Eleanor returned home.

Sir Edgar coughed meaningfully. 'Is everything all right, my dear? Are you feeling unwell?'

Eleanor became conscious that Master Rudhale was staring at her intently. His cheeks had taken on a ruddy glow, the scars' fine white furrows standing out across his face. His hands moved to brush away creases from his wine-coloured tunic, unlaced at the neck to expose the glint of fine hairs on his chest. He planted his feet firmly apart, his head tilted slightly on one side as he studied her reaction. If he had indeed been surprised by her appearance, he had recovered his equilibrium much quicker than she was managing to do. Her training since childhood in the behaviour required of a lady flooded back into Eleanor's mind.

'Not at all, Father. Please forgive me, Master Rudhale. My journey was long and I am forgetting my manners. How lovely to meet you,' she said with a polished smile and a slight emphasis on the word *meet*.

On firmer ground her nerves settled and she inclined her head automatically with grace that would make her mother proud to witness.

Rudhale bowed deeply again, once more exhibiting the easy grace with which he had moved on the ferry.

'Lady Peyton, I am at your service.' His voice was deep and dripped honey. He spoke with a sincerity that would have fooled Eleanor if she had not already encountered him. He brushed a stray strand of hair back from his eyes and gazed directly at her through lashes almost indecently long on a man. A smile danced about his lips and Eleanor's heart pounded with the intensity that had so confused her at their first meeting. She looked away, lost for words and unnerved by the reaction he provoked inside her.

'Eleanor, you're very late and I'm afraid I am neglecting you,' Sir Edgar broke in. 'William, please be so kind and pour my daughter some wine.' He motioned Eleanor to take the steward's seat by the fire. She sank down gratefully and stretched out her leg, glad to take the weight off her ankle. The short journey to Sir Edgar's rooms had put more strain on it than she had realised.

'Tell me, my dear, was your journey difficult?' Sir Edgar asked. Without waiting for an answer he addressed the steward. 'I do worry about my daughter travelling so far alone. No one knows whom one might encounter on the road, but she insists!'

From the corner of her eye Eleanor saw Rudhale stiffen and the steward's broad shoulders tensed, his hand halfway to the open bottle nestling between piles of scrolls and parchments on the table. Eleanor glanced at him over Sir Edgar's shoulder as he twisted his head towards her. Briefly their eyes locked. Rudhale raised one eyebrow questioningly, as though issuing a challenge to Eleanor to explain what had happened.

Her mind once again conjured the memory of him holding her close in such a disrespectful manner. And the kiss he had demanded. Even as she bristled at the memory a warm flush began to creep up the back of her neck as she stared at the full lips. Alarmed at the feelings that rose up inside her she ran her hands through her hair, pulling the long plait across her shoulder and away from her neck, hoping to cool herself.

It was clear that Rudhale had not been aware who she was on the ferry, but even so his manner had been unseemly. The man deserved to have his insolence revealed and it was on the tip of Eleanor's tongue to tell her father everything. She looked back to Sir Edgar. His brow was furrowed with concern and she hesitated. An encounter with an unknown man whilst travelling alone would be the ideal pretext for Sir Edgar to curtail her independence. Unhurriedly she held her hands out to the fire, taking her time before she answered, enjoying making the steward wait.

'Nothing eventful happened, Father. The river was flowing fast and the wind made climbing Kynett's Hill hard for the horses, otherwise I would have been here an hour ago. Apart from that our journey was the same as it always is.'

A triumphant grin flitted across the steward's face. It reminded Eleanor of an extremely self-satisfied cat and her stomach tightened with annoyance that she had passed up the chance to reveal his conduct. She expected him to leave now that she had arrived, but to her consternation he made no attempt to leave the room. Instead he drew up a low stool and sat between Eleanor and her father. Now she looked closely at his clothing she noticed the thin band of orange-and-green piping around the neck of his tunic, signalling the livery of Tawstott. As he handed her the wine cup, she held his gaze.

'Master Rudhale, how long have you been in my father's service? He has not mentioned you to me.'

Sir Edgar spoke before Rudhale could answer. 'Rudhale has been in my service for a little over five months, though he grew up in the town here. His father was my falconer until his death two years past. You must remember old Thomas Rud-hale, Eleanor?'

Eleanor wrinkled her forehead. Although she knew the name, hawking had never been a favourite pastime of hers and she spent little time in that part of the estate. The face finally crawled into Eleanor's mind. A quietly spoken man who rarely strayed from the mews, his belt and jerkin hung about with bags and odd-looking equipment. Another memory surfaced, too, however: a young man slouching around the outbuildings. Eleanor's eyes flickered to the steward. Surely that youth, too thin for his height with dull floppy hair, could not be the one who stood before her now, arms folded across his broad chest and a wolfish smile playing about his lips?

'Yes, I remember,' Eleanor said slowly. 'I'm sorry for your loss.'

'We all are. Never was a man so good with a goshawk,' Sir Edgar barked, clapping his hand on the steward's shoulder.

'Unlike his son,' Rudhale remarked darkly, tracing a finger meaningfully down the deep line of his scar. 'Father sent me to work as usher to a merchant in the north in the hope I could make my fortune and keep my eyes.'

Eleanor's eyes followed the path of his finger.

Taking that side of his face alone he looked like a cutthroat, but the ugliness was tempered by his almost sapphire eyes and enticing smile. Rudhale watched her carefully, as though testing her reaction to his deformity. Determined not to respond, she fixed her eyes on his.

'You seem rather young to be steward of such a large household,' she remarked.

'William may be young, but he comes highly recommended,' the baron explained. 'He and Edmund shared lodgings for a while.'

'Edmund remembered me when this position arose.' Rudhale smiled. 'Sir Edgar was good enough to trust Edmund's testimony. You are right though, few men my age could hope to attain such a prominent role, but I hope I am proving my worth.'

Eleanor narrowed her eyes, digesting the information as Sir Edgar hastened to assure Rudhale of his value. Her brother had a habit of choosing friends who shared his tastes for drinking and women. From Rudhale's behaviour on the ferry it would seem he was yet another good-for-nothing reprobate of the sort that Edmund would naturally find delightful.

She took a large sip of wine, swallowing her annoyance down too. The wine was spicy and sweet and Eleanor relaxed as the warmth wound down to her belly. Sir Edgar placed great importance on keeping a good cellar stocked and Rudhale was clearly capable of rising to the challenge. Eleanor held the cup to her nose and inhaled deeply. She raised her eyes to find the steward watching her carefully, his blue eyes fixed on her as though he was assessing her evaluation. She took another mouthful.

'It's good,' she commented appreciatively.

'It's seasoned with ginger and aged in whiskey casks,' Rudhale explained as he refilled Eleanor's glass. 'I am trying to persuade your father to buy half a dozen barrels in preparation for the midwinter feast.'

'You're giving a feast?' Eleanor stared at her father, unable to keep the astonishment from her voice. She forgot her irritation with the steward in the light of this news. Sir Edgar was notoriously reclusive and it was a family jest that if his wife permitted him to, he would live within the confines of his library on a permanent basis.

Sir Edgar frowned and threw himself heavily into the chair opposite Eleanor. He pulled fretfully at his greying beard, no longer the vibrant red Eleanor remembered from the previous winter.

'I have no choice, my dear,' he growled. 'Unfortunately Duke Roland is rumoured to have made damaging losses at cards and dice. Whether or not that is true I don't know, however he has decided that he will be spending the winter months touring his lands and living off the generosity of his tenants-in-chief. As his nephew by marriage, I am being granted the great honour of having his retinue here for two weeks. He expects a feast to celebrate the passing of the shortest day.'

'Father!' Eleanor's eyebrows shot upwards at the incautious manner in which her father spoke of his liege lord in front of the steward. Her lord as well, she reminded herself, as Baldwin had also owed fealty to Duke Roland. She glanced across to where Rudhale was now busying himself replacing scroll boxes on the shelves that lined the walls. Sir Edgar must have read her thoughts because he leaned across and took her hand.

'Don't fear for what William here might think. He knows he is serving a cantankerous old man and, like the rest of you, I expect him to humour my moods. I trust his discretion absolutely.'

Rudhale nodded his head in acknowledgement. He placed the final caskets on the shelf and Eleanor found her eyes drawn to his slim frame as he reached with ease to the high shelves. Rudhale crossed the room and picked up the bottle from the table. He refilled their glasses and returned to lean against the fireplace beside Eleanor, his long legs crossed at the ankles and the firelight turning his blond locks as red as Eleanor's own.

'I suspect your mother might have had something to do with her uncle's decision,' Sir Edgar continued. 'She sees certain advantages to having guests. The duke will be bringing a number of his court with him. Your sister is of an age where she needs to be seen in society and your brother should be married by now. For your part, Eleanor—'

'I myself will be returning home as usual as soon as I am permitted, Father,' Eleanor broke in sharply, anticipating what was coming next. The room, already stifling, grew hotter. She stood abruptly, walked to the window and leaned back against the cool panes. 'You told me nothing of this in your letter. I will not be paraded around like one of your prize mares. I am done with all that!'

'For *your* part,' Sir Edgar continued, with only the slightest hint of reproach in his voice, 'I would be grateful if you would provide a dozen or so casks of oysters for the feast. I have never found any finer than those from Baldwin's fisheries. I am sure you would wish the duke's party to be well fed and there could be business in it for you, too.

If you will insist on living independently, I must at least try to aid you where I can.'

'Oh!' A prickle of heat flickered across Eleanor's throat. 'Of course, Father. I'm sorry, I didn't mean...'

'Oh, yes, you did,' Sir Edgar chided gently. 'I don't say I blame you, but that is a conversation for another time.'

Eleanor glanced at Rudhale. The steward was now bent over the fire, adding logs to the diminishing flames. He gave every impression of appearing unaware of her blunder, though the deliberate way in which he went about his task left Eleanor in no doubt that he had been listening to every word. A burst of irritation shot through her that she had let her guard down in front of him. She crossed the room and refilled her cup before offering the bottle to her father and finally the steward. Hoping to break his self-possession, she addressed him with a demure smile.

'This wine really is very good, Master Rudhale. I can tell you must have taken great pains to ensure its safe arrival!'

She had the satisfaction of seeing him blink a couple of times as he worked out the meaning behind her words, before he broke into a broad grin, his blue eyes gleaming. Even that had not appeared to disconcert him. He raised his cup to her and drained it.

'May I compliment you on your taste, Lady Peyton. It needs time to settle really; being thrown around in a saddlebag has done nothing for it, but you can tell the quality, can't you? How can you resist such a glowing recommendation, Sir Edgar?' Rudhale asked the baron smoothly. 'Will you write me an authorisation to purchase the remaining supply? I will attend to it first thing tomorrow. Master Fortin intends to travel to Bristol, then to Gascony, within the week and I would like to catch him before he leaves.'

'Abroad, eh? Is he planning to trade? It's a good time now we are at peace once again and there are fortunes to be made, I don't doubt it.' His mood warmed by the wine, Sir Edgar cheerily gave a wave of the hand. 'Certainly, William, it's a good vintage and it would be churlish of me to deprive you of your income.'

Eleanor wrinkled her forehead, aware she was missing something.

Rudhale smiled at her. 'I have some personal interest in the matter, Lady Peyton. My last position was as pantler in the household of the wine merchant I acquired this from. When I left his employment he allowed me to invest a small amount in his business. If I can benefit both my previous and current employer, it is all to the best.'

'And yourself?' Eleanor asked.

'Of course,' he replied. 'It may never make me wealthy, but only a fool would turn his back on the opportunity to add to his coffers.'

He moved to the table. Taking a quill in his left hand, he began scribbling rapidly on a sheet of parchment with confident strokes. Watching, Eleanor mused on Rudhale's references to his previous positions. An usher, a pantler and now a steward: each position was more influential and well remunerated than the last. So Rudhale was ambitious, but also happy to move on before too long? She wondered if his time in Tawstott would be equally brief.

Sir Edgar affixed his seal and Rudhale folded the document carefully before slipping it inside his jerkin. Eleanor followed it with her eyes, her mood lifting a little. With any luck the man would see to the task personally and be gone again by morning.

'If you will excuse me, I must leave you now. Dinner will be almost ready. Having been absent for three days, I would like to supervise the final preparations myself.' With a bow to the baron he excused himself. He paused before Eleanor and looked deep into her eyes. 'Now she has arrived I would like to give Lady Peyton a good impression of my competence.'

Eleanor smiled coolly and held out a hand. The steward hesitated briefly before taking it in his and raising it. Did his lips brush her hand for slightly longer than necessary, or with slightly more pressure than decorum allowed? Eleanor wasn't sure. She inclined her head and bade him farewell, watching until the door closed behind him and fervently wishing the next two months would pass quickly.

# Chapter Three

William Rudhale's smile lasted for as long as it took to him to leave the room, then melted away to be replaced with a grimace. He breathed in a lungful of cool air and held it for a moment before exhaling deeply, admonishing himself for his lack of foresight. He had known for weeks that Lady Peyton was expected any day. Why had he not made the connection between Sir Edgar's daughter and the woman on the ferry? Her hair alone should have given him enough of a clue; that intense shade of copper was so rarely seen that it would have been remarkable if the woman were *not* related to Sir Edgar.

Somehow he had forgotten that the widowed daughter must be younger than him. If he had pictured her at all, it had been a plain, pinched face atop a shapeless, thickening body swathed in black. Lady Peyton was as far removed from the dumpy, elderly woman in his imagination as it was possible to be.

He had spent most of his ride from the ferry to Tawstott happily reliving the sensation of the enigmatic woman's slim frame pressing tightly against him. He had let his imagination have free rein with what he would do if they were to meet again. Certainly she would not have refused his kiss a third time, he would have made certain of that.

A shiver of desire rippled through him at the memory of the slender frame with such soft, tempting curves. He shook his head ruefully. No point spending too much time thinking about them. It was clear that Lady Peyton most definitely had not expected to encounter him again and, judging from her expression, she was not at all pleased to do so!

Will strode along the dimly lit corridor at a leisurely pace, the cold air providing a welcome blast of sobriety after the stuffiness of Sir Edgar's library, and made his way to the kitchens. With an assured manner he gave orders, noting with satisfaction the efficiency with which they were carried out.

*'Rather young to be a steward,'* Lady Peyton had said, the scepticism clear in her voice. Will's pride pricked for a moment. It was true enough

that he was young, but what of it? The lady would find no fault tonight, he determined. He busied himself testing dishes and tasting wine. Satisfied with the quality of the food, he gave his praise to the cooks, then issued orders to the serving maids, bestowing charming smiles on them as he did. He smiled to himself as they blushed and scurried away giggling.

Will made the short journey to the Great Hall where two long tables were laid for the household members, one down either side of the room, leading to the raised dais where the family would sit. A man was lounging by the fire at the far end of the room. Perched on an iron stand was a small, hooded kestrel. As Will entered the hall the bird screeched. Sir Edgar's current falconer pushed himself to his feet and hailed Will with a cheery wave of a bottle.

Will greeted his younger brother with a frown. 'Rob, I've told you before, keep your birds out of here. How long have you been here? You're not usually this early for meals.'

In response the sandy-haired man reached inside his jerkin and produced an embroidered yellow scarf. He twirled it above his head before holding it out to Will for inspection.

'Eliza Almeny finally gave me her favour…and

a little more besides.' Rob grinned impishly. 'I won the wager and you owe me five groats!'

The wagers had begun years ago when Edmund had loudly stated to their fellow drinkers that Will's grotesque scars would ruin his ability to catch any woman. His pride injured, and still smarting from the damage to his face, Will had risen to the challenge. By the end of the evening he'd charmed the tavern maid into his bed and discovered that a ready wit could make a woman overlook most imperfections, especially when a quick tongue was combined with a thorough dedication to using it in a variety of inventive ways.

He'd won from Edmund his drinks for the next week and since then the wagers had been an amusing game between the two men. When he returned to Tawstott to find Rob mooning over the miller's daughter, Will had seen no reason not to include him in the fun.

Will raised his eyebrows at his brother. 'Five groats? I said three, you swindler!'

Rob laughed. 'Yes, but you wagered I wouldn't manage to kiss her before midwinter's night. I've done more than that and I'm three weeks early so I believe I deserve more. Besides...' he paused and his grin became suddenly bashful '...I'll need the extra now I'm going to be a husband!'

Will's face broke into a surprised grimace. 'A husband, is it! Then you do indeed need more, though mayhap I should give the money to Eliza, as it seems she's been the one to ensnare you rather than the other way about!'

Rob tipped the bottle towards his brother. 'You say that now, but you may feel the same one day,' he said with a sympathetic smile that made Will's stomach twist.

Will shook his head and frowned darkly. 'You know I have no intention of marrying,' he said emphatically.

'Remind me, in that case, is the next wager to be yours or Edmund's?' Rob grinned.

Will's eye roved to the serving maid who was lighting thick beeswax candles in the sconces. He winked at her and she fumbled her taper, a blush spreading across her cheeks. The girl held no real attraction for him and his action had been instinctive.

'Perhaps I'm getting a little tired of this sport.' Will sighed. 'I think no more wagers for me.'

'In that case you may as well marry.' Rob laughed.

'However much you try convincing me otherwise I see no benefit in laying all my eggs in one nest,' Will said.

Rob rolled his eyes. 'How many women do you need to bed before you convince yourself you aren't a grotesque?'

Unconsciously Will's fingers moved to his scar. He caught himself and balled his fist. He reached for the bottle in Rob's hand. It was empty, of course.

'I meant to save you some, but you were longer than I expected,' Rob said. 'Sir Edgar kept you a long time tonight.'

'I would have been finished sooner, but we were interrupted,' Will explained. 'Lady Peyton arrived in the middle of our discussion and delayed matters.'

Rob let out an appreciative whistle. 'Is she as beautiful as ever, and as prickly?'

Will walked to the dais and straightened a couple of goblets, keeping his eyes averted from Rob. Prickly wasn't how he would describe the way Lady Peyton had felt in his arms. In fact, she had been more appealing than any woman he had encountered in a long while.

'I don't remember how beautiful she was before,' Will answered finally, raising his eyebrows. 'I haven't lived here for almost five years and when I left she was not yet a woman grown.'

He tried to keep his voice light as he considered

the woman young Eleanor Fitzallan had become, but experience told him Rob would not be easily deceived. Sure enough Rob followed him across the floor, pursing his lips suspiciously. Will poured them both a drink. He raised his cup in salute and drained it in one. It was not as fine as the one he had shared with Sir Edgar, but was at least as potent. A warm feeling began to envelop his head again and the knots in his shoulders eased. He regarded Rob over the lip of his cup and refilled it.

'Yes, she's beautiful,' he admitted. He thought back again to their first meeting and his lips twitched. When she had rounded on him with such indignation on the ferry it had taken all his self-possession not to silence her fury with a kiss! Will ran his fingers through his hair, thanking his good fortune he hadn't done so.

'I think prickly *would* be a fair description,' he conceded.

'I always imagined taking a tumble with her would be akin to falling into a holly bush!' Rob laughed.

Will snorted noncommittally, wondering what his brother would say if he knew how close to the holly bush he had got. The way her green eyes had widened as he'd pulled her close to him had sent a throb of raw desire through his entire body that even now threatened to return.

Enticing smells drifted from the kitchen so Will struck the large brass gong sharply. Whisking away their goblets, he took his position by the double doors to greet the household.

Presently the family and household servants began to make their way into the hall. Sir Edgar and Lady Fitzallan led the procession followed directly by Edmund Fitzallan escorting Lady Peyton on one arm and Anne Fitzallan, fourteen and the youngest of Sir Edgar's children, on the other. Will bowed deeply as Sir Edgar led his family to the table on the dais, but could not resist casting a surreptitious look at Lady Peyton. She caught his eye and her step faltered. A rose-coloured flush appeared enchantingly on each cheek. She nodded her head the smallest degree that manners would permit and Will hid a smile, turning instead to greet Edmund and Anne.

Throughout the meal Will's mind was firmly on his duties, determined to ensure everything ran smoothly. Once or twice throughout the evening he sensed Lady Peyton's eyes on him as he explained the ingredients of a particular dish to Sir Edgar, but if ever he looked directly at her she whipped her head down.

Before the sweet dishes were brought out Sir Edgar stood and left the table. The atmosphere took on a more informal air in his absence as members of the household dispersed or moved into groups and the hall became pleasantly alive with the sounds of voices and dice games.

Will found a spot on the end of a bench and allowed himself a moment of satisfaction that the evening had been accomplished smoothly. He watched as the three women and their attendants moved to seats by the fireside. Lady Fitzallan and Anne began to devour a plate of honeyed figs, but Lady Peyton seated herself slightly apart from her mother and sister, her body perfectly still and her eyes downcast. The air of melancholy surrounding her was almost tangible and Will's heart lurched at the sight.

Edmund broke his reverie as he threw himself on to the bench and slung an arm around Will's shoulder. Will greeted him with a distracted smile, the intrusion into his thoughts unwelcome.

Edmund picked up a bottle of wine and filled two goblets to the brim. 'You look weary, Will,' he commented. 'Was my father particularly demanding tonight? Did he agree to buy the wine?'

'No, he wasn't—and, yes, he did. He recognised the quality straight away. With a little more money to invest I could earn well from this vintage alone,' Will answered. He sighed deeply. 'It's a pity my stake is so small.'

They drank contentedly for a while, discussing the upcoming feast, Rob's successful wager and impending marriage. Rob retrieved his kestrel from the perch by the fire with a bow and a few brief words to the ladies, then joined his brother and friend. Lady Peyton's eyes followed him as he crossed the room and Will saw her expression change to a frown as she saw where he was heading.

'Why does my dear sister keep glaring at you?' Edmund asked suddenly, turning his head to Will. 'Every time she glanced your way during dinner she looked as though she wished she had a sharper knife. Surely you can have done nothing in the hour or two she has been here to incur her displeasure?'

'You must be imagining things, Edmund. What could I have done?' Will asked innocently. He took a deep draught from his goblet.

Rob leaned forward on his bench. 'Will, you're hiding something, I can tell.'

Will sighed. He had intended to keep his encounter with Lady Peyton to himself, but now the matter had arisen of its own accord. The wine had relaxed his mood enough that he had a sudden impulse to share his tale.

'We have met before tonight, though not in the best circumstances,' Will admitted, a wry smile crossing his face. 'Today I nearly caused her to drown. I'm fortunate not to be packing my bags as we speak!' He described the encounter on the ferry and his requests for a kiss. By the time he had finished his tale Rob was open mouthed in disbelief. Edmund's face was twisted into an incredulous smile.

'I swear, Edmund, if I had known she was your sister I would never have behaved in such a manner,' Will insisted. 'I intended no offence.'

Edmund swigged his wine with a careless shrug and raised an eyebrow. 'None taken. The thought of my dear sister in such disarray has brightened up an otherwise tedious day. In all honesty I wish you had kissed her, Will. I wish anyone would, in fact.'

Will and Rob exchanged a glance of surprise at Edmund's words.

'It would do Eleanor some good to be reminded that she's a woman. She has been widowed so long I fear she has forgotten,' Edmund explained. 'She's had a sad life,' he said sorrowfully.

'Here's the target for our next wager,' Rob crowed delightedly.

'No, it isn't,' Will said sternly. 'I'm done with all that and, even if I weren't, I'm not putting my position here in jeopardy. I've worked too hard to get it.'

'That would be the challenge, of course: to charm her without causing any risk to yourself.' Rob smiled.

'Coaxing a serving girl between the sheets is one thing. I have no intention of risking Sir Edgar's rage by seducing his daughter,' Will insisted.

'I wouldn't want her seduced completely,' Edmund protested quickly. 'I wouldn't play games with her virtue so carelessly. A kiss, though, that would be a different matter and one that is unlikely to endanger your employment.'

'A single kiss? That's hardly any challenge,' Will scoffed. He looked once more to where Lady Peyton sat staring solemnly at the fireplace. Her slender form was in silhouette and Will could make out the shape of the contours he had so recently held close. He remembered the purse of her lips as she had glared at him. Would they be as soft to kiss as he imagined them to be? A prickle of excitement ran down his spine at the thought.

Edmund eyed him for a moment. A familiar mocking glint flashed across his eyes. He stood up, wobbling slightly, and patted Will on the back. 'Your limited charms won't be enough to win my sister over anyhow. She'd never look twice at you.'

Lady Peyton was listening to her mother speaking but, as though she had felt Will's eyes upon her, she glanced across, seeing the three men staring in her direction. Her green eyes narrowed suspiciously. Will remembered those clear, wide eyes scrutinising him in Sir Edgar's library as she had hinted at their encounter. She could have told her father everything and yet something had stopped her. He had seen interest there, he was sure, and he had most certainly seen the flush in her cheeks when she was in his arms.

His jaw tightened as he recalled her declaration that she would never kiss him. She had been so confident of her assertion that his sense of pride flared at the thought of such a challenge.

As he poured another round of drinks, playing for time, Lady Peyton rose from her seat. She crossed the hall—still not putting the weight fully on her foot, Will noticed. Edmund hailed her with a cheery goodnight and she bent unwillingly while Edmund planted a drunken kiss on her cheek. Her eye fell on Will. He inclined his head towards her and she gave him a nervous smile. He watched her depart, her skirt swaying gracefully despite the unevenness of her step, emphasising her narrow waist and the curves of her hips.

'You've got a fancy for her, haven't you, Brother? I can tell,' Rob said. 'Well, you can put her out of your mind. It's common knowledge she has no time for any man.'

'Rob's right. I'd be happy for you to kiss her. I might even welcome you as a brother-in-law, but you'd be on a hiding to nothing,' Edmund agreed. 'I reckon Mother will be looking at the duke's entourage for husbands for my sisters.'

'Why should that concern me? I'm not looking for marriage,' Will said. 'I'll leave it to Rob to exceed the terms of the wager so foolishly.' Of course a noblewoman such as she would have her eyes on a mate of equal status. He sat back in his chair, arms stretched behind his head. 'Very well, I'll bet five groats I can kiss her by midnight on the night of the midwinter feast.'

Rob laughed, 'You're aiming too high this time. In fact, I'm so sure you'll fail that I'll make it ten groats.' He chortled.

'Ten from me, too,' Edmund agreed.

Will sucked his teeth thoughtfully. Twenty groats was almost a month's salary, much more than any wager previously. He could ill afford to lose such an amount. To win it though was tempting indeed. Visions of Master Fortin's ship laden with wine barrels passed before his eyes. Twenty groats more to invest and for what hardship? Doing something he wanted to do anyway.

Why was he even hesitating! A widow must miss some comforts of marriage after all.

'One kiss, nothing more? And you assure me I will not incur your father's wrath?' he asked once more.

Edmund nodded. 'How would Father ever find out? Eleanor would never tell him. On the lips, mind,' he said. 'None of this virtuous hand-raising or brotherly cheek-brushing.'

Brotherly cheek-brushing was the last thing on Will's mind. He drained his goblet and slammed it down on the table.

'I'll do it. The wager is on!'

# Chapter Four

An insistent knocking at the bedchamber door dragged Eleanor from her sleep much sooner than she would have liked. She buried her head beneath the warmth of the covers, but the rapping became louder until it had the rhythm and intensity of a drum and she could ignore it no longer. She climbed out of bed with a groan. Her foot was still tender as she hobbled to the door.

Anne stood with one hand raised, caught mid-knock.

'I thought you were never going to wake up,' the younger girl said petulantly, twisting a lock of her strawberry-blonde hair around her fingers. 'You left the hall early enough last night to have had more than enough rest.'

Eleanor smiled and beckoned her in, relieved it was only her sister and not her mother. Lady Fitzallan had definite opinions about the hour her daughters should be dressed by. Even after running her own establishment for years Eleanor found herself squirming at the thought of a scolding. She half-hopped back to the bed and climbed in, stretching her leg out.

'Open the shutters, please, Anne,' she instructed and watery daylight flooded into the room. Eleanor peered down at her ankle, wincing at the sight. Released from her tightly laced boot, the foot had swollen overnight and an ugly bruise crept from her instep across and round her anklebone. No wonder it hurt to walk on. Anne gasped in disgust at the sight of Eleanor's ankle and climbed on to the bed, leaning heavily against her sister and drawing the thick blanket close around them both.

'You said nothing of this to Mother last night,' Anne exclaimed accusingly. 'How did you do it?'

Eleanor reached down and gave her ankle an experimental prod. A biting pain shot across her foot as she touched the tender flesh. It would take days to heal, she was certain of it. Her anger at Rudhale's ludicrous actions on the ferry returned in a rush.

'I slipped on the ferry crossing the Taw and twisted it,' she explained crossly. She threw herself back against the pillow in annoyance. 'It was not my doing. I was almost knocked overboard thanks to the reckless behaviour of…' Her voice trailed off cautiously. Last night she had passed up the chance to tell her father what had passed between herself and the steward. She could hardly now share that with Anne, at least not if she expected it to remain secret any longer than it took for the girl to leave the room.

Anne was watching her closely, her hazel eyes wide. 'Of who?' the girl asked eagerly.

'A stranger on horseback. No one important,' Eleanor continued. Her irritation mounted as she recounted the incident. Anne's reaction was not at all what she had expected, however. Her sister's eyes shone and she clutched Eleanor's arm passionately.

'Eleanor, that's the most exciting thing I've ever heard!' Anne's voice was a high-pitched squeal. 'He saved you from the water and pulled you into his arms, yet you didn't kiss him? How could you have resisted him?'

'How could I have resisted an arrogant man who thinks he could demand such an intimacy from a woman travelling alone?' Eleanor asked in surprise. There were six years between them and sometimes she forgot how silly Anne could be.

Anne snorted and hugged herself tightly, her face wistful. 'A kiss from a dashing stranger! It's like something a troubadour would sing about. It's so romantic, Eleanor. Was he handsome?'

The steward's face rose in Eleanor's mind and an unwelcome blush began to creep around her neck at the memory of his eyes flashing in her direction. She bit her lip and reached for the comb that lay on the table.

'I don't recall,' she said frostily, pushing down the memory of the way her heart had thumped. 'Besides, however handsome he was, it would not excuse such rudeness.'

Anne took the comb from Eleanor's hand and began to run it through the tangles of her sister's hair. 'So he *was* handsome!' Anne said triumphantly. 'Promise me that if it should ever happen again you will not refuse,' she begged.

Eleanor's heart lurched at the thought. She caught the direction her thoughts were leading and scolded herself. The steward's manner towards her in Sir Edgar's library had been courteous and there was no reason to believe he would be so brazen in future. It most certainly would not happen again.

'I would do no such thing,' she said calmly. 'And neither would you unless you wanted to ruin your reputation.'

Anne pouted. 'That's easy for you to say. You've

already had one husband and I'm sure you could catch another any time you chose. I've never had a suitor, not properly, and Mother isn't even looking for me. No one will ever marry me!'

Eleanor took her sister's hand and smiled. 'You're three years younger than I was when I married Baldwin. There's plenty of time for suitors.'

Anne's face lit up. Eleanor bit her lip thoughtfully. Anne had been only ten years old when Baldwin had come into Eleanor's life. How could she begin to explain what it felt like to be presented to a stranger ten years her senior and informed she would be his bride? 'Don't be too keen to give your freedom away, it will happen soon enough,' she said earnestly. 'Let's not talk any more of this though. Dinner seems a long time ago and I want some breakfast.'

Leaning on her sister's arm for support, Eleanor made her way to the Great Hall. Unlike the evening meal, breakfast was a more informal affair with members of the household coming and going as their needs and duties dictated. By the time Eleanor and Anne arrived the servants and the girls' parents had long since departed—Lady Fitzallan to her solar and Sir Edgar no doubt to his library—so the hall was empty. The two girls settled on to the padded seat in the window alcove and set about devouring the remaining bread and ale. Their earlier conversation was forgotten as they swapped tales of what had passed since their last meeting.

The door opened and Eleanor's heart sank as William Rudhale entered. She had hoped him to be miles away by now, riding back with his wine order. Rudhale did not seem to notice the women at first. He stood on the threshold and glanced around the room, his brow knotted with concentration.

'William!'

Anne's unexpected cry of greeting brought Eleanor out of her reverie. She frowned at her sister, but Anne was watching the steward too intently to notice, her cheeks reddening visibly.

On realising he was not alone the steward gave a start, but his face broke into a charming smile. He walked to them in long, confident strides and bowed deeply. Eleanor studied him surreptitiously. The last time she had seen him he had been well into a flagon of wine with Edmund. Unless her brother had greatly changed his habits, by rights this morning Rudhale should be suffering from a sore head and longing for a darkened room. Instead he looked fresh and well, his hair curling about his collar and his beard trimmed close. He was dressed plainly in a dark-blue tunic and black breeches. The leather belt that drew his waist was ornately stamped: the only touch of vanity in an otherwise sober outfit.

'Good morning, William. I didn't see you yesterday,' Anne said, her words rushing out in a tumble before anyone else could speak. Her eyes glowed. 'I looked for you when I was riding, but Tobias wasn't in the stable. Will you be riding today? I shall be.'

As she heard the excitement in Anne's voice a terrible realisation struck Eleanor. Her sister was attracted to Rudhale. With a head filled with tales of romance and bandits, naturally Anne would find such a well-looking young man attractive. His scar would no doubt only contribute an air of danger and add to his appeal rather than detract from it. If only she had told Anne the horseman's identity and warned her away when she had the chance.

Eleanor leaned forward and stared at the steward, watching his reaction as a fox might watch a rabbit. Her sudden movement caught Rudhale's attention. His eyes slid to Eleanor's and widened as he obviously realised the conclusion she had arrived at. He shook his head in a gesture of denial. The movement was so small as to be almost imperceptible, but his meaning was clear. He was aware of Anne's feelings, but did not reciprocate them.

Rudhale smiled politely at Anne, his hands stiffly by his side. 'I'm sorry, Miss Anne,' he said formally. 'I hope you enjoy your ride, but I have so much to do today after arriving back so late yesterday evening.' His tone was polite, but his face showed none of the vitality it had contained when he had demanded the kiss on the ferry. Eleanor sat back against the window frame, her shoulders dropping slightly with relief. Anne sighed with dissatisfaction.

'Perhaps your sister will accompany you,' Rudhale suggested, smiling at Eleanor with a good degree more warmth than he had her sister.

'She can't. She's injured her foot,' Anne replied. She sighed heavily. 'Ah well, I shall have to ride alone and hope I encounter a dashing horseman like Eleanor did yesterday!'

Eleanor's mouth dropped open at her sister's indiscreet words. Rudhale's eyes lit up and he looked at her with interest.

'Those were not my words as well you are aware, Anne,' Eleanor said sharply. Her stomach curled with embarrassment. The thought that Rudhale might believe she had described him as such was excruciating. 'I think I shall return to my room. I have some business to attend to.' She lowered her feet to the floor, wincing slightly. Anne moved to help her, but Rudhale stepped forward.

'Allow me to assist you, Lady Peyton,' Rudhale said gallantly. 'It would be a shame for your sister to delay her ride.' He held an arm out to her.

Eleanor opened her mouth to refuse him, but changed her mind. The necessity of needing his help won out over her reluctance to be in his company. They walked silently side by side, Rudhale supporting her weight as though she was little more than a child. He slipped his arm around her waist as she leaned heavily against him. His hips brushed against hers and the contours of his broad chest were unmistakable through his tunic. Try as she might, Eleanor could not ignore the way her heartbeat quickened at his touch.

'I thought you were leaving today,' she muttered as they left the Great Hall.

'Other matters prevented me going personally so I sent a messenger. I trust dinner lived up to your expectations last night, Lady Peyton?' Rudhale asked as they walked slowly along the corridor.

'Perfectly, Master Rudhale,' Eleanor said coolly, 'Though I'll admit they were low to begin with.'

Rudhale stopped walking. He cocked his head, a small frown furrowing his brow. 'How so, my lady?' he asked. 'You do me an injustice.'

'An injustice?' Eleanor folded her arms across her chest and gave a short laugh of disbelief. 'What indication have you given me that you are anything more than an irresponsible fool?' she asked scathingly. 'Your behaviour yesterday was hardly to your credit. Leaving aside the injury you caused me, if my father knew what you had demanded do you think you would continue in his employment for long?'

Rudhale's gaze became iron hard. 'Contrary to what my appearance might suggest I am not in the habit of "demanding". I merely suggested it because when a beautiful woman ended up in my arms it would be foolish not to!' He crossed his own arms and planted his feet apart, mirroring Eleanor's stance. 'And you did not tell Sir Edgar what happened when you had the opportunity,' he pointed out. 'Why is that? What stopped you revealing my improper behaviour? It can't be simply because you thought me dashing, though I owe you thanks for that compliment.'

A knot of irritation blocked Eleanor's throat, choking her retort. Truly the man was more arrogant than she had believed possible! 'Believe me, Master Rudhale, I do not find your behaviour "dashing". That was my sister's word as I already explained. Nothing could be further from the truth.'

Rudhale was grinning again. Really, did the man find everything in life amusing?

Eleanor smoothed her hair back, conscious that she was losing her composure in front of him.

'I did not tell my father purely for my own ends. I have spent too long battling to be allowed my independence for some fool to ruin that for me. The fact it benefitted you is purely coincidental. Now you may help me to my room or leave me to manage by myself, but I do not wish to speak of this any further.'

Lady Peyton began to limp away, leaving Will staring at her slender back. The encounter was not going how he had pictured it when he had first seen her in the Great Hall. He had congratulated himself on succeeding in getting her alone so quickly, but he had not anticipated her being quite so cold. Seeing his chance to lay the groundwork for the wager about to disappear, Will caught her by the arm. She glared at him once again. He held his hands up and fixed her with a disarming smile.

'I think it is fair to say we did not begin on the

best footing, my lady,' he said, inclining his head towards her ankle. Her face softened at his jest, but she bit her lip, as though she was amused, but did not want to admit such a thing. He stored the information away for future use.

'Shall we start again?' he asked. Lady Peyton said nothing, but when he held an arm out again she took it. A small thrill of victory ran through Will. Their progress to Lady Peyton's chamber was slow, but that gave him all the more time to win her over.

'I noticed when you came to dinner that you were limping. Is it very painful?' Will asked, filling his voice with concern. 'I hope it doesn't interrupt your activities too greatly, though I'm afraid it will stop you riding for a few days at least.'

Lady Peyton shook her head. 'It aches, but I have no plans to ride,' she replied.

'I hope it is better before the midwinter feast. It would be a shame if you could not dance.'

'I don't dance,' she answered, bowing her head and increasing her speed slightly. In the dimly lit corridor her face was obscured by shadows, but something in her tone caught Will's attention. A hint of regret nestling amongst the aloofness, he thought.

'I thought all ladies could dance,' he said, raising one eyebrow.

The muscle in her arm tightened involuntarily under his. 'I didn't say I couldn't. I choose not to,' she said curtly before lapsing into silence.

They had reached her bedchamber. Lady Peyton untwined her arm from Will's and opened the door. A crumpled green-velvet coverlet was visible on the bed and Will's mind began to wander down paths it shouldn't. Moving a touch closer, he rested one arm on the door frame and bent his head over Lady Peyton, fixing her with the intense gaze that never failed to leave his targets breathless with desire.

'Lady Peyton, I owe you an apology,' he breathed huskily. 'What I did on the ferry...what I asked of you...I was wrong to do so.' Her green eyes widened in surprise. This was almost too easy. 'I have no excuse other than that I was swept away by your beauty.'

Will dropped his eyes to the ground as though ashamed, before raising them to look at her once more through half-closed lids. Instead of the rapt expression he expected, Lady Peyton looked outraged.

'Swept away?' she said disdainfully. 'It's fortu-

nate indeed your horse did not miss his landing if
you are swept away so easily!'

'I mean no offence,' Will answered calmly. 'It
is a compliment to you that I was overcome by
sentiments stronger than my sense of propriety.'

'I want no such compliments, Master Rudhale,'
Lady Peyton exclaimed. Two pink spots appeared
enticingly on her cheeks. 'If I must suffer to live
under the same roof as you, the greatest compliment you can pay me is to believe me when I say
I wish you to stay out of my presence as much as
possible.' She spun on her heel and half-flung herself into the room, slamming the door behind her.

Will stood alone in the corridor, scarcely able to
believe what had just happened. He fought back a
laugh of glee. Truly she was wonderful.

There had not been a woman yet who had resisted Will's attempts at seduction—few even
tried. Now he was more determined than ever that
a woman as captivating as Eleanor Peyton would
not be the first!

## Chapter Five

Her heart thumping, Eleanor banged the door closed behind her and leaned back heavily as though Rudhale might attempt to barge his way through at any moment. She raised a hand to her neck and was unsurprised to feel her skin hot to the touch, a telltale prickle of a blush creeping across her chest. Her hand was trembling and she clenched her fist tight.

Jennet was emptying Eleanor's travelling chest with her back to the door. At the sound she jumped, her head twisting round to where her mistress stood.

'You startled me, my lady. Is something the matter?' she asked in alarm.

Eleanor smiled faintly at the absurdity of her behaviour and shook her head. The steward might be egotistical and his words far too personal for comfort, but there was no reason to suspect he would commit so violent an indiscretion. Really, she was not herself this morning.

She crossed the room and sank on to the low folding stool in front of her window, rummaging on the ledge among the boxes until she found the green glass bottle containing her favourite scented oil. She dabbed a drop on her temples, inhaling the fresh aroma of lemon balm, and slowly her composure returned.

Jennet came and knelt at her side. 'My lady, do you remember the man on the ferry—?' she began. Eleanor cut her words off before she could continue.

'I know.' She nodded. She took Jennet's hands. 'You must not tell anyone what happened. I have spoken to him and told him I will not discuss the matter again...'

Her voice trailed off as she thought back to the conversation. Never before had she spoken in such a manner to anyone, least of all a man! She reminded herself that until she met the steward there had never been any cause to do so.

Even so, she could not blot out the vision of Rudhale's eyes penetrating her with such open, honest desire. He had made his attraction perfectly clear and it unsettled Eleanor deeply. Even more troubling was the constriction in her belly whenever she was in his presence, as though a fist was wrapping her stomach around itself and pulling her closer to his reach whether she willed it or not.

'My lady?' Jennet prompted.

Eleanor realised with a start that she had been staring at the wall, seeing nothing for who knew how long. She shook her head and smiled at Jennet.

'I could not have made myself any clearer. If Master Rudhale has anything of the gentleman about him, that should be the end of it,' she finished.

Drawing a deep breath she picked up a book and began to read. Becoming engrossed in the subject, she soon forgot about Rudhale. When a knock at the door brought her mind back to the present, it never even occurred to her to worry whom it might be.

Jennet rushed to the door and the wise-woman from Tawstott Town followed her into the room. Eleanor beamed at the thickset, wispy-haired woman dressed in black. Joan Becket had brought all of Lady Fitzallan's children into the world. A close friend of Lady Fitzallan, she still maintained an interest in the lives of the three who had survived.

Crossing the room, she curtsied to Eleanor and

kissed her hand. 'Eleanor, good to see you again. Someone told me you've got yourself injured.' Mistress Becket smiled.

Eleanor's hand instinctively moved to her ankle. Mistress Becket's eyes followed her action and she nodded.

'Well, let me have a look and I'll see what I can do.'

Eleanor lifted her foot on to a stool and unrolled her stocking. Anne must have told their mother, of course. The girl was incapable of keeping anything a secret. Eleanor frowned to herself. No doubt she would be called to explain what had happened before long.

The examination was quick and a mild sprain the verdict. Mistress Becket smeared a foul-smelling poultice of crushed comfrey and nettle leaves over Eleanor's ankle. She bound it tightly with thin straps of flannel and stood back with a smile.

'Walk lightly for the next few days. Borrow a stick from your father and you won't have to spend your days hiding away in here.'

Eleanor reached for the purse that lay on her table, but Mistress Becket held up her hands.

'The payment has already been settled,' she told Eleanor as she wiped the remaining mixture on a cloth and packed it into her basket.

'Did Mother pay you?' Eleanor asked, surprised.

The old woman's eyes twinkled. 'Not her,' she said with a grin.

'Who, then?' Eleanor asked curiously. Mistress Becket's fees were not cheap and Anne was unlikely to have the funds or inclination to pay. Becket smiled as she reached the door.

'Why, by the person who asked me to attend you, of course,' she said with another grin. 'Master Rudhale.'

Eleanor leaned back in her chair, her mind in a whirl. She ordered Jennet to find her a crutch as the wise-woman had recommended. She could barely contain herself while she waited. The words on the page jumbled themselves in disordered sentences. She tried to calm herself with embroidery, but found the threads knotting under her touch. Twice she stabbed her finger and she finally flung the cloth on to the bed and settled for staring out of the window at the clouding sky until the maid returned.

Eleanor found the steward in the rear courtyard supervising deliveries of grain. He had his back to Eleanor and at first was unaware of her presence. She had intended to confront him immediately, but instead held back, curious to see him at work. She watched as he gave orders to the two servants. He spoke in a quiet voice and from the expressions on the faces of the other men he commanded their respect. He stood with his wax tablet in hand, tallying up the sacks as they were hefted from the delivery carts and carried into the granary.

The sky had been darkening steadily and large drops of rain began to fall. Rudhale slipped his note tablet into the leather satchel that crossed his chest and, joining the two servants, hefted a sack across his shoulder. He lifted the burden without apparent effort and an unexpected shiver ran along through the length of Eleanor's body as she recalled him lifting her equally as easily on the ferry.

Despite the bitter coldness of the day, he was wearing no cloak over his wool doublet and the contours of his torso were evident beneath the slim-fitting garment. An unwilling smile formed on Eleanor's lips as she watched. Rudhale turned towards the granary and noticed Eleanor for the first time. The steward's expression had been one of concentration, but as he saw Eleanor his eyes widened and his face relaxed into a grin. She forced the smile from her face, unwilling for him to see it. Still carrying his sack, he strode to Eleanor.

'I did not expect to see you here, my lady,' he said in surprise. 'Is there anything I can help you with?'

'I need to speak to you,' Eleanor said firmly.

Rudhale glanced at the sky. 'As you can see I am rather occupied and you are at risk of getting a soaking for the second day running. Might I suggest you return to the house and I will find you once I am done?'

Eleanor folded her arms and looked at him defiantly. 'No, I want to speak to you now. Leave the men to work without you.'

To Eleanor's surprise Rudhale shook his head. 'No, I'm sorry, Lady Peyton, but this is too important. I cannot afford to have a month's worth of grain drenched, even for you.'

He walked to the granary, his shoulders set under the weight of his burden. Eleanor watched him go, his dedication to the task unexpected. She took a step back towards the house, then wavered. The rain was coming down faster now. She had no wish to get wet, but no man would order her around in that fashion. She stood her ground, leaning on the stick for support and wishing she had brought a cloak.

Rudhale returned from the building empty handed after a few moments and found her still standing there. With a stern look he dipped his hand into his satchel and handed the wax tablet to her.

'Stay if you must, but if you insist on waiting at least be of assistance to me.' He nodded his head towards the granary. 'Stand in the entrance and tally the sacks.' He walked on without waiting for her response and heaved another sack from the cart on to his shoulder.

Eleanor wavered, her pride rebelling at the way he ordered her, but if she returned to the house she did not know when they might meet again so she made her way to the granary and stood inside the entrance of the stone building. She did as Rudhale asked, adding her own precise marks next to the neat lines of his tallies. Her sense of organisation took over and she happily instructed the servants and steward how best to proceed. The cart was soon emptied and the sacks stacked neatly on the stone shelves in the granary.

After a few words of thanks, Rudhale sent the cart driver and servants on their way. He walked back to Eleanor and stood beside her, brushing his hands briskly down the length of his arms and torso to brush the worst of the rain off. Eleanor found herself following the movement closely. She raised her eyes to meet his. Droplets of water glistened in his beard and hair. He cocked his head to one side and ran a hand through his hair, watching Eleanor closely. She held the tablet out and he took it. His fingers touching lightly against her hand for the briefest moment and Eleanor shivered.

'Thank you for your help,' Rudhale said. 'You have saved me a degree of trouble. I am in your debt.' He walked into the granary and shifted a sack further on to the shelf.

His words reminded Eleanor why she had come and she followed him inside. The storeroom was shadowy, the only light from the open door and the small holes around each wall. The air was sweet with the scent of grain and she took a deep breath.

'It is I who am in your debt,' Eleanor said. 'I have come to settle it now.' Her hand moved to the pouch on her girdle. 'How much did Mistress Becket charge you?'

Rudhale raised an eyebrow at her words. 'You owe me nothing,' he said. 'I summoned her to attend you. I will pay for it.'

'I didn't ask you to do that.' Eleanor put her hands on her hips and glared at him. 'What right do you have to act on my behalf in such a way?'

Rudhale moved closer to her. 'I did it because I could see you were in pain and did not believe you would take care of it yourself. I'm right, aren't I?'

Eleanor's mouth dropped open. She closed it quickly and took a step back, surprised at the gentleness in his voice. 'Even so, that is no business of yours.'

'The responsibility for the injury was mine,' Rudhale said firmly. 'The decision to ask Mistress Becket was mine. The cost will be mine also.'

Eleanor dug her hand into her pouch and produced a groat. She held it out to Rudhale. He folded his arms and set his jaw, eyeing Eleanor defiantly.

'Take it, for goodness' sake,' she exclaimed, her temper rising. 'I don't want your money. I can afford to take care of my own affairs.'

'Your father pays me well. I am not as poor as you suppose,' Rudhale said scornfully.

'That isn't what I meant!' Eleanor grimaced as she realised how her words must have sounded. She lowered her voice and said, 'I refuse to be under obligation to any man.'

At her tone Rudhale's expression changed. He looked at her quizzically. 'There is no dishonour in doing so,' he said, his voice earnest. He looked away as though deep in thought, and when his blue eyes slid back to Eleanor's they gleamed. Eleanor's throat tightened.

'If you wish to repay me, you could do so in another manner,' Rudhale suggested. 'As your ankle will be healed soon, you can dance with me on the night of the midwinter feast.'

A long-buried sense of yearning struggled inside Eleanor. The now-familiar sense of indignation she felt in his presence fought back. The indignation won. She squeezed the coin tightly into her hand.

'I told you before, I never dance. I certainly won't with you.'

'Why not?' Rudhale moved closer again and this time Eleanor did not move away. Rudhale lowered his voice. 'Are you ashamed to be seen with a servant, or is it my face that prevents you?'

'Neither!' Eleanor cried indignantly. 'Do you imagine me so proud?'

'What are you afraid will happen if you do?' Rudhale breathed.

Eleanor swallowed. 'I am afraid of nothing,' she said boldly. She ignored the voice that whispered how much of a falsehood her denial was and looked him squarely in the face. She held the coin in front of her once more. When the steward ignored it, Eleanor placed it on the shelf beside the grain sacks.

'Since my marriage ended I have looked after myself. I do not intend to cease now. Take the money or leave it. It's all the same to me.' She walked out of the granary and back to the house,

using all her willpower not to turn to check if Rudhale had picked up the coin.

Will watched Lady Peyton depart. He scratched
his beard thoughtfully. Every instinct told him she
found him attractive, so why was she so determined to deny the fact? He picked the coin from
the shelf where Lady Peyton had placed it. It was
still warm from her touch. He rolled it between
his fingers, contemplating his next move. This
was the second time in one day the infuriating
woman had left him standing alone. As long as
she kept retreating he could never begin to break
down her reserve.

Complimenting her beauty had not worked. Calling the wise-woman should have softened her attitude towards him. She lived alone, with no male
company or protection. By rights she should be
longing for someone to take care of her. Instead
she had insisted on that ridiculous notion of independence. Clearly he would need to use different
tactics in this conquest.

He walked back to the house, examining the
completed tally. Lady Peyton's hand was neat and
businesslike. He recalled the way she had directed
the servants, more enthusiastically than he had

seen her do anything so far. A grin spread across his face as a plan began to form in his mind.

Sir Edgar was poring over a large ledger when Will entered his library. He shut the ledger with a bang and grimaced at Will.

'Duke Roland's visit is going to bankrupt me, I fear,' he grumbled. 'The costs keep mounting.'

'There is much to be done before the visit,' he agreed. 'I should be happy to have twice the assistance I have now.'

'Well, I can ill afford to hire anyone else,' Sir Edgar cautioned. Will's heart leapt with glee. The baron had practically introduced the subject himself.

Sir Edgar picked up his quill and tapped the end irritably against the table edge. 'My only hope is that my wife finds husbands for my daughters and makes the expense worthwhile, although I can scarcely afford dowries at this time. Eleanor will have to provide her own, though I'm sure she would be more than happy to do so. Never have daughters if you can help it, young man!'

This was even better, Will thought triumphantly. He fixed his face into a sympathetic smile. 'It is about Lady Peyton that I have come to see you...' he began.

'Eleanor, what of her?' Sir Edgar peered at Will warily. 'You don't wish to marry her, do you?' He laughed as he spoke, though Will thought he could hear a note of hope in the baron's voice.

'I would not presume to reach so high,' Will declared. 'I merely came to say that I have noticed Lady Peyton seems rather...' he searched for a word that would not offend '...rather listless and vexed. I wondered if she might need something to occupy her.'

'I'm sure she does,' Sir Edgar agreed. 'If I only had the time or finances to fill her days, I'm sure she would be much happier.'

Will sighed, then his face lit up. 'I have an idea—!' he began, then broke off. 'No, it would never do,' he said with a regretful shake of his head. He walked to the window and gazed out. From the corner of his eye he could see Sir Edgar leaning forward with interest.

'If you have something to say, tell me,' Sir Edgar instructed.

With mock reluctance Will spoke. 'I have a suggestion that might satisfy all our needs.'

He outlined his idea to Sir Edgar. The baron sat back in his chair, hands together across his belly. 'Excellent idea, William,' he said finally. 'Would you find Eleanor? I shall tell her immediately.'

'May I suggest Lady Peyton is led to believe the plan is yours alone? After all, it was you who gave me the inspiration and I would not wish to take the credit.'

'Nor the condemnation if it does not meet with Eleanor's views?' Sir Edgar asked shrewdly.

The two men's eyes met and an unspoken acknowledgement passed between them. The baron recognised his daughter's temper, too. An unprecedented twinge of sympathy seized Will at the thought of Lady Peyton's brother and father both conspiring against her. Little wonder she preferred to live elsewhere.

Still, that was not his problem. He had less than three weeks to win his wager. Whistling cheerfully, he made his way in search of Lady Peyton, picturing the look on her face when she learned of his plan.

# Chapter Six

'Have you succeeded yet?'

Will had been so engrossed in his musings as he made his way from the north wing that he had not noticed Edmund Fitzallan standing in the hall-way until his friend shouted after him. Despite the weather Edmund was dressed in his heavy riding cloak and hood. Will experienced a momentary pang of envy, wishing he too could spend his days at leisure. He didn't need to ask what Edmund referred to.

'After less than a single day? I'm flattered you credit me with such ability!' Will leaned against the stair banister and inspected his fingernails, assuming an untroubled expression. 'I haven't yet, but I will. In fact, I'm in search of your sister now—do you know where she is?'

Edmund raised his eyebrows and laughed.

'Would I tell you if I did? I might as well throw my stake down the well if I'm going to help you.'

'It's hardly much of a help,' Will replied. 'Helping would be telling her of my excellent character and suggesting she finds comfort from widowhood in my arms. Besides,' he added, 'your father sent me.'

Edmund jerked his thumb towards the stairs. 'I haven't seen her, but try the solar. Mother will be there as usual. It's possible Eleanor might have decided to join her. If she has, she might even be pleased to see you as a result!' He opened the door and turned back with a grin. 'Don't take too long over the matter, Will. There's a new dairymaid over at Collett's farm and I'm eager to try a taste of her cream.'

'Then do so,' Will replied, wincing slightly at Edmund's words. 'You needn't delay on my account.'

Edmund laughed. 'What, and waste the chance to win my money back?'

Will smiled and crossed his arms, 'So you do believe I'll succeed!' he crowed.

The frown Edmund gave as he left kept Will amused as he climbed the stairs to the solar, Lady Fitzallan's domain at the top of the south wing. As Will entered the light, airy room and bowed, Lady Fitzallan lifted her moss-green eyes to notice him. She was not the kind of woman who would wrinkle her nose, but Will always had the distinct impression that if she were not the well-bred niece of a duke she would have done whenever she saw him.

She was sitting close to the fire, her tapestry frame close beside her. Anne sat on a low stool by her feet, a lute in hand which she laid on her lap as she saw Will. Three maids completed the picture of domestic harmony. They had paused in their task of sorting coloured wools and buried their heads together amid hushed giggles when they saw who stood there. Will and Edmund had spent happy evenings drinking and laughing in their company during Will's first month in Tawstott. He hoped the information would not find its way to Lady Peyton, otherwise he might as well pay Edmund and Rob this very day!

Lady Peyton was sitting in the window seat, removed from the company. Her grey woollen dress almost veiled her against the stone wall, a stark contrast to the brightly coloured clothes of her mother and sister. Only her copper-coloured plait prevented her from disappearing entirely. Her feet were drawn up and an embroidery ring lay on her lap though she was staring at the rain. She glanced across when the door opened. Will might have imagined it, but he swore the briefest flash of a smile crossed her face before she looked determinedly out of the window once more.

'May I help you, Master Rudhale?' Lady Fitzallan asked coldly.

'I have a message for your daughter—' he began. Anne's lute fell to the floor with a clatter.

'For Anne? Well, deliver it,' Lady Fitzallan said crisply, frowning at her daughter.

Lady Peyton had turned her head at Anne's reaction. Now she looked at Will, suspicion flashing in her green eyes.

'It is for your elder daughter, my lady,' Will explained. He bowed to Lady Peyton. 'Your father wishes to speak to you, my lady.'

'Tell my husband he must wait, Eleanor is engaged at this moment,' Lady Fitzallan replied before her daughter could respond. Lady Peyton's brow furrowed and Will recognised the temper he had borne the brunt of. He hid a smile and adopted a humble expression as he crossed the room to the window.

'He expressly told me he wishes you to come now,' he said.

Lady Peyton looked past him to the huddle of women.

'I'll come,' she said.

She unwound herself from her seat as Will bent to pick up the crutch that lay at her feet and held it out. Lady Peyton took it, her eyes gleaming and her lips twisting into a conspiratorial smile. Together they left the room.

A welcome blast of cold air hit Eleanor as she left the room. The solar was always far too hot and she had been in danger of falling asleep. She took a deep breath.

'You looked like a lost sailor who needed rescuing from a sea of boredom,' Rudhale murmured as they walked along the corridor.

He wore his customary cocksure expression, as though he viewed himself as a knight errant who had saved Eleanor from certain death rather than a slightly tedious afternoon of sewing.

'What a vivid image. Perhaps you should become a bard when you tire of stewardship,' she suggested.

'I've done many jobs in my time, but I'll admit that isn't one I've considered.' He fixed her with a wicked smile. 'Perhaps I need something to inspire me. Or someone.'

Eleanor blushed at his insinuation. She gave him a hard stare to disguise her discomfiture. 'Isn't it rather beneath you to deliver a summons?' she asked. 'Has Father run out of messenger boys?'

Rudhale raised his eyebrows, though Eleanor could not tell if he was pretending to be offended or if her words had really stung him.

'He asked me to find you,' the steward said. 'I like to take care of important tasks myself wherever possible.'

He sounded sincere, but almost out of habit Eleanor rolled her eyes. Seeing the gesture, Rudhale frowned.

'Do you doubt me, my lady? Haven't you seen enough to convince you I take my duties seriously?'

He sounded genuinely offended now and a needle of shame pricked Eleanor's conscience. Certainly this morning in the granary he had shown more conscientiousness than she would have expected and the meal last night had been excellent. She looked down at her hands, knowing she was being unjust.

'I apologise,' she said quietly. 'Other than our first meeting I have no grounds to doubt you.'

Rudhale nodded his head in satisfaction. His face softened once more and he held out a hand to Eleanor. Recognising the peace gesture, she accepted his arm.

'You seem to have done many different jobs?' she asked curiously. 'Is it the places you tire of or the roles?'

Rudhale looked thoughtful. 'A little of both, perhaps. I have no ties to bind me and one should never pass up the opportunity to experience something new.' He tipped his head to one side and raised an eyebrow, leaving Eleanor wondering what he wanted to experience with her. Rudhale changed the subject, however.

'Aren't you curious why Sir Edgar wants you?' he asked as they walked along the dimly lit corridor.

'Do you know?' Eleanor asked suspiciously. She had thought nothing of it, but now she was alert. She pursed her lips thoughtfully.

The steward tilted his head in acknowledgment. 'I do. I could tell you if you wish,' he suggested teasingly.

'And what would the price of that information be?' Eleanor asked. Her mind went back to his suggestion of a suitable form of payment on the ferry. Before he could answer she said, 'I am more than happy to hear it from my father's own lips. Yours may stay closed.'

Rudhale laughed. 'Do you believe this is some ruse to get you alone?' He cocked his head to one side. 'Is that what you hoped?' he asked with a wily smile.

Eleanor lifted her chin and glared at him. 'Of course not,' she declared, before relenting slightly. 'Though another half-hour of listening to the maids gossiping and I may have taken the chance anyway.'

Rudhale's eyes crinkled at the corners. Eleanor's stomach curled around itself. She dropped her head and walked faster.

The staircase was narrow and the two moved closer together. Momentarily their shoulders brushed, before Rudhale released Eleanor's arm and stood back to let her pass. As she stepped, her crutch slipped on the oak floor. Her ankle gave a twinge and she drew her breath sharply. Instantly Rudhale's hand shot out to her waist, steadying her, fingers spreading wide across her back. His arm was as firm as a rock and a shiver passed through Eleanor's body as she leaned against him. She allowed him to take her weight and hoped he could not tell the sensation his touch had produced in her.

'It would be much more convenient if my parents would inhabit rooms next door to each other instead of at other ends of the building,' she said crossly as she descended the staircase.

'Different floors, different rooms and different interests? It isn't uncommon,' Rudhale remarked lightly.

Eleanor gave a vague murmur of agreement. She had often wondered about her parents' marriage. The ambitious baron had courted and won the niece of a duke, but Eleanor had never known if there was anything beyond the attraction of the dowry. Would her own marriage have been the same? she wondered. Forty years of indifferent conversation and dutiful lovemaking? What had she said to Edmund? *Safe and peaceful?* And utterly devoid of passion. Not for the first time she thanked her stars that the prospect of that was over and done with. Her conscience stabbed her, reminding her of the price Baldwin had paid for her freedom and she winced with guilt.

'Not that I ever intend to marry, but it occurs to me that if I needed to separate myself from my wife that much, the marriage would not be worth speaking of,' Rudhale said thoughtfully.

'You don't intend to?' Surprised, Eleanor glanced at him.

Rudhale gave a careless shrug. 'How long do you think desire would last if your choice was ill made? Why take the chance?'

It was almost as though he had read her thoughts. The certainty with which he spoke of irritated her however. Eleanor's cheeks coloured and the blood thumped in her ears.

'At least if you did marry the choice—and the mistake—would be yours to make,' she replied, more bitterly than she'd intended. 'You will never be sold off for financial advancement, or your family's position. It's easy to speak of love when that is the only factor you need consider.'

It was the first time she had voiced her feelings to anyone so clearly. How did Rudhale constantly provoke her to be so unguarded?

'I didn't mention love,' Rudhale said smoothly. He fixed Eleanor with an unyielding look, his lips curling into a hard smile. 'And it's easy to speak of money when you have it.'

'Is that why you won't marry?' Eleanor asked.

A momentary expression of hardness flitted across Rudhale's face. 'My reasons are my own,' he replied curtly. Eleanor blinked in surprise and, seeing her expression, Rudhale's face softened once more.

'Your father will be waiting. We should hurry.' He strode down the passageway, leaving Eleanor behind and burning with curiosity.

* * *

Sir Edgar was standing looking out of the window when they arrived.

'Ah, you found her, William, well done. Eleanor, good of you to come so quickly,' he said. Rudhale bowed and left the room, closing the door softly behind him.

'Eleanor, as you know our guests will be arriving shortly. There is a great deal to prepare and time is running short.' Sir Edgar gestured to the table that was piled high with rolled scrolls and heavy books. 'You will assist William in making the arrangements.'

'I will *what*?' The exclamation burst from Eleanor before she could stop herself. She folded her arms and looked at her father in astonishment. Whatever reasons she could have imagined, this had never occurred to her.

'You heard me,' Sir Edgar said. 'William is capable, but is stretched to his limit already.' He took one of Eleanor's hands and patted it. It was the same gesture he had done to cajole her ever since her childhood, and despite herself Eleanor smiled. 'Also, it is my opinion that you need something to occupy your days, my dear. It seems to me to be the perfect solution.'

'Father, I don't know…' she began hesitantly.

She stopped as a suspicion occurred to her. 'Does Master Rudhale agree to this?'

'Of course,' her father said airily. 'William is willing to do whatever it takes to make this occasion a success. It reflects on him, too, you see.'

That was true enough. Eleanor wondered if perhaps she was being unfair after all. The few times Rudhale had spoken seriously had been when she had called his abilities as steward into question. Her mind became so tangled whenever he was around that she could well be attributing blame where there was none. But still, the thought of spending more time in his company was unsettling.

'Why does it have to be me?' she asked. 'Why could Edmund not work with him? They are friends after all.'

Sir Edgar gave a mirthless laugh. 'You know I love your brother dearly, as I love all my children, but credit me with knowing you all well. Edmund lacks the character and inclination to accomplish what I require him to do. I would go so far as to say, the wisest thing he has done this far is to befriend William and bring him into my service. At least he will be sure of sensible counsel when he succeeds to the title.'

'I barely know Master Rudhale,' Eleanor protested, clutching for any more ways out of the situation. 'It wouldn't be appropriate for me to spend time alone in his company.'

Sir Edgar tilted his head and gave Eleanor a thoughtful look. 'Eleanor, you are in danger of becoming a recluse. You need to become accustomed to the company of people again. William is a fine young man and very conscientious in his duties. It will do you good to spend time with him. The more I think about this, the more I see only advantages.'

He nodded to himself in satisfaction. Eleanor's heart sank, knowing his mind would not be changed. She sighed her agreement, dropped a curtsy and left the room.

Rudhale was leaning against the wall opposite Sir Edgar's library. His long legs were crossed at the ankles and he was whittling something with a short knife. He stowed them in the pouch at his belt and smiled at Eleanor. She recalled the hints he had dropped as they walked to Sir Edgar's study. In a rush her suspicions regarding the part he played returned. Eleanor put her hands on her hips. She stared at the steward angrily.

'Was this your idea?' she asked.

He stared at her and spread his arms wide. 'My idea? How could it have been? Do you think I have so much influence over your father? You must regard my abilities higher than I thought. I am not sure if I should take the compliment to myself or be offended by the slight on my employer.'

Eleanor narrowed her eyes. The steward's face radiated innocence. Too much innocence by far. She crossed the space between them, her crutch tapping sharply on the stone floor, punctuating the silence with irritated bursts that perfectly echoed her mood.

'I don't believe you,' she said. 'You had something to do with it, I am sure of it.'

'I merely commented to your father that if he could spare me anyone to assist, I would be most grateful. I may have remarked that you appeared in need of distraction. If Sir Edgar chose to combine those two facts, I can hardly be held responsible for that, can I?'

Eleanor cursed inwardly. She knew he would never admit it.

'Lady Peyton.' Rudhale inclined his head and smiled down at Eleanor. The unsettling feeling rose in her stomach again. 'I will not hold it against you if you prefer to return to your woman's work. I shall tell your father you prefer to spend your days sewing with your mother and sister.'

Still holding Eleanor's gaze, Rudhale circled

around her so he was now outside Sir Edgar's door. He continued smoothly, 'I am sure he will understand and I shall manage as best as I can. I would not want you to feel under obligation to do this if you feel the task is too daunting.'

Too daunting! Eleanor's pride flared at the implied insult and blood rushed to her cheeks. The jibe about woman's work had been bad enough, but she would not stand by and be held as incapable.

'Wait!' she cried.

Rudhale paused, his hand halfway to the door. Eleanor straightened her shoulders and looked him squarely in the face.

'I'll do it. I will work with you.'

Rudhale nodded and Eleanor saw a glint of triumph in his eyes as though he had known all along she would agree. She cursed inwardly, realising how easily she had been tricked. She bit her tongue. It was too late now to take it back.

'Good,' Rudhale said. 'Now I am afraid I must leave early in the morning. I am returning to Frome to oversee the wine order and will be gone for two nights.'

With a bow Rudhale sauntered away. Eleanor watched him leave. She returned to her room thoughtfully. An emotion she had not felt for so long surfaced, so unfamiliar it took her a moment to name it. Then it came to her.

Anticipation.

# Chapter Seven

Master Rudhale had left Tawstott Mote by the time Eleanor woke the following morning. She had slept badly, her head muddled by a dream in which Sir Baldwin silently tallied up the months since his death on a wax tablet that melted in the rain. Arriving in the Great Hall, her mood was not improved by finding Lady Fitzallan waiting with a disapproving face.

'There is something for you,' she announced, indicating a note leaning against a candlestick on the high table. The writing was not a script Eleanor was familiar with and she decided it could only belong to Master Rudhale. She studied the fold of paper curiously, half-wondering if it would contain declarations of affection, or propositions of an indecent nature.

She broke the seal and read the brief message. It was a list of tasks that needed to be accomplished before the arrival of the guests, annotated with suggestions of how to go about matters. The tone was formal but polite. Other than the implication that Eleanor needed such detailed instructions the letter contained nothing improper whatsoever. She smiled wryly at her own foolishness. Really, she needed to master her imagination where the steward was concerned.

She looked up to find her mother watching her closely.

'Why is that servant communicating with you?' Lady Fitzallan asked sternly.

Eleanor explained the situation Sir Edgar had thrown her into.

'Your father insists on employing someone of low birth in such an important position and that is his decision. It is intolerable, however, that he should expect you to spend time in his company.' Lady Fitzallan sniffed. 'You refused, of course.'

It was a statement, not a question.

'No, I agreed,' Eleanor said, lifting her chin and meeting her mother's eyes. Lady Fitzallan's eyes bored into her daughter.

'I manage an estate and work with my own steward on a daily basis,' Eleanor said calmly. 'I am more than happy to work with Master Rudhale.'

Lady Fitzallan straightened her back even further and looked frostily at her daughter. 'If you ever hope to wed again, your time would be better spent resting so that when Duke Roland's entourage arrive you do not look so sallow and tired. Otherwise a low-born servant will be the best suitor you can hope to attract.'

'Master Rudhale is not merely a servant!' Lady Fitzallan's tone was so contemptuous that Eleanor spoke without thinking. She added quickly, 'I have no intention of attracting any suitors, highborn or otherwise. I am perfectly happy as I am.'

Lady Fitzallan stood. 'Remember to whom you are speaking, Eleanor! I will forgive your tone, but this subject is not finished with.'

She swept from the room, leaving Eleanor sitting alone. Yesterday Sir Edgar had hinted that she needed to become more used to men; now her mother's words sent a chill through her. There would be further conversations she had no doubt, though she would evade them as long as she was able.

Moodily Eleanor turned the paper over in her hands. Both parents had now invoked Rudhale's name in their criticism of her lack of husband. No doubt the steward would be unsurprised at Lady Fitzallan's reaction. Eleanor had noticed the coldness in her mother's voice when he had brought the message yesterday. She wondered what Rudhale would say if he knew Sir Edgar suggested Eleanor use him to familiarise herself with men.

She imagined what her father would say if he knew how familiar the steward had proposed they become and laughed softly. The young boy sweeping the hearth jumped at the sound and looked at her questioningly. Eleanor shook her head and he continued with his work. Her mood brightening, Eleanor reread the letter and began to plan her course of action.

For the next three days it did nothing but rain. Ordinarily the women of the household were confined indoors, but thanks to Rudhale's list Eleanor was able to escape the trial of spending her days with the other womenfolk in the solar. She borrowed Sir Edgar's litter and paid trips to the town and estate farms, silently thanking Rudhale for the means to escape the house.

Eleanor threw herself into the tasks with pleasure. Rooms needed to be allocated for the guests and their servants and entertainment arranged for the evenings. It was little wonder the steward had required assistance. She did not even mind Edmund and Anne teasing her whenever they came across her investigating the contents of the linen stores or fretting over the quantities of fine beeswax candles. Lady Fitzallan continued to voice her disapproval, but with so much to command her attention, Eleanor was able to avoid her mother's presence as much as possible.

'William will have no job to return to if Eleanor has her way,' Edmund remarked to Sir Edgar on the third afternoon. They sat by the fire as Eleanor walked slowly around the Great Hall, gesturing with the crutch she now barely needed as she supervised the vast iron candelabra being loaded with candles and hoisted aloft.

'I'm sure Eleanor has no designs on William's station, but mayhap *you* could learn something from her dedication to the task,' the baron warned his son with a wink. 'If you are not careful, William will be seeking a position in her household and leaving us before you are baron.'

An odd flutter passed through Eleanor's stomach at the thought of Rudhale joining her household. Edmund scowled and Eleanor smiled at their joking, happy to be busy. She added her own notes to Rudhale's list in preparation for his return, secretly satisfied that he would find no fault with her labours when he returned that evening.

* * *

From mid-afternoon onwards Eleanor found herself on a path that inevitably led to the court-yard or Outer Hall. Once she even made the short journey to the stables to enquire whether enough room had been set aside for the visitors' mounts, but found no returning rider there. When the rain grew heavier and she could no longer remain out-doors, she settled on to a low seat in the Outer Hall, finally admitting to herself that she was waiting for Rudhale to return.

She read his message once more, determined to catch him as soon as he entered, reasoning that the sooner he was informed of all she had done, the easier his mind would be. The slate sky dark-ened to ink, but Rudhale did not come.

By next morning the rain had become a driving sleet that penetrated to the bone. Rudhale still had not returned by mid-afternoon and Eleanor had neither the pretext nor inclination to spend her time in the draughty Outer Hall.

She was standing at the top of the stairs in the north wing, a frown on her face, when footsteps behind her made her heart stop. The corridor housed the sleeping quarters of the male servants, though all were busy at work and at this time of day the rooms should have been deserted. She turned to see who it was and almost collided with her brother.

'I did not expect to find you here,' Edmund said, grinning at her surprise. He narrowed his eyes. 'Are you meeting a secret lover?'

'Don't be so foolish!' Eleanor said scornfully. She sighed. 'I fear we don't have enough space for the duke's retinue to sleep. Already the men will be sharing six to a room.'

She returned her attention to the plan in her hand as Edmund came to stand beside her. He took the parchment and studied it. 'You haven't filled this room,' he commented, pointing to the room marked as Rudhale's.

Eleanor glanced towards the chamber in question. 'I did not want to presume Master Rudhale would be willing to share with strangers. It does not befit his position, nor does sharing with the common servants. I think I shall have to leave the matter for him to sort on his return.'

'Oh, I'm sure William won't have any difficulty in finding somewhere to lay his head for a few nights.' Edmund grinned. He raised an eyebrow and smiled at Eleanor. 'In fact, I'd go as far as to say he needn't warm the same sheets more than once if he chooses.'

Edmund's meaning was clear and Eleanor blushed. She snatched the parchment from her brother's hand and crumpled it.

'He's your friend. Let him share your chamber.' She swept her skirts into her hand and descended the narrow staircase leaving Edmund alone, his gleeful laughter following after her.

After that, some of the pleasure went out of Eleanor's tasks. She quarrelled with Anne, snapped at Jennet and had to bite her tongue when Lady Fitzallan began once more hinting that Eleanor's appearance was lacking in charm. This last barb stung her deeply. She was tired from her efforts, of course, but a glance in the polished bronze mirror assured her that she was far from being pale and ill looking. Her cheeks contained more colour and her eyes were brighter than ever.

Mother was being malicious, she told herself as she walked to Sir Edgar's library. Her father was absent so she helped herself to a book from his shelf. She studied the title with interest: *The Romaunt of the Rose*. Lady Fitzallan would no doubt disapprove of her daughters reading such frivolous material, so as an afterthought she took a larger book as well.

She carried them to a seat in the Great Hall and settled on to one of the padded seats in front of the roaring fire. She became so engrossed in the poem, her cheeks flaming and her heart racing at the words, that she barely heard the door swing open. It was only when it slammed shut with a heavy thud and footsteps echoed across the stone floor that Eleanor realised she was not alone. She glanced up to see a hooded figure heading towards her and recognised the wine-coloured travelling cloak the steward had been wearing on the ferry.

Guiltily she slipped the book of poetry under the folds of her skirt and pulled the larger volume on to her lap. She composed her features—naturally the heat of the fire would explain any untoward colour in her face—and called his name. 'Master Rudhale!'

Will stopped and lowered the hood of his cloak. He had been sure the hall was empty when he entered, however Lady Peyton was sitting by the fire. She was dressed yet again in a grey gown and was half-concealed by the shadows. Her eyes followed him across the room as he walked towards her. She gestured to the seat opposite hers and Will sank into it wearily, dropping his bag at his feet.

'My apologies, I did not notice you, my lady.' Perhaps it was his imagination, but her disposition seemed brighter. Her cheeks were flushed, as though she had been exerting herself, though quite how when she was sitting here alone, he could not imagine. 'You should wear colour more often,' he said boldly, 'you are in danger of disappearing altogether.'

Lady Peyton's lips curled into a small smile. 'Something akin to your cloak?' she asked. 'I don't believe that would become me.'

Will unclasped the buckle at his neck and swung the garment from his shoulders. He stood to hang it on the iron hook by the fireplace and held his hands to the fire. The ride had been hard and his limbs were stiff and cold.

'Perhaps not,' he conceded with a laugh. 'If you had asked I would have brought you something from town, though. A veil, perhaps, or ribbons?'

'What makes you think I need finery?' Lady Peyton asked, her voice suddenly guarded.

Will's eyes ran over her dress and up to her hair, pulled back into a plain knot at the back. 'No reason, other than I thought you might wish for something brighter. Perhaps I shall bring you something anyway next time I go. Grey is too dull for midwinter.'

Lady Peyton pulled herself up haughtily. 'I wear grey out of respect for the memory of my husband.'

To Will it was as though a door had slammed behind her eyes. He bit down his exasperation.

'Well,' he said, reaching for his bag, 'if you would not accept a gift, will you at least take a cup of wine with me? I have been riding half the day and would welcome something to warm me through.'

Will walked to the table and filled two cups. As he handed one to Lady Peyton their fingers momentarily touched. Hers were warm and left the sensation of heat on his skin where they brushed against him.

'Did you complete your business?' Lady Peyton asked politely.

Will grinned triumphantly. 'I did.' He leaned forward in his chair, eager to share his news. 'My old master indeed plans to send a pair of ships to Gascony to buy from King Henry's new vineyards. He's offered me the chance to invest. If I can get together a large enough stake, this could be my chance of making my fortune.'

'Will you manage, do you think?' Lady Peyton asked.

'I hope to be able to,' Will replied. *If I win my wager, that is,* he added to himself. He reminded himself that there was still much groundwork to be done in that respect and smiled at her warmly.

'And then what? Would you travel to France?'

'Not if I can help it. Sailing is too slow. I prefer

to do my travelling on horseback,' Will said. 'A few months working on the river barges between Frome and Bristol was as close to a sailor's life as I want to get. Wherever I go next it won't be by boat!'

Lady Peyton regarded him seriously. 'Next? Are you already thinking about leaving? You don't seem able to stay anywhere for long.'

Will smiled. Could it be she would be sad to see him leave? That was progress. 'Not just yet, though you're right, I haven't yet found the place that can anchor me.' His eyes flicked to his travelling cloak. 'I'm not sure I ever will,' he admitted.

'Or the person?' Lady Peyton asked.

Will looked into her clear, green eyes. 'Or the person,' he agreed gruffly. As he glanced down his eye fell on the book on Lady Peyton's lap. Her sleeve obscured the title and he grinned, sensing an opportunity.

'You read,' he remarked.

Lady Peyton nodded. 'Does that surprise you? I could hardly have understood your note if I did not.'

'For pleasure, I mean.' Will settled back into his chair. He stretched his legs out until they were almost touching the folds of her skirts. 'I'll wager

I can guess what you have been reading,' he suggested. 'Not the title, but the subject at least.'

'What would the stake be?' Lady Peyton asked suspiciously. She leant back against the wall and folded her arms across her body, hugging the book to her chest. Will tried not to stare too noticeably at the soft mounds of her breasts, pushed up and just visible over the edge of the volume.

'The same thing I asked for before.' Will grinned. 'A single kiss.'

Lady Peyton rolled her eyes to the ceiling and huffed. The gesture was so unexpected from a high-born lady that Will burst out laughing. She glared at him.

'I decline your terms,' she said. 'Why are you so insistent?'

'Because you are beautiful and I'd like to kiss you. Why does the thought scare you?' Will countered.

Lady Peyton sat upright. She kept the title hidden, Will noticed with delight. 'It doesn't scare me,' she said firmly.

Will leant forward. So close that he could see the flecks of green that danced in her eyes.

'Then accept the wager,' he breathed.

He lifted his cup, holding her gaze, and took a deep draught of wine. He waited, letting silence sit between them. Lady Peyton frowned and bit her bottom lip. Will pictured himself slowly tasting it and his heart quickened.

'Not for that prize. Name another, Master Rudhale,' Lady Peyton insisted.

'I see you no longer have your crutch so I judge your ankle must be healing. For a dance then,' Will said. 'If I win, you promise the first dance at the midwinter feast will be with me. And call me by my name,' he added on impulse.

'Very well. And if *I* win, you will not ask me again to kiss you,' Lady Peyton replied.

A ripple of triumph stirred in Will's belly. A dance invariably led to so much more. He nodded and raised his cup in salute to her. She did the same and they both drank, eyes meeting over the top of their cups.

'You were reading poetry,' he announced. 'Some tale of love and trials of knighthood. Of advances spurned and hearts broken. All women love poetry and I have yet to meet one who can resist the prospect of love triumphant.'

Lady Peyton's face froze. 'All the women you have known?' she asked icily.

'Very few,' Will assured her hastily. *And fewer still who mattered.* The thought took him by surprise. He held his hand out. 'The book, if you please.'

Without speaking, Lady Peyton held the book towards him obediently. He opened the hidebound volume and read the title aloud.

'Geoffrey of Monmouth. *Historia Regum Britanniae.*'

'Not all women have time for foolish love stories, Master Rudhale,' Lady Peyton said softly.

Will laughed gently through his disappointment. 'I shall leave you to your kings, my lady,' he said, handing the book back. He bowed, picked up his bag and left the hall. Lady Peyton had appeared pleased to see him and his spirits were high even though he had lost the wager.

Will knew nothing of Sir Baldwin, but the man must have been a very paragon of manhood for his widow to be grieving so deeply still, but surely by now she must be craving another man's touch. He had promised not to ask her for a kiss, but what did that matter? There were so many ways of asking that did not require words, after all.

## Chapter Eight

'I tell you for the last time: I will not countenance a peacock!'

Eleanor folded her arms and stared defiantly at Master Rudhale.

'It is too…too…'

'Too grandiose?' the steward suggested.

Eleanor nodded. Even for a duke's feast the idea of so over-elaborate a centrepiece would be too gaudy.

Rudhale gestured to the rough sketches of beasts and birds that littered the table between them. His eyes glinted with amusement. 'Which animal would suit your nature, I wonder? A timid doe, or perhaps a soft brown rabbit?'

Eleanor's lips curled into a smile at his teasing. Rudhale had disputed almost every decision she had made in his absence. Ordinarily she would have bridled at such a challenge to her authority, but somehow his arrogance had softened. He had done it with such good humour that she had not minded and found herself responding in kind. She conceded some, he gave way on others and two days had passed with Eleanor enjoying every tussle.

They had been arguing for an age into the late afternoon as they sat in the Great Hall rejecting design after design. Eleanor was almost beyond caring what form the marchpane centrepiece would take, but the discussion had been a welcome diversion on a gloomy day and she was determined to win the battle of wills.

'The peacock represents yourself, I suppose?' she countered with a wicked smile.

'As if I need such adornments!' Rudhale looked at her with playful indignation and brushed imagined dust from his plain linen tunic.

Eleanor's eyes followed the passage of his hands as they moved across his broad chest. She found herself wondering what it would feel like to brush her fingers across the firm contours and her throat constricted. Disconcerted by the thought, she folded her arms and spoke with mock severity. 'If I had known you to be so argumentative, I would have worked swifter while you were absent and made all the plans alone.'

'If I had known how rapidly you would have run through my list, I would have made it shorter and left you instead to weave with your mother!' Rudhale mused. 'Forcing me to bed down with your brother indeed!'

Eleanor's smile dropped and she looked away from him, picking the first sheet her hand rested on. Quite why Edmund's allusion to Rudhale's bedfellows caused her any concern at all was something Eleanor preferred not to consider. Of course the steward could have—and probably did have—any number of women with a click of his fingers. She pushed the image to the back of her mind, feeling a brief swell of satisfaction that she had not added to the numbers.

Rudhale left his seat and walked round the table to stand behind Eleanor. He leaned over her shoulder and studied the sheet in her hand. Eleanor looked at what she was holding for the first time. A pair of turtledoves stared back at her, their heads together as they sat atop a fruit-laden tree. Her throat tightened briefly as she gazed at the devoted lovers. Rudhale took the paper from her.

'We are agreed?' He smiled, though Eleanor had not spoken. She nodded. He leaned back against the table beside Eleanor, his hand almost touching her own. 'I knew I could rely upon you to find the perfect choice, my lady.' His face grew serious, taking Eleanor by surprise. 'I give you my thanks for your help. In this and all you have done to aid me.'

He inclined his head towards her respectfully. The muscles in his throat tightened, revealing a contour that was smooth and taut where his beard ended. Eleanor's eyes traced the line of Rudhale's neck down to where the tangled ends of his hair brushed against the hollow of his collarbone, visible at the laced neck of his tunic. The steward cleared his throat quietly and with a start Eleanor realised she had been staring at him in silence for who could tell how long.

'For three years I have been mistress of my own household. Did you doubt I would be capable of organising such affairs?' she said brusquely to cover her embarrassment. Rudhale's eyes widened at her tone and shame flooded her. 'I give you my thanks, too, for asking me to help you,' she said more gently. 'It was you who thought of it, wasn't it, not Father?'

'I had no doubt you would be perfectly capable of following my suggestions.' Rudhale nodded. He raised one eyebrow, his blue eyes dancing again. 'I am completely sure you could admirably fulfil anything I asked of you.'

Eleanor's heart quickened and she regarded him suspiciously. However seemingly innocent his words Eleanor was sure they had a double meaning. She scolded herself for the unjust thought. Since Eleanor had won Rudhale's wager the steward had kept his promise to cease asking for her attentions. In the hours they had spent secluded together making preparations, his attitude had never been less than courteous. Unexpectedly she found herself almost regretting she had not been obliged to dance with him after all.

Rudhale's eyes abruptly slid sideways. His hands closed tightly about the edge of the table, then he stood and moved away. Eleanor twisted in her chair to find Anne standing in the doorway.

Anne looked from Rudhale to her sister and her cheeks flamed. Rudhale bowed his head in greeting and her eyes glowed. For a moment she looked both a child and a woman and a knot of anxiety tightened in Eleanor's stomach.

Anne walked to the table and stood beside Eleanor's chair in the place Rudhale had vacated. 'Mother sent me to find you,' she told Eleanor. 'She wants to speak to you.' She reached for the paper in Rudhale's hand and cocked her head to peer at it. 'May I see?' she asked coyly, moving closer to him. Rudhale held the paper out to her stiffly.

'Anne, go and tell Mother I will come shortly,' Eleanor said crisply. 'We have not quite finished here.' The younger girl's shoulders sagged as she left the room without a backwards glance.

Rudhale drew Eleanor's chair back to help her rise. She faced him, their bodies close, barely an arm's reach between them.

'Master Rudhale, before I leave I must speak to you about a delicate matter. I suspect my sister is... That she...' She looked away, feeling awkward. 'I think she has certain feelings towards you.'

Rudhale ran both hands through his hair and nodded. 'I believe you are right,' he admitted ruefully.

'Have you given her any hope in that regard?' Eleanor pressed on, feeling bolder.

The steward folded his arms across his broad chest. 'Not in the slightest,' he declared. He gazed at Eleanor through half-lowered lids, fixing her with a frank smile. 'I swear to you I have no interest in your father's younger daughter.'

Eleanor's heart gave an unwilling flutter and

she could not ignore the hint behind his words this time. She exhaled angrily. 'Do not jest about this!'

'I know you have a poor opinion of me, but your sister is a child! I have never given her any indication her feelings are reciprocated,' Rudhale said earnestly.

Eleanor stalked past Rudhale. She paused at the door and whipped round to face him. 'Do more than that,' she said firmly. 'Make it clear they are not.'

Lady Fitzallan was waiting when Eleanor entered the solar. As she sat on the low stool beside Anne, Lady Fitzallan clapped her hands and dismissed her maids.

'I have received a letter from my uncle's wife,' Lady Fitzallan announced, fixing her daughters with sharp green eyes. 'Her Grace informs me that there will be three knights who are in a position to marry. They are coming with the hope of choosing brides. I expect you both to accept an offer of marriage if one is forthcoming. Anne, you will clearly be entering into a rather longer arrangement, but, Eleanor, I see no reason why matters cannot be concluded speedily.'

Eleanor's stomach heaved as though a fist had been driven into it.

'I see every reason!' she burst out.

Lady Fitzallan rose from her seat. 'Anne, leave us.'

Anne left the room with a backwards glance at Eleanor who stood rigid, her hands knots of tension at her side.

'I refuse to be part of this! What does Father say?' Eleanor asked, her voice tight in her throat.

'Your father is in agreement that you need a husband,' Lady Fitzallan said. She reached a hand to Eleanor's shoulder, but the gesture could barely have been any less comforting. Eleanor shrugged out of her mother's reach.

'Sir Baldwin was the best connection your father was able to make at the time, but he was hardly what I had hoped for you. This is a great opportunity to marry well. I want a good marriage for you, Eleanor. A good man. In another year or two you will be too old to be considered by anyone worth having.'

'I do not care to marry anyone *worth having*,' Eleanor said stubbornly. Her legs shook as she stood in front of her mother. 'I am still in mourning. I do not wish to marry again.'

Half a head taller than Eleanor, Lady Fitzallan glared down, bright spots of anger appearing on her high cheekbones. 'After all this time? You have grieved for Baldwin for longer than most wives and yours was not even a true marriage!'

Tears began to fall, smarting on Eleanor's cheeks. The tears she cried were as much for the girl whose future had died alongside her husband as for Baldwin himself.

'True or not, it is the only marriage I intend to have,' she retorted, wiping her hand harshly across her face.

'You always knew this time would come. Baldwin's estate needs an heir. It is your responsibility to provide one. It was by our leave and Duke Roland's that you were allowed to remain living at Rowland's Mount and the lands did not revert immediately. The only reason your marriage was not declared invalid was because there was no one else to manage his lands and it suited everyone involved,' Lady Fitzallan said calmly.

'And it suits me still,' Eleanor said. She screwed her fists tighter in an attempt to keep her voice from trembling. 'I married to make family connections once and I would rather live alone and die a maiden than spend the rest of my life with someone I do not love!'

Without waiting for permission to leave she stormed out of the solar. At the bottom of the stairs she stopped and leaned against the wall,

her head and palms pressed against the cool stone.
Her heart pounded in her chest. Jennet would be
waiting in her room and the thought of her maid
fussing around was more than Eleanor could stand
when she craved solitude.

She made her way through the house, searching
for somewhere she could sit and regain control of
her emotions, but every space she found was occupied. At home she would walk along the shore, but
there was nowhere as peaceful here. Conscious of
her red eyes she kept her head down as she hurried
through the Great Hall and headed for the courtyard. Dimly she heard Master Rudhale call her
name, but she shook her head and waved a hand
as though to brush him away.

The sun, which had barely broken through the
heavy clouds all day, had nearly disappeared
below the archway, turning the buildings grey. Eleanor shivered as the icy wind hit her. She almost
went back for her cloak, but the sound of voices
and laughter drifted to her from the Outer Hall.
She shook her head and made her way round the
side of the house to the walled garden where she
hoped to find some protection from the weather,
and threw herself on to a stone bench.

Eleanor pulled a sprig of rosemary and fitfully
ripped the leaves off one by one, letting them

drop on to the ground with a trembling hand. She drew her knees up to her chest and hugged herself tightly to ward off the cold. She stared into the shadows and her stomach twisted again as she thought of the argument with her mother. Her eyes swam with tears that were hot in the biting wind. How long would it be before she was missed and summoned back to the house? She drew deep breaths, fighting the urge to run to her chamber, pack her belongings and return home.

'Lady Peyton?'

The voice was low and unexpected. Eleanor gave a start. She spun round to find William Rudhale standing by the far end of the bench, a large bundle under one arm. Eleanor bowed her head quickly, unwilling for him to see the evidence of her tears, and wiped them away with the back of her hand.

'Why are you here?' Eleanor asked suspiciously. 'Did my mother send you to find me?'

'Nobody sent me,' he answered softly. 'You looked distressed so I decided to follow you.'

He gestured to the bench and raised an eyebrow. After a moment's hesitation Eleanor nodded and the steward sat down beside her.

He unfurled the bundle that he carried and Eleanor recognised his voluminous red cloak.

'I thought you might need some shelter from the

wind. It is no weather to be out in without something to keep you warm.'

Eleanor's lip trembled and she bit down on it.
'Thank you,' she whispered, her voice catching
in her throat.

Rudhale leaned across and gently wrapped the
cloak around Eleanor's shoulders. Their eyes met
and he gave a slight smile, as though being caught
in the act of a kindness embarrassed him. He
brushed a stray lock of hair from her cheek with
fingers that left a trail of heat across her skin.

At this gesture of kindness, Eleanor's emotions
finally overwhelmed her. She put her head in her
hands and burst into sobs, not caring that the steward saw or what he might think. Her frame shook
with each fresh rush of tears. She was dimly aware
of Rudhale's arm slipping around her shoulders as
he drew her head down on to his chest.

Eleanor stiffened momentarily as the unfamiliar
closeness provoked feelings that were much more
alarming than her grief. Rudhale's hand found a
home in the small of her back and she melted willingly against him. She could not say for how long
she cried, conscious only of warmth, of Rudhale's
soothing wordless murmurs as she let her sadness
flood out, and of the comfort of his strong arms
around her body.

\* \* \*

Will leaned against the back of the stone bench and looked thoughtfully down at the head nestled against his chest as he waited for her tears to subside. He had answered Lady Peyton's question truthfully, if omitting certain motives could be called truth. When she had half-stumbled through the Great Hall his mind became alert and he had followed her. A woman in such obvious agitation would need consoling and Will knew well that when a pair of arms might offer initial comfort, a pair of lips usually provided the final solace.

Now he was unsure. He did not know what had caused her sorrow, but whatever Lady Fitzallan had said to her daughter had struck deeply. He frowned and stroked a hand in small circles across Lady Peyton's shoulder blades protectively.

Will bent his head and caught the scent of lemon balm in her hair. He closed his eyes and inhaled deeply, drinking in the sweetness, and tightened his embrace, drawing Lady Peyton closer. She shifted against him, her body half-twisted so they were face-to-face. Her slender frame heaved with each breathy sob, inadvertently pushing her full breasts invitingly against Will's chest. Will's breath stuck in his throat as longing rushed through him.

Lady Peyton's movements became smaller as

her weeping gradually ceased until she rested motionless in Will's arms. Aware of every curve of
her body that touched his, Will reluctantly loosened his hold. Lady Peyton sat upright, but made
no move to escape his embrace. With fingers that
prickled at every touch Will gently brushed a stray
hair from her cheek.

He should kiss her now. He sensed she would
not resist. He could almost taste her lips as he bent
his head towards her, but as he did Lady Peyton
looked into his eyes. Even in the half-light her eyes
were a vivid green. They were rimmed with red
from weeping and so full of anguish that within a
hair's breadth of winning his wager Will stopped.

'Tell me what's wrong,' he said softly.

Lady Peyton's face twisted with misery and she
looked away, shaking her head. She stood, but Will
caught her hands. They were icy cold and tiny in
his warm grasp.

'Let me help you,' he urged, tugging her beside
him once again.

She shook her head, tears brimming once more.
'No one can help, there is nothing to be done.'

Will listened in silence as she told him of Lady
Fitzallan's announcement.

'When my husband died I gained freedom that
I never expected to have. Have you any idea what

it is like to spend your life knowing that your destiny is in someone else's hands?'

Will laughed mirthlessly. 'Every day! I work for my living, my lady. Serving your father buys my bread. My only freedom is the choice to starve!'

'But not for ever,' Lady Peyton answered. 'You'll be rich one day when your wine venture succeeds. Your chance of independence lies ahead of you, Master Rudhale.'

'I'm touched by your faith in me.' He smiled. 'With luck I shall be my own master one day. Luck and money, that is!' He ran his thumb across the palm of Lady Peyton's hand. She squeezed his hand briefly in response and Will felt the flicker of desire spring to life once more. For one fleeting moment he found himself envious of the as-yet-unknown noble with the wealth and title to win her hand.

'Would it be so bad to marry again?' he asked.

'I never expected love, but I thought I would be content. Now I am alone, but I have peace.' Lady Peyton withdrew her hands and sighed. Her eyes were bright and tore at Will's heart. 'I don't even know why I am discussing this with you. You've never married.'

'No,' Will answered. His heart twisted. A lump formed in his throat, causing his voice to sound unusually thick to his ears. He looked at the woman who had poured her secrets out to him and an urge to confide in her overcame him. Impulsively he told her what he had admitted to so few in his life.

'Though I almost did.'

## Chapter Nine

Eleanor blinked. Moments before she had been engulfed with sadness and despair. Now she burned with interest.

'You were married?' she asked in surprise.

The idea was so unlikely. Try as she might, Eleanor could not imagine the steward heading eagerly towards matrimony, nor could she picture the sort of woman who had persuaded him there.

'No, I said I was *almost* married,' Rudhale replied, his face solemn. He closed his mouth abruptly. His lips were pressed together tightly, barely visible beneath his beard.

'But you did not go through with it?' Her heart gave a twinge of envy at the ease with which men could extricate themselves from such situations. 'Perhaps you could teach me how to escape an undesirable betrothal,' she said darkly.

A shadow crossed Rudhale's face. 'I should not

have mentioned it. My past has no bearing on your situation. You are no longer a child, though. If you do not wish to remarry, then say so.'

'I did,' Eleanor pointed out archly. She leant back beside Rudhale on the bench. 'It isn't that easy. Baldwin died without an heir. The estate has been in his family for four generations, but if I have no children it will revert to Duke Roland's control. How can I let that happen?'

'Your children would not be his heirs, though,' Rudhale pointed out.

'No,' she conceded with a sad smile. 'But it is the best I can do to stop it passing to a stranger. Besides, it isn't just Baldwin's estate, it's my home. I don't expect you to understand; you have no ties anywhere.'

Rudhale's brow knotted and his hands found Eleanor's once more. She was not certain he was even aware of the movement, but at the gesture Eleanor became suddenly self-conscious.

She had cried in front of this man, spilling out confidences that must be of no concern to him. Worse than that, she had permitted him to hold her so intimately. More than merely permitted: she had wanted his touch from the moment he had put the cloak around her shoulders. She cast her eyes downwards, caught in the memory of Rudhale's hands on her body in case he inadvertently saw the desire his gesture of comfort had awakened in her.

Even as Eleanor's heart raced, her belly churned at the thought that if anyone had found them together in such a manner it would have been ruinous for them both. Her eyes darted from side to side, as though she might see people hiding behind every bush and she hastily withdrew her hands from Rudhale's.

He wrinkled his forehead in confusion, then laughed abruptly, though there was no malice in his tone. The sound cut through the silence and once again Eleanor glanced around.

'Don't worry, my lady. No one is going to find you doing anything untoward.'

'But if someone should come…' Eleanor began.

Rudhale held up a hand to stop her. 'Then I shall say you and I were gathering greenery to decorate the hall. Who would dare contradict me?' He reached behind him and twisted a small twig of yew from the hedge and held it to his breast, his face a picture of innocence. 'See. Now your honour will be safe.'

He looked so comical Eleanor couldn't help smiling. 'Even so, I must get back before I am missed,' she said. She gathered her skirts in one hand and made to stand, but Rudhale caught her gently by the arm.

'Your eyes are still red,' Rudhale said. 'Wait a while longer or people will indeed question what has occurred. You're warm enough, aren't you?'

Eleanor nodded and settled back alongside him on the bench. Her unease faded as they sat in silence. Rudhale shifted and his arm brushed against Eleanor's. She felt her breath catch in her throat, aware of every movement he made. Wrapping his cloak closer around her body, Eleanor took a deep breath and caught a scent that she had first noticed while she had been in Rudhale's arms: wood smoke and something else, both spicy and earthy, that reminded Eleanor of the deep brownish-red of autumn leaves. She had not been close enough to him before to detect it, but now she would always associate it with the steward instantly.

She glanced thoughtfully at Rudhale, who was methodically stripping the leaves from the yew branch and paying her no attention. He had been about to kiss her, Eleanor was certain. She had recognised in his eyes the same hunger she had seen on the ferry and the passion that was simmering below the surface. Something had stopped him and she could not say if she was relieved or sorry. Being in his arms had been more than simply comforting and she could not have sworn that this time she would have refused his attempt so wholeheartedly. Her heart skipped a beat and she shifted slightly, widening the gap between them to a more fitting distance.

'Thank you for your cloak, Master Rudhale. It was a kind gesture.' She hoped her voice did not sound as unsteady aloud as it did in her ears.

'You are welcome,' the steward said with a smile. 'And my friends call me Will.'

'Are we friends?' Eleanor asked, a note of uncertainty creeping into her voice. 'I know so little about you.'

Rudhale raised an eyebrow questioningly. 'Perhaps not, though I would like us to be.' He spread his hands wide, leaning against the back of the bench. 'What would you like to know?'

His openness was unnerving. Eleanor's curiosity at his earlier revelation rose up again and her words tumbled out before she thought better of them.

'Will you tell me about your betrothal?' she asked impulsively.

She realised as soon as she spoke that the question had been a mistake. Rudhale's face turned to granite. He sat abruptly forward and placed his chin in his hands. His hair as usual was loose and covered his face. Wishing she could bite the words back, Eleanor shifted uncomfortably beside him.

'There is little to tell. It ended before I left Tawstott to go north.' His voice was low but clipped.

He would have been almost the age she was now and she had not expected it to have happened here. She knew she would be looking around Tawstott Town, wondering who the woman was for ever.

'Why did you leave her?' she asked.

Rudhale stood abruptly, turning his back on Eleanor. When he faced her again his eyes were cold. Eleanor gripped the edge of the bench, surprised at the change in him. 'My marriage would have been—was from start to finish—a mistake, and it is not one I intend to repeat.'

'Forgive me, I meant no offence,' she mumbled.

Rudhale's eyes bored into her, ice blue in the fading light. He held an arm out to Eleanor. 'It's colder now and you will have been missed. We should return.'

They walked in silence back to the house. Rudhale held his arm rigid, his form so different from the warm embrace Eleanor had so eagerly yielded to. It was merely a courtesy and shame set her cheeks on fire. She'd had no right to pry. As they neared the courtyard Rudhale stopped.

'With your permission I shall leave you here, my lady. I have business with my brother.'

'Of course,' Eleanor said. Rudhale dropped his arm, but Eleanor did not relinquish her hold. He looked at her with distrust.

'I owe you an apology. I had no right to demand such information from you,' Eleanor muttered. 'It was a poor way to repay your kindness.'

Rudhale's expression softened. 'You owe me no apology. Some things are best not dwelt upon, that is all.' He bowed. 'Goodnight, Lady Peyton.'

'Goodnight…William,' Eleanor said quietly.

Rudhale paused mid-bow. He lifted his eyes to Eleanor's. A slight smile played about his lips. He straightened and, without another word, walked back through the archway in the direction of the mews. Eleanor watched until he vanished into the night. Hugging his cloak around herself tightly, she walked the final steps to the house.

In the Outer Hall Eleanor removed William's cloak, hanging it over a peg where he would find it on his return. From the Great Hall the sounds of conversations and laughter drifted to her ears. She arranged the folds of fabric carefully, feeling slightly guilty that she had not thought to return it to William before he set out to the falconer's dwelling. He could have asked for it back, of course, though he had not appeared to feel the cold. She remembered the heat of his body as he held her and a hot shiver ran up her spine.

There was a brief lull in conversation in the Great Hall and the sound of lute playing filled the air. Eleanor slipped through the door and made her way to the dais at the end, excusing her lateness.

Lady Fitzallan turned cold eyes on her daughter as she passed by. Had her mother told Sir Edgar of their quarrel? She kept her head bowed and quickly ate the thick rabbit stew that was placed before her. As soon as the meal was over she excused herself, despite her mother's request that both daughters join her by the fire.

Wearily Eleanor made her way to her chamber, glad to finally be alone. The room was damp and chilly so, after ordering a fire to be lit, she wrapped herself in her warmest fur-trimmed mantle and climbed on to the bed. After a few moments she climbed down again and walked to the window. She placed her candlestick carefully on the ledge, sat on the low stool and began to unpin her hair, half her mind on her task and one eye on the view of the moat, the stable...

And the mews...

* * *

'Let me in and give me a drink, Rob,' Will instructed through chattering teeth. 'I'm in sore need of something to warm me through.'

Between leaving Lady Peyton and arriving at the hut attached to the mews, it had started to sleet. Now, cloakless and getting wetter by the minute, Will was beginning to regret his decision.

Rob gawped at finding his brother shivering in the dark. 'No wonder, if you've come this far in only your tunic.' He laughed. 'Are you trying to make yourself ill?'

Will pulled a low stool close by the hearth as Rob poured him a tankard of ale and grasped it between stiff fingers. He leaned towards the flames, allowing the heat to penetrate his cold limbs. He did not regret giving his cloak to Lady Peyton— the expression in her glistening fern-green eyes as he had almost kissed her more than paid off his gamble of following her—but he wished he'd had the foresight to find her own.

Rob joined his brother by the fire, a glove in his hands that he had been busy stitching. Will watched the needle move deftly through the thick leather as Rob embroidered the sleeve with stitches of gold cord.

'How is the peregrine faring?' Will asked. 'Will

she be ready to present to the duke on midwinter's day?'

Rob nodded. 'She's a fine bird. Sir Edgar will have no need to worry about the quality of his gift.'

'You'll feel no shame yourself, I'll warrant.' Will smiled with genuine pleasure at the prospect of his brother's success. 'Perhaps before long you'll be a duke's falconer instead of a baron's. If you are lucky, you'll make your fortune and there's no telling how far you might rise.'

Rob shrugged. 'I'm happy where I am. I never had your ambitions.'

Will stood and paced around the low-ceilinged room with its familiar furniture, crowded shelves and hooks laden with equipment. He had spent his childhood days here, learning the craft at his father's side, and it was as much home to him as their cottage in Tawstott had been. He had hated every moment of his apprenticeship and had burned to escape, but now a pang of melancholy hit him. The hut had barely altered in the five years since he had left Tawstott. Almost unconsciously he ran a finger along the line of his scar.

'It's strange to think that in another life, this would have been mine.'

'You would never have stayed,' Rob pointed

out. 'You'd have found some other opportunity to leave.'

'True enough. You've always been more content than me. I envy you that really.'

A pair of wide, dark eyes flashed unexpectedly through Will's mind. Five years since he had seen them for real, but he could still picture the owner perfectly. He drained his tankard in one hard swig and held it out to Rob for refilling. He looked at his brother gravely and sat back down.

'I told Lady Peyton about Amy.'

Rob whistled through his teeth and reached for the flagon of ale, filling Will's tankard almost to the brim. 'Well, that's one strategy I would never have thought of, but I suppose it could work. How much did you tell her?'

'Barely anything, but still more than I should have said.' Will frowned at the memory and the unspoken accusation in Lady Peyton's voice. His lip twisted into a grimace. 'Or perhaps less. She asked me why I abandoned Amy. She naturally assumed I had dealt badly by her.'

'And you told her what?' Rob asked, narrowing his eyes.

'I told her nothing,' Will said shortly. 'I have nothing to explain or justify. My past is no business of hers.' He frowned, remembering Lady

Peyton's assumptions. 'She'll be gone before long and most likely married soon. As long as I win my wager it matters not what she thinks of me.'

Rob topped up the tankards again. 'And how are you progressing? Two or three days is your usual measure. Are you finding it harder than expected? You don't have many nights left before the feast.'

Will placed his tankard on the hearth and folded his arms. A day or two earlier the question might have caused him a degree of anxiety, but tonight he was more confident than he had been before. Although he had still not won his kiss he had come the closest yet.

'It's taking more time than I anticipated. I've never met a woman so guarded. She's determined not to allow any man into her life.' Will conjured up the rise and fall of Eleanor Peyton's body as she had pressed against his chest. Did she really have no understanding of the effect her touch had on him?

'She isn't a common tavern wench or dairy-maid,' he explained. 'She needs gentler treatment. She won't simply fall on to her back at a snap of my fingers, any more than one of your birds would fly to your hand straight off without training.'

Rob laughed and pointed at the scar on Will's

face. 'If you'd learned to handle birds with such sensitivity years ago, you'd have been a better falconer.'

'And if I were, I'd have stayed here, married Amy, grown old and dull and never thought of wagers or leaving Tawstott.' Will brushed his fingers lightly over his cheek once more. 'I should thank the hawk that gave me this.'

He stood and put the tankard on the table. 'I should get to bed. I still have much to do before Duke Roland arrives, even with the help of the lovely Lady Peyton. Perhaps the duke will be in need of a new steward and I'll climb higher yet.'

Rob elbowed his brother in the ribs. 'Or perhaps Lady Peyton's new knightly husband may and you can spend your days serving her instead. Wouldn't that be amusing?'

Will smiled, though he found the idea anything but. He walked back to the house, huddling against the wind. As he neared the stone building he stopped and stared up at his home. Lights burned dimly in the windows of the house, giving it a friendly appearance, and a feeling of satisfaction warmed his bones.

Rob was right. Will would never have been happy leading the life of a falconer, however pres-

tigious the establishment he worked in. Leaving
Tawstott had granted him more opportunities than
he could ever have dreamed of. He had not been
joking when he talked of hoping for a position in
the duke's household. He had risen so far already
and the thought of further advancement tugged
his heart enticingly. The knowledge rankled momentarily that however high he climbed he would
still be dependent on the whim of one master or
another. No matter! When he won the wager he
could invest in the vineyards and make a tidy income.

He whistled happily as he walked back, head full
of plans until a light burning in a window on the
upper floor caught Will's attention. It took him a
moment to recognise whose room it was. Impulsively he took a step towards it, but stopped as he
made out the silhouette of a figure in the window
frame. Briefly he wondered if Lady Peyton was
watching for him. He pushed the thought aside,
dismissing it for the foolishness it was.

How high would he have to climb before a
woman such as Eleanor Peyton would look at him?
He'd need more than a meagre income from a
vineyard for that! He knew what would happen:
he would win the kiss—he held no fears in that

regard after tonight—and collect his stake. Will would be richer by twenty groats and Lady Peyton would leave Tawstott, whether to marriage or not. If she remained as guarded as she was, she would no doubt want nothing more to do with him after such an indiscretion.

As he strode back to the courtyard the thought crept up on him like an assailant in the night that perhaps at the cost of her friendship he had not set the stake high enough.

# Chapter Ten

A pale shaft of morning sunlight stole through the window of Eleanor's bedchamber. Eleanor inhaled deeply, drawing in air so fresh and chilly it hurt as it filled her lungs. She shivered slightly and pulled the coverlet higher around her shoulders. Her breath hung in the air like smoke. She listened to Jennet humming as the maid lit the fire and watched the light make its way slowly across the wall, savouring the peace. In less than a week Tawstott would be full of visitors and every moment would be taken up with obligations. The events of yesterday hung over her like a cloud and she knew she would have to face her mother before the day was out.

When her breath stopped appearing in small puffs Eleanor sat staring out of the window where last night she had sat until the candle had burned to a stub. After days of drizzle and sleet the wind had changed direction overnight, driving the oppressive grey clouds away. The sky was cloudless and for the first time since Eleanor had arrived home the rolling hills and moorland beyond Tawstott Town were clearly visible and inviting. Jennet chatted idly as she brushed Eleanor's hair and left it to fall in waves to her waist.

'And Maud says that if Master Rudhale is pleased he might...'

The name leapt out at Eleanor from Jennet's narrative and she jerked her head upright.

'I'm sorry, my lady, did I hurt you?' Jennet fussed, pulling the brush away.

Eleanor waved a hand, flustered that the steward's name had caused her to react in such a way.

'No. I'm sorry, Jennet, my mind was wandering and I wasn't listening fully. I was looking at the hills and remembering how much I used to love riding there.'

Jennet looked over Eleanor's shoulder at the frost-covered fields and wrinkled her nose. 'I don't like horses,' she said.

Eleanor smiled. Jennet didn't like many things that involved being anywhere other than safely indoors. An unexpected urge to be on horseback tugged at Eleanor's heart. It had been over a year

since she had ridden longer than the short trot
from Rowland's Mount to her village.

She rolled her foot around in a small circle
thoughtfully. It was less painful and the bruising
was almost gone. In fact, she had not used her
crutch for two or three days and last night when
she had stormed out into the garden it had not even
crossed her mind to expect pain.

Eleanor lifted the lid of her clothes chest and
pulled the contents on to the bed. Her heart sank.
None of the three dresses she had brought with
her would serve to ride in and the only gown suitable was from before she was widowed. Her figure had not changed much in three years and the
dress would still fit, but it was deep blue with thick
lines of orange braid along the sleeves and hem. It
presented a stark contrast to the browns and greys
lying beside it and Eleanor hesitated at the sight.

Since Baldwin's death she had worn only sombre
tones. She picked the dress from the bed, pursing
her lips thoughtfully. The dress itself was not too
bright: if Jennet could unpick the braid that would
be less likely to cause comment. She remembered
Master Rudhale's comments that she should wear
colours and her cheeks flamed. *William*, she reminded herself with a twitch of her lips and her
scalp prickled, sending small ripples of excitement

down her spine. What would he say if he saw her in such a gown?

'Perhaps I can wait until tomorrow instead,' she said. She folded it carefully, passing it to Jennet, and changed into the brown gown and fur-trimmed surcoat. While Jennet bound her hair back into a knot, Eleanor's eyes drifted to the door. Usually in the mornings an errand boy appeared bringing notice of what tasks William had planned, but she had received no such message today. Perhaps her questions had offended him after all. She hoped not.

Eleanor thought about the figure she had seen striding back to the house in the dark the night before. When he had paused and stared directly at her window Eleanor had tensed, experiencing a stab of panic as though she had been caught spying. William had been too far away and it had been too dark to make out his face, but she could picture his expression clearly. Of course it had not been her he was looking at, but even so she had shrunk back at the thought he might have caught her watching him.

'Tell me again what you were saying about Master Rudhale,' Eleanor asked Jennet, as lightly as she could manage. She knew barely anything about him beyond his casual references to his former positions, but if there was gossip Jennet was sure to know. 'Is he well thought of by the servants?'

Eleanor blushed at the directness of her question, but Jennet had the deviousness of a chicken.

'Oh, yes, among the women certainly,' she answered breezily. 'He's ugly, of course; how could he be otherwise with that horrible scar, but somehow that makes no odds to him.'

Eleanor leaned forward, eyes narrowed. 'What do you mean?'

Jennet wrinkled her forehead and shut her mouth tightly. Eleanor nodded, prompting her to continue, burning with curiosity. His revelation last night had been wholly unexpected and she was itching to know more of his past.

'They say he has a new woman whenever he chooses,' she told Eleanor in a scandalised whisper. 'Half the girls in the town hope to marry him because he's the most powerful of your father's servants and might be rich one day. I think he just enjoys playing with them because as soon as he's about to capture a heart he loses interest. They tell he's a wondrous good kisser, though!'

Eleanor's stomach squirmed. She folded her arms tightly across her chest and stared out of the window once more, digesting what Jennet had said. She had laughed more in Will's company than any time she could remember and the past few days had made Eleanor almost forget his behaviour on the ferry. Last night she would have kissed him and joined the ranks of foolish women when she should have known better. Her heart fluttered at the memory of his lips close to hers, their bodies entwined. William had so nearly fooled her into believing him honourable and she had almost fallen for his tricks.

'Well, no more,' she muttered under her breath. 'I think I shall let Master Rudhale tend to matters without my assistance today,' she announced curtly. 'I have my own business to attend to.'

She set about composing a letter to her own steward at Rowland's Mount, telling him of the oysters required for the feast. She sealed the letter and drummed her fingers on the table, her stomach starting to churn. There was no delaying any further: she had to go and see her mother. She stowed the letter in her pouch to deliver to Sir Edgar later and, leaving Jennet to make alterations to the riding dress, made her way to her mother's solar.

*Just say you don't want to marry*, William had said, as though that would be an end to the matter. Clearly for him it had been, Eleanor thought enviously. She stopped outside the door to the solar and drew a deep breath, gripping the fabric of her skirt in her fists to stop her hands trembling. Her anxiety was unfounded however. Lady Fitzallan was not there and the only occupants were Anne and her maid.

'Mother is ill today,' Anne announced. She fixed Eleanor with a meaningful look. 'She said her head aches too much to leave her room after your behaviour yesterday.'

Throughout their childhood the girls had been subject to their mother's sudden ailments, brought on usually by some imagined offence. The correct procedure was to apologise extensively and follow Lady Fitzallan's demands until she recovered. Now a small crest of rebellion lapped at Eleanor's guilt and she made a decision. She would treat today as a reprieve and that could wait until tomorrow. She smiled brightly at Anne.

'Then you and I shall let her rest and amuse ourselves today.'

The time passed pleasantly, and when Anne suggested a walk in the gardens Eleanor readily agreed. She returned to her room and collected her cloak, then made her way down to meet her sister. Entering the Outer Hall she stopped in dismay. Anne was not alone. William was with her.

Every muscle in Eleanor's body tensed at the sight of them standing close together, Jennet's tale of the steward's many seductions fresh in her mind. She observed the scene more closely and relaxed a little. William was wearing his cloak and riding boots and over his shoulder he carried a large, leather bag. His cheeks were red with cold and his hair loose and tangled. He had clearly been returning from an errand when Anne had intercepted him. Although Anne leaned in towards William, her head raised to speak, he in turn stood rigid, his arms by his side.

As Eleanor walked towards them William turned and saw her for the first time. The smile with which he greeted her was so open and warm that Eleanor began instinctively to return it until she reminded herself she was no longer going to allow him to have such an effect upon her. She bit back the smile and nodded her head warily towards him, feeling unnerved by his gaze upon her.

'Good day, Lady Peyton. Anne has been telling me you are going walking about the grounds,' William said warmly. He lowered his voice conspiratorially. 'I was suggesting you gather some greenery to decorate the hall.'

Eleanor glared at him, but he only grinned back infuriatingly. 'What a good idea,' she said, fastening the clasp of her cloak about her neck. 'Anne, are you ready?'

Anne smiled up at William. 'Why don't you come with us?'

'I'm sure William…I mean Master Rudhale has far better things to do,' Eleanor said firmly, at the same time as William answered with a careless,

'Why not?'

They stared at each other, the steward's blue eyes issuing a challenge that made Eleanor's heart quicken. She looked away and shrugged in defeat. William pushed open the heavy oak door and allowed his companions to pass through. As they walked towards the carp pond William dropped to Eleanor's side.

'I'm glad we met,' he whispered discreetly. 'I've been thinking of you. I was hoping to see how you fared today.'

He was close enough that their cloaks brushed and Eleanor's heart began to race, more conscious than ever before of the powerful form concealed beneath. She cast her eyes down. 'I am well, thank you' she replied coolly.

William raised his eyebrows at her tone. 'If you are concerned about last night, you have nothing to fear. I know how to keep a confidence, and if you are worried that what passed between us was somehow inappropriate—'

Eleanor cut him off abruptly. 'Last night is of no concern to me. I told you to make it clear to my sister that she has no hope of winning your affections and yet I find you together.'

'Do you expect me to simply ignore her when she speaks to me from now on, or throw the fact in her face cold-heartedly? Am I so cruel in your eyes?' William's eyes flashed angrily. 'There are ways of softening such news so that it does not hurt or humiliate.'

'I'm sure you are well practised in the matter,' Eleanor replied tartly before she could help herself, remembering Jennet's words. William jutted out his chin and his eyes glinted.

'Prove it to me,' she challenged.

'As your ladyship wishes,' William said drily. He left her side and strode ahead to where Anne was throwing pebbles into the water and began speaking to her in a lively voice. Eleanor scuffed her foot moodily in the dirt. She followed slowly and stood close enough to overhear while seemingly spellbound by the long shadows of the bulrushes that grew in clumps around the water.

'Are you looking forward to the feast?' William

was asking. 'There will be so many new people for you to meet. Duke Roland is bringing his newly invested knights, I believe.'

'It's so exciting. Mother hopes to find us both husbands,' Anne said. She cocked her head with a smile, looking for the entire world like a grown woman. 'I might be married soon and will leave here for ever. Would you be sorry for me to leave?'

'I would be a bad friend to begrudge you such happiness,' William replied. His eyes drifted to Eleanor, who dropped her head to avoid his gaze. Slightly louder he continued, 'I hope you find a good husband in one of these knights.'

'You think I should accept one of them?' Anne said. Disappointment tinged her voice and her smile vanished. Eleanor's heart gave a twinge.

William smiled kindly. 'You are very young to be thinking of marriage, but if you find one of them pleasing you should certainly consider him. One day you will meet the man who cares for you and he will think himself lucky indeed to have your love.'

'A man who cares for me? One day,' Anne said plaintively. Her lips twisted downwards as she realised the implication of William's words. She blinked hard and her voice took on a sharp edge.

'And what of Eleanor? Do you wish a knightly husband for her, too?'

Eleanor looked up at her name. Her eyes met William's over the top of Anne's head. He looked taken aback by the question and said nothing. He held her gaze intensely, his eyes burning into her with unconcealed desire. Time seemed to slow. Eleanor's blood began to pound in her ears and she was unable to tear her eyes from his.

'I hope that Lady Peyton finds the happiness she is searching for however she chooses,' William said eventually.

Silence hung thickly in the air. A sudden lump blocked Eleanor's throat and tears prickled her eyes. 'I never said I was searching for happiness,' she muttered.

'Then I imagine you are unique in that respect,' William said, his face disbelieving. 'Few of us are fortunate to be so content with our lot. I am afraid I must leave you both now,' he said abruptly. 'I have spent far too long neglecting my duties this afternoon.' He bowed to Anne, then walked to Eleanor. Pausing to lift her hand to his lips, he asked in a low voice, 'Will that suffice to prove my compassion?'

His touch sent crests of longing rising in Eleanor's belly crashing over her flesh. 'Thank you,' she whispered.

William walked off without looking back. Anne stared after him until he had rounded the corner, then faced the lake, her shoulders drooping. Eleanor walked to her side and reached a hand to her sister's shoulder. Anne shrugged it off violently and whipped around to face Eleanor.

'You made him say that, didn't you?' she hissed.

'Me? What makes you say that?' Eleanor asked.

'Oh, don't pretend you had nothing to do with it,' Anne raged. 'I know you did and I know why. It's because you mean to have him for yourself!'

A slap to the face could not have shocked Eleanor more. Her mouth dropped open as the unfairness of Anne's words struck her to the bone.

'Anne, that's ridiculous,' she whispered hoarsely.

'No, it isn't,' Anne cried. 'I'm not the child you both think I am.'

'Well, you behave like a child at times,' Eleanor snapped. She lowered her voice and tried to mould her face into a calm expression. 'I understand you're upset, but you are imagining things. Master Rudhale means nothing to me.'

Anne laughed bitterly. 'Is he Master Rudhale now? You called him William before!' She pointed a finger at Eleanor. 'I've seen how you look at each other and I know what it means.'

'We don't look at each other in any way!' Eleanor protested. She ran a hand across her forehead, cursing herself for her blunder over his name. She lifted her chin. 'By all accounts the man is an unscrupulous seducer with a heart of rock. I did not want you to be hurt or ruined, but if you choose to think the worst possible motive of me that is your business!'

She turned on her heel and stormed off, leaving Anne to make her own way back to the house. Out of sight she stopped and leaned back against a tree. Her hands trembled and her knees threatened to give out from under her. It was not only the quarrel that had shaken her. Anne had been unerringly right in her accusation. William *had* made no secret of his interest in her. She had not discouraged him fully, but had chosen instead to spend more and more time in his company.

She remembered the excitement and anticipation that surged through her when he had held her in his arms and her knees almost gave way as sensations she had thought never to feel threatened to overwhelm her. She let out a moan of frustration at her own folly. After his conduct on the ferry she should never have agreed to assist him; she should have avoided him at all costs. Anything rather than allow the longing to build inside her until the thought of not kissing him was agonising.

Anne ran past towards the house, oblivious to Eleanor standing beside the path. The sun was beginning to set and Tawstott was cast into shadow, looming oppressively as Eleanor looked towards it. Sadness welled up in her and the thought of returning was unbearable. She closed her eyes and breathed deeply, forcing herself to be calm. She nearly succeeded when a plan abruptly burst into her mind. She wiped a hand across her eyes, drew her shoulders back and began to walk back to the house.

Sir Edgar was sitting at the desk, poring over an old book as Eleanor entered his library. He frowned at the interruption and Eleanor's nerve almost failed her. She took a deep breath and looked him in the eye.

'I have made a decision, Father. I'm going home. I'll leave at first light.'

## Chapter Eleven

Sir Edgar leaned forward, frowning deeply. 'Duke Roland and his retinue are the most important and influential guests I have had stay in many years. His good graces could mean patronage for Edmund, a superior husband for Anne, all manner of advantage to all of us. If you choose to leave, it will make matters extremely difficult for me. I know you understand the obligation I am under and how untoward it would appear if you are absent.'

Eleanor shook her head and forced a smile to her lips. She swallowed down the lump of anxiety that threatened to choke her words. 'You misunderstand me. I don't mean to stay there, merely for a night or two. There are things I need to do. Matters I want to take care of that I would rather do in person.'

'What matters? Sir Edgar asked, pursing his lips.

'The oysters,' Eleanor said. She pulled the letter to her steward from her pouch and passed it from one hand to the other. 'I don't think I made myself clear enough in my letter and I want to ensure Duke Roland eats only the finest I produce. No one knows as well as I do which to pick. Also—' She broke off and looked down at the ground, aware that another reason was needed. Her eyes landed on the dull, brown gown she wore. 'I want to bring back a dress I forgot.'

Sir Edgar raised his eyebrows. 'A dress? You wish to travel for eight hours in either direction to collect a dress?'

'For the feast,' she explained. 'Something brighter and more fitting for a dance. And my jewels.'

'You have not given this proper thought. How can you return to Rowland's Mount? The house will be shut up and almost all the servants gone,' Sir Edgar pointed out.

Eleanor wrinkled her nose in irritation. Sir Edgar was correct. The plan had come to her so suddenly that she had not fully thought through what it would involve, only that she had a desperate urge to leave Tawstott Mote.

'I'll stay in the inn in the village,' she answered confidently. 'Nell will have rooms.'

Sir Edgar regarded her sceptically. 'Your mother told me what passed between you yesterday. Tell me the truth, is that why you wish to leave?'

Eleanor met her father's gaze evenly. 'I won't deny that has played a part in my decision. I am not myself. I've upset Mother and this afternoon I quarrelled with Anne. Master Rudhale—' She broke off abruptly and bit her lip, aware that she had almost said too much.

Sir Edgar pushed himself from his chair. 'What of William? Have you fallen out with him, too? He was telling me only this morning how valuable your assistance has been. He spoke of you very warmly.'

'He did?' To hear he had spoken in such terms to her father surprised her. There could be no advantage to him in that. Of course William had been complimentary to her face since they began working together. At the time Eleanor had been pleased and taken it as recognition that she was completing her tasks efficiently. Since Jennet's words that morning she had suspected it to be merely one more tool in his attempt to seduce her, but now uncertainty gnawed at her.

'I mean to say Master Rudhale will not miss me for a day or two,' Eleanor continued. Whatever his motives might be, she hoped fervently that would prove true. Each encounter left her emotions more in disarray and resisting him was becoming harder. If he was truly as fickle as Jennet had implied, a few nights of her absence should be enough to ensure he found a new quarry by the time she returned and she would be safe. Her own longing was an infatuation that would pass quickly enough without nourishment to feed it.

She sighed deeply and put a hand to her head, mimicking Lady Fitzallan's posture of frailty. She found the mime all too convincing. 'I feel uneasy about what the next weeks will bring and I fear it will make me ill,' she said in a wavering voice.

Sir Edgar walked around the table to his daughter and guided her to a chair by the fire. 'I am sorry if the thought of another marriage distresses you. You knew it was inevitable and your mother and I are acting in your best interests.'

'My best interests are being left in peace to do what makes me happy,' Eleanor replied.

'Are you even sure you know what that is?' Sir Edgar asked, settling himself into the chair opposite her. 'If you had truly loved Baldwin, I could understand your reluctance, but you never had the time to grow more than passing fond of each other. I blame myself for that.'

The concern was clear in Sir Edgar's voice and Eleanor sensed his waning opposition.

'I thought I would have longer to become accustomed to the idea,' she said quietly. 'I cannot remain here, knowing I have such expectations on my shoulders.'

She leaned across and took his hands. 'Please, Father, let me go. I promise I will return before the duke arrives.'

Sir Edgar was silent, his eyes fixed on the flames. Eleanor held her breath, the tension almost making her dizzy. If he said no, she would not be able to bear it.

Finally Sir Edgar spoke. 'These are my terms: I will permit you to leave tomorrow, but for one night only. That will give you ample time to conduct your business and return by nightfall the following evening. You will travel with an escort, of course. My carriage is faster than yours.' He paused and fixed Eleanor with a stern look. The elation she had begun to feel died away. Sir Edgar continued, 'In return for this, you will agree not to reject any offers you receive without considering the benefits they bring.'

'You cannot make me accept a husband as you did before. I am not a child any longer. I am a widow in the eyes of the law.' Eleanor folded her arms, surprised at the words that had burst from her. She had to stop herself grinning, thinking what William would say when she told him what she had said. She remembered she did not intend to speak to him more than necessary and the elation died inside her.

'You are right, I cannot compel you. Nevertheless, those are my terms,' Sir Edgar said firmly. 'The men who will be coming are rich and hold influence with Duke Roland. Think what life as a lady of court would be like.'

'I have no interest in a position at court,' Eleanor pointed out.

Sir Edgar said nothing. He simply folded his arms, mirroring Eleanor's posture.

Eleanor's mind worked rapidly. It was not what she had hoped for, but one night was better than none. She doubted even William could lose interest completely in that time, though she had to hope it would be enough to start the wane. Sir Edgar had said she had to consider any offers of marriage, but considering an offer did not mean she had to find it to her taste.

While Eleanor was thinking, a ray of late sunlight streamed through the window, painting the walls pale gold. She stared into it, remembering her earlier wish to go riding, and her mind was made up.

'I agree to your terms, but I have one more request. I don't want your carriage. I would like to ride there instead. The roads are too bad, especially in this weather. The journey will be faster on horseback and I can easily carry everything I need. If you could spare me a carriage and driver, you can spare me horses and a groom to be my escort, can't you?'

Sir Edgar's eyes widened at her words and Eleanor nodded encouragement, her eyes pleading with him not to refuse. He broke into a sudden laugh. 'I never could resist you, my dear. Very well, I agree. I'll arrange for a messenger to ride to the inn directly.'

Eleanor kissed his cheek and rose to leave. As she opened the door Sir Edgar called after her.

'Last year you would never have wanted to ride. You're changing, Eleanor.'

Eleanor almost had to stop herself skipping in triumph as she made her way back to her chamber. She burst into the Great Hall, a smile on her lips, and slowed. Edmund and William were sitting at a table close to the fireplace, a flagon on the table between them as the maids scurried back and forth, giggling and casting their eyes at the two young men.

William was scribbling furiously on a parchment, engrossed in his task and his head bowed, hair loose and concealing his face as usual. Edmund called after her. She glanced over her shoulder to return his greeting, not wanting to stop, and as she did her eyes met William's. He had lifted his head, paused in the act of writing, quill motionless on paper. His eyebrows lifted in an expression of curiosity and his lip twitched.

Eleanor wondered what he saw in her to give rise to such interest. She felt the too-familiar sensation of her heart beginning to race beneath his gaze. Discomfited, she blinked and looked away, hurrying from the room with as much decorum as she could manage.

As Eleanor climbed the staircase to her chamber Sir Edgar's observation came back to her and she paused thoughtfully. Was she changing? Of course not, her father was being foolish. There was nothing to change. She was happy as she was and would be happier once free of Tawstott, threats of marriage and thoughts of William Rudhale!

Will had not noticed Lady Peyton pass by him until Edmund had called after her. At the sound of her name, he glanced up from his letter and found their eyes locked together. Her face was flushed and her eyes gleamed. She held his gaze, her lips parting unconsciously, then she turned and was gone. Will's eyes followed her as she made her way rapidly down the length of the hall. She held her head high and the graceful movement of her hips caused her skirts to sway enticingly, hinting at the shapely limbs beneath.

Edmund called a serving girl to bring him fresh wine. She crossed the room jauntily, a coquettish smile on her face and a wiggle in her walk, making no secret of her interest in the young men. She bent over the table to remove the empty flagon, flashing her deep-brown eyes and giving both men a glimpse of the top of her breasts spilling out of the tightly laced bodice. Will thanked her briefly, her dark eyes reminding him uncomfortably of Amy. He looked back to the doorway once more, his mind on the woman who had just passed through it and the green eyes that had regarded him with such sadness.

The previous night she had cried in his arms with a despairing grief that made his heart lurch. When he had left her in the grounds barely an hour ago she had been withdrawn and cold towards him. The spirited woman Will had bickered and laughed with over the past week had transformed back into the aloof stranger he had first met with anger barely concealed below her surface. Now once more there was colour in her cheeks and almost a dance in her step. Something had caused such a series of marked changes and Will wanted to know what.

Pushing his chair back, Will packed his parchment and quill into his bag, determined to discover the cause. He bade farewell to Edmund, brushing aside his friend's queries as to the state of the wager with a non-committal laugh, and walked out the way Lady Peyton had entered the room. The sun had set and it was bitterly cold once more so he doubted she had been outside all this time. Will made his way to Sir Edgar's library, certain he would find the answer to the mystery there if he could prise it from the baron.

'William, as ever you arrive at the opportune moment,' Sir Edgar declared as Will closed the door behind him. He was seated at his desk, a paper in front of him. He pushed his signet ring into the wax and sealed the document before holding it out to Will. 'Find me a messenger and have them set off for the inn at Rowland's Mount immediately. Lady Peyton is returning home in the morning.'

The room darkened around Will. He stared at the paper in his hand, realising he was holding the solution to the puzzle. And what a solution it was.

'She's leaving?' he asked foolishly, his mouth twisting down. The twenty groats were lost. He would never kiss her now. Never feel those soft curves beneath his hands again. More than that, he would never again hear Eleanor's laugh and see the tilt of her lips as she smiled. The thoughts were so quick to follow each other he could not tell which came first.

'Not permanently. Don't fear, Will, you won't lose your aide for long,' Sir Edgar answered. Will thanked his stars that the baron had attributed such a meaning to his reaction.

'She says she has business to attend to, though I think that is merely a pretext,' Sir Edgar continued. His face split into a smile. 'I believe Eleanor is not as averse to the idea of marriage as she pretends to be because she wants to gather dresses for the feast.'

A man with less self-possession would have let his jaw drop at such news. Will forced his to remain closed, though a flame of jealousy flickered deep within him. For all her talk of independence and unwillingness Will should have guessed she would not resist the lure of a rich husband. He'd never known a woman who wasn't attracted to the prospect of wealth and why should Eleanor Peyton be different? His fist tightened unconsciously around the document as long-buried bile resurfaced.

'I'll send the fastest rider,' he said. 'Shall I give orders for Lady Peyton's carriage to be readied at first light?'

Sir Edgar pulled his beard and grimaced. 'She isn't taking her carriage. Nor mine. She insists on riding.'

'Alone!' Will's mouth did fall open at this. 'That's far too dangerous. You can't allow her to—' he began, aghast, before recalling who he was talking to and biting his words back.

Far from showing displeasure at Will's words, Sir Edgar smiled. 'Not alone, though I am sure Eleanor would see nothing wrong with such a notion. I can still exert *some* influence over her at least. She's taking a groom as escort.'

Visions of Sir Edgar's servants flashed through Will's mind. Too old. Too scrawny. Too lascivious. He rejected each candidate without a second thought. None of them would keep Eleanor safe enough for his liking.

'Let me go with her,' he said.

'A single man and an unmarried woman. I'm not sure propriety allows it,' Sir Edgar said doubtfully.

'A widow and her father's closest servant. Propriety could not question that, surely?' Will answered.

'Can you spare the time so close to the feast?'

Will folded his arms and planted his feet firmly. 'I will gladly spare it. I can ride faster than any of your men and I can protect Lady Peyton better, too, should such a need arise.'

Relief settled on to Sir Edgar's face and he nodded his agreement. 'I put her in your hands, William.'

Will's evening passed in a flurry of activity. He sent Sir Edgar's messenger on his way with an instruction to obtain the finest rooms in the inn. He gave the stable lad orders to ready his stallion Tobias and the finest mare available for Lady Peyton, wondering what sort of horsewoman she would prove to be. Almost as an afterthought he called into the kitchens and packed a bottle of wine, a bag of sweet apples and a round of cheese for the journey.

Finally he made his way to his chamber and sat by candlelight to sharpen his sword. As he began rhythmically sliding the whetstone down the length of the blade it struck him that there was an added advantage to his offer to escort Lady Peyton. He had won himself two days alone in her company. They could not fail to become closer on the journey. His wager was not yet lost. He shook his head in wonderment that he had not thought of it earlier.

He stowed his sword, pulled the tunic over his head and rolled his shoulders back wearily before removing the rest of his clothes and sluicing himself down with icy water. The room was cold and his bed chilly. Slipping hurriedly between the sheets, he wished he had a companion to warm them with him.

*What sort of lover are you, Eleanor Peyton?*

He lay idly imagining what it would be like to have her alongside him, limbs intertwined, her hands caressing his body. He had almost drifted into a satisfied sleep when his eyes shot open as a thought struck him. Her distress had prevented him kissing her yesterday and now her safety on the journey had been his prime concern. He was experiencing something he neither expected nor wanted to feel.

He was starting to care.

* * *

The sky was cloudless but barely light when Will led Tobias from the stable to the courtyard. He paused to adjust the bridle to his liking, patting the stallion's nose. The stable lad walked ahead, leading a chestnut mare to where Lady Peyton waited, muffled in a heavy grey cloak with a voluminous hood that masked her face.

Will hung back at the corner, watching as she mounted the mare with ease, swinging her leg over the saddle and giving Will an inadvertent flash of blue beneath the sombre cloak that made him grin in surprise.

Will led Tobias towards her. 'Good morning, my lady,' he said with a smile.

Lady Peyton lowered her hood and stared around the deserted courtyard. 'Where is my groom?' she asked suspiciously.

In answer Will mounted his horse. 'I offered my services.'

Lady Peyton flashed Will a look of pure hatred that took him by surprise. She let out a sharp oath and dug her heels into the mare's flanks, spurring it away and leaving Will in her wake.

# Chapter Twelve

'I think fortune will be on our side with the weather,' William observed as they trotted through the almost deserted street of Tawstott Town. He flashed her a smile that Eleanor refused to acknowledge.

She looked around. The first insipid rays of sun were beginning to appear over the tops of the low buildings where the townsfolk were beginning to start their day. It was going to be one of those rare winter mornings when the ice-kissed trees cast long grey shadows. Perfect for riding. On any other day Eleanor's heart would have sung with joy, but now she gripped the reins tightly, gritting her teeth to stop tears of frustration springing to her eyes.

How could Will have known her plans? *How?*

She could guess the answer, of course. Her father would have asked him to arrange matters.

What she could not say for certain was whose idea it had been for William to be her escort, though she was willing to wager she knew the answer already. His esteemed steward! So well regarded that Sir Edgar would entrust Eleanor to his care. She snorted angrily, causing William to throw her a questioning look.

'I hope you slept well last night, my lady. Today is going to be a long and tiring ride,' William remarked, seemingly unconcerned by Eleanor's outburst.

Did he think she was not aware of that? She knew better than anyone what the journey entailed. They were going to her home after all.

'Then we had better not waste time on idle talk,' Eleanor said with a toss of her head. She refused to speak to William any further, rebuffing any attempts at conversation until he finally stopped trying. Nor would she look in his direction as he rode alongside her, instead keeping her gaze steadfastly fixed on the road ahead.

As soon as they reached the edge of the town Eleanor spurred her mare faster, hoping to leave William behind but his stallion kept pace with ease.

Almost two hours passed before the anger churning in Eleanor's belly settled into mere irritation at

William's presence. The horses made light work of the journey, clearly relishing the sharp air and chance of exercise. Eleanor still did not speak and the only sounds to break the silence were the cawing of crows and the pounding of hooves on the frozen ground.

They broke into open ground, heading up the steep hill that would take them down towards the river and Eleanor risked a sidelong glance at William. Grudgingly she admitted to herself that he was an excellent rider. His hood was thrown back and his face was serene. His hips moved with an easy motion—man and horse in complete harmony. Beside him Eleanor felt like a novice, unable to catch the rhythm to her satisfaction. Her thighs were already aching after so long since her last time in the saddle and even through thick winter gloves her hands stung when she grasped the reins. William looked across and caught her eye. Embarrassed to be caught watching him, she spurred the horse on with an irritated yell.

When they reached the summit of the hill William pulled on his reins and wheeled his mount around. Eleanor drew her horse to a stop and looked at him with suspicion. He reached into the saddlebag and produced a couple of apples, pass-

ing one to Eleanor and biting into the other enthusiastically.

'How are you faring, Lady Peyton?' he asked.
'If you are finding the ride hard, it isn't too late
to turn back and return to Tawstott. I could have
Sir Edgar's carriage ready in no time at all if you
would prefer.'

Eleanor sniffed contemptuously. However un-
pleasant the ride might be, admitting to such a
thing was absolutely out of the question. Pride
notwithstanding, if they returned Sir Edgar would
almost certainly say there would not be time to
make the journey. The prospect that she would
be back at Rowland's Mount before dusk gave Eleanor the motivation she needed to keep moving
on. She fed the apple core to her horse and with a
crack of the reins set off once more. She was glad
when the river finally came into view and she
would be able to rest for a while as they waited
for the ferry.

At the river William dismounted and held a hand
out to Eleanor.

'I can manage by myself,' she said, the thought
of taking his hand making her stomach curl into
knots she was determined to ignore.

She hastily swung her leg around to dismount,
but as she jumped to the ground the trailing hem

of her skirt caught on the ornate horn of the saddle. She reached to untangle the cloth, but instantly William was behind her. He took hold of the mare's bridle and reached his other hand around Eleanor to free her.

Eleanor bit down an oath as William leaned in close, his breath warm against her neck. Once more she caught the warm scent she recognised and she shivered at the sensations the memory evoked. If she lifted her head now, his lips would be within her reach. Hastily she looked in the opposite direction, commanding her heart to stop racing.

'Stand still,' William instructed as he deftly unhitched the skirt.

Her skirt fell free and Eleanor turned to face him. William kept his hands on the bridle and saddle, his arms surrounding Eleanor. He stared down at her, his blue eyes brimming with worry. The memory of what they had almost done in the garden hit her once more and a sharp stab of longing almost took her legs from under her.

'You look weary, my lady,' he said softly.

'I'm fine,' Eleanor muttered.

She pushed past William and walked unsteadily to the water's edge. William hitched the horses to a post and came to stand by her with folded arms as Eleanor waved her arms fruitlessly to try attracting the attention of the ferryman on the far bank. She sighed and shook her head in defeat. With a grin William reached under his cloak and produced a hunting horn. He raised it to his lips and gave three sharp blasts. The ferryman waved and began to ready his vessel, ushering the waiting passengers aboard. William raised an eyebrow at Eleanor.

Irritated she marched back to the horses and fed them handfuls of oats while the craft made its slow progress across the water. William once more followed her. He scratched his horse between the ears, then ran his hand through his own tangled locks.

'It's going to be very dull if you ignore me for the entire journey,' he said.

'I did not ask you to come,' Eleanor retorted.

'No, you didn't,' William said calmly. 'Nevertheless I am here, though it is clear you wish I was not.'

Eleanor leaned back against a tree and stared at her feet, at a loss as to what to say. To admit his presence was indeed unwelcome would be to invite the question why. All he could have learned from her father was a string of half-truths. She couldn't explain her need to get away without re-

vealing that he had played a part in her decision
to flee Tawstott.

'Why did you come?' she asked instead.

'To protect you, of course,' William answered.
He sounded surprised that she had to ask. 'What
other motive do you suspect me of?'

'I don't need your protection,' Eleanor said, ignoring his question. 'I agreed to a groom accom-
panying me because my father insisted I did not
travel alone, but I am more than capable of taking care of myself. She pulled her cloak back to
reveal the slender dagger that was buckled at her
waist, smiling at William triumphantly.

William's eyes travelled to her weapon. He gave
a loud bark of laughter. Eleanor's cheeks flamed.
She drew the dagger from its scabbard and bran-
dished it aloft.

'I won't hesitate to use this if I need to.'

William stopped laughing abruptly and his face
became solemn. 'I'm sure you won't, if you can get
close enough and your assailant is polite enough
to wait for you to make your move.'

'Do you think I don't know how to use this?'
Eleanor cried indignantly, taking a step towards
him, dagger still held before her. 'I don't need you
to protect me!'

William's eyebrows knotted together in annoyance. He muttered something under his breath and threw his cloak back across his shoulder. For the first time Eleanor noticed a plain leather-bound scabbard buckled to his right side. He reached across with his left hand and unsheathed the weapon. The blade sighed gently as he withdrew it from the scabbard. The sword was plain, the pommel and crossguard lacking any of the etching or ornamentation that would adorn the weapon of a nobleman, but the edges of the blade were sharp and left Eleanor in no doubt that it could kill.

'You say you know how to use your dagger? Then defend yourself, my lady,' William said, his voice deathly quiet.

He took a step away from Eleanor and turned his back on her. Eleanor opened her mouth to ask what he meant, but with a speed that took her by surprise William twisted the sword about his wrist and spun round.

Before Eleanor could react William had the sword held full at arm's length, pointing at her breast. The tip was barely a hand's breadth from touching her dress. The words died on Eleanor's lips and the only sound that came out of her mouth was a soft whimper. Her head jerked up in shock to discover William watching her intently, his face fiercer and more determined than she had ever seen him look.

'Look where your dagger is now,' he commanded sternly, his eyes blazing, 'and tell me how you would defend yourself against anyone who truly meant to do you harm?'

Eleanor looked down. Though she held her own weapon at full reach, the tip barely reached the crossguard of William's sword. Her knees shook as she realised he was right.

'That is why I asked to be the one to accompany you,' William said. His eyes were as hard as the iron he wielded, blazing with intensity that made Eleanor's head spin. 'I am quicker than you, stronger than you and if anyone tries to hurt you, my blade will *not* stop at their breast.'

At his words the dagger dropped from Eleanor's wavering hand. She wondered if William would be as quick to reach her should she faint. Surely he would not let her fall, but would catch her in those powerful arms. Such strength they must contain, to hold the sword perfectly motionless and pointed at her heart! An unwitting sigh escaped her lips at the thought of them crushing her against him once again. Her heart was racing far too fast that it must surely burst from her breast.

Cries of alarm came from somewhere nearby, followed closely by the drumming of hooves.

'Move away from the lady or I'll run you through,' came a shout of warning.

Neither Eleanor nor William had noticed the ferry reaching the bank. A man was running from the craft towards them. He drew his sword as he approached and flourished it at William.

'Drop your sword or I'll execute you here and now!'

It occurred to Eleanor how the scene must look to a stranger and a hysterical laugh bubbled in her throat.

The man raised his sword and gestured at William, who let his weapon fall to the ground and took a step back.

'You have nothing to fear now, my lady,' Eleanor's rescuer said confidently. The man's voice was crisp and refined. He looked of an age similar to William. He, too, had blond hair though his was neatly tied at his nape and he was half a head shorter. His cloak was fur trimmed and spoke of quality.

William gave a meaningful cough and Eleanor blinked as though waking from a dream.

'Thank you for your aid, sir, but I am in no danger,' Eleanor said hastily. By now the other travellers had disembarked and were milling around watching the drama play out.

Her rescuer's handsome face clouded with confusion at Eleanor's words, but he rallied. 'Have no fear. You need see no bloodshed to upset your sensibilities. I will take this villain into my custody and see he receives the swiftest justice as soon as I reach the nearest town.' He surveyed the clearing. 'Are you travelling alone, my lady? Where are your menfolk?'

'I don't have any fear, truly,' Eleanor insisted again. The reference to menfolk set her teeth on edge, but after William's dramatic demonstration of her inadequate defence she let it pass. She gestured to William. 'This man is my companion. He was behaving like a fool, but I assure you I am perfectly safe in his company.'

William flashed a look of annoyance at Eleanor at her description. The stranger lowered his weapon cautiously before returning it to its elaborately decorated scabbard. 'I would advise you to choose your servants with more care in future.'

'He isn't—' Eleanor began, but the man was addressing William.

'I misunderstood your intentions towards your mistress. You should consider your actions more carefully in future before someone takes your head from your neck.'

William gave a curt nod before hefting his sword across his shoulder and striding over to where the horses waited. Eleanor retrieved her dagger and slipped it back into its sheath.

She turned to follow William, but the man knelt before her and seized hold of her hands. Taken by surprise she did not resist the liberty.

'My name is Sir Martin of Allencote. I would ask your forgiveness for my actions too, my lady but I do not regret them. I will not allow a woman of such beauty to be molested in such a way,' he said earnestly. 'My heart is glad that you are safe.'

Eleanor blushed at his words, though an unworthy thought crossed her mind that if she had been less beautiful would the man have left her to her fate? Out of the corner of her eye she saw that William had unhitched their horses and was waiting, his face stern. She thanked Allencote warmly, easing her hands free. The ferryman was holding another horse, a fine white charger, its bridle and saddle decorated with fine silver knotwork. A discreet coat of arms showing a leaping stag was emblazoned on the panniers.

Allencote rose to his feet and took hold of his steed's reins. William came to stand beside Elea-

nor, his shoulder almost touching hers in an attitude of protectiveness. She hid a smile.

Allencote mounted and wheeled his steed
around. 'Farewell, my lady, I must be on my way,
but perhaps we shall meet again,' he said, a note
of hope in his voice. He dug his spurred heels into
the horse's flanks and sped away in the direction
Eleanor and William had arrived from.

'Lady Peyton, the ferry is waiting,' William said
gruffly. He led the horses on to the craft and held
both sets of reins in one hand as he fumbled for
his moneybag.

'I'll pay the fare,' Eleanor said, reaching for her
pouch and beckoning for the ferryman to her.

William scowled. 'I am not so poor that I need
your assistance to pay my way.'

Eleanor blinked in surprise at the ferocity in his
tone. 'You would not be making this journey if it
was not for me. This is my indulgence so I will
pay for it,' she said firmly. William walked to the
side of the ferry and stared out across the river.

Eleanor paid the ferryman and walked to where
William stood. He did not look at her.

'You're angry with me,' she said softly.

'And rightly so.'

'I did not ask him to intervene,' Eleanor said.

'I don't care about that,' William said, his jaw

tensing. 'Any man worthy of the description would have done the same, but I will not be called a fool by anyone.'

'You behaved like a fool!' Eleanor answered, her temper rising.

William looked round at her, his expression dark.

'You drew a sword on me,' Eleanor exclaimed. Her lip trembled suddenly. 'You could have killed me.'

The rage on William's face melted away. He put his arms on Eleanor's shoulders and pulled her round to face him. Ripples of exhilaration coursed the length of her arms at his touch.

'I would never risk harming you,' he said forcefully. 'Never! I know how to use a sword. I wanted you to understand that I am capable of defending you, but I handled the matter clumsily.'

Eleanor smiled weakly. She remembered the expression of determination she had seen on his face and a tremor passed through her body. 'I do understand…and I accept your protection.'

'Let's call a truce,' William offered. 'Today started badly, but need not continue so.'

Eleanor smiled in agreement. They stood side by side, shoulders touching as the ferry jolted into motion. She looked back at the riverbank, unable to banish the vision of William staring at her along the length of his sword. In that instant the joking, amiable companion she had spent weeks with had vanished, replaced by an altogether more commanding figure, his face serious and his intent deadly. There was no doubt in Eleanor's mind that he was more than capable of protecting her from anything and the knowledge did more than comfort her. It excited her in a way that nothing before ever had.

# Chapter Thirteen

The river was fast-flowing and the ferry tilted alarmingly as the current caught it. Lady Peyton wobbled and Will instinctively put an arm around her shoulder to steady her. She glanced briefly up at him before her eyes returned the bank they had left. She made no move to pull away from him, instead leaned against him, their bodies touching from hip to shoulder. Every fibre of Will's being felt more alive at the feel of her nestling against him. He wondered how long he could legitimately hold her close and if she was aware of the feelings that churned deep within him.

He knew that for many nights to come he would regret the way Lady Peyton's face had drained of colour at the sight of his weapon. How could he have been so short-sighted? He had not realised how near she had come to breaking down until she rounded on him so angrily on the ferry. It

had taken all his control not to take her into his
arms there and then, to banish her ordeal with an
embrace. He pulled her closer protectively as the
ferry gave another lurch, deciding he would not
release her just yet.

'Who do you think he was?' Lady Peyton asked
unexpectedly.

Will frowned. Had her mind been on the blond
knight all the time she had been in his arms? Feeling foolish, Will withdrew his arm from her shoulder.

'I did not catch his name,' he replied.

'Martin of Allencote,' Lady Peyton murmured.
She fixed Will with solemn eyes. 'You didn't like
him. I'm sorry for his manner towards you.'

Will waved a hand, affecting more carelessness
than he felt. 'I cannot blame him. I would have
done the same had I seen what he thought he saw.'

'Yes, you would,' Lady Peyton said. Her voice
was warm and Will's heart throbbed. 'I hope you
never have to though. I wouldn't like you to put
yourself in danger.'

'I'm not a nobleman, my lady,' Will replied, his
throat tightening, 'but I can use a sword as well as
any knight.' He glanced back towards the bank.
'I can fight as well as Sir Martin of Allencote, I'd
wager,' he muttered to himself.

'I wonder where he was travelling?' Lady Peyton mused.

Did she expect him to come galloping back? Will wondered moodily. Or perhaps it was hope she felt. Rich, handsome and chivalrous: such a man would impress any woman when he behaved in so gallant a manner. Why would Lady Peyton be any different?

'I wonder if he's part of Duke Roland's entourage?' she continued.

Will's jaw clenched at the possibility that Allencote might be heading straight for Tawstott at this moment. His bearing, clothing and horse all spoke of nobility. It was not beyond the bounds of possibility that he could be one of Duke Roland's retinue.

'It's doubtful,' he said lightly. 'He'd be flouting the laws of hospitality to arrive so early.'

Lady Peyton nodded. 'It would be an unlikely coincidence to chance upon a stranger on your travels only to find them waiting in your house.' Her eyes danced as she spoke, her humour obviously returning. 'Don't you agree?'

'Indeed it would. I'm afraid you will have to look elsewhere to find your wealthy husband,' Will joked.

He regretted his words instantly as Lady Peyton

stiffened and drew a sharp breath. 'When have I ever given you the slightest indication that I want a rich husband?' she asked indignantly.

Will held his hands out in a gesture of remorse. 'You haven't,' he said. 'It was a poor jest. You have told me repeatedly that you want no man at all. I apologise.'

Lady Peyton nodded, then abruptly walked to where the horses were tethered. Will stared at the river, the emotions that assailed him as violent as the rolling crests. Eleanor Peyton had denied more than once that she wanted a man, but her body spoke a different tale. Even in their first encounter on the ferry he had recognised something waiting to be awakened within her. Will had not imagined her quickening breath whenever he took her in his arms, nor the craving in her emerald eyes as she looked at him. Now those eyes had looked with interest at another man and Will was disconcerted to find he did not like it in the slightest.

They rode hard on the other side of the river. Lady Peyton soon found her stride, so much so that Will had to practically force her from the saddle mid-afternoon to allow the horses to rest.

'Must we stop?' she asked impatiently, pacing

back and forth as the animals ate their fill, her eyes sliding repeatedly to the sun.

'You know we have to,' Will told her firmly. 'There is no sense in tiring the horses. They'll only go slower if we don't let them rest.'

He produced his package of cheese and a couple more apples. 'Here,' he instructed, 'eat something or you'll be close to dropping, too.'

Lady Peyton looked as though she was about to refuse until Will fixed her with a firm stare. She took his offering, devouring the cheese with a swiftness that was most unladylike.

By the time Will had finished his final mouthful Lady Peyton was in the saddle once more. She cracked the reins and cantered off, cloak billowing behind her before Will had even mounted Tobias. He raced after her, drawing close until they were side by side. Lady Peyton glanced across and Will raised his eyebrow before urging Tobias faster and overtaking her. Her cry of challenge came like music to his ears as the miles flew beneath their hooves.

They stopped again when the woods began to thin and the road branched into two directions leading away down either side of the river. Lady Peyton dismounted and disappeared into the undergrowth with a mumbled excuse. Will followed her example and headed in the opposite direction. When he returned she was already mounted, though her cheeks were pale and she looked tired.

'Don't you want to rest a while?' Will asked.

'No, let's keep moving. We're at the estuary now. We're almost there.'

'Why are you in such haste? We'll be there soon enough,' Will said, producing his wine flask.

Lady Peyton looked at the sun that was well into its downward journey. 'I want to go to my house tonight,' she explained. 'If we leave it too late I won't be able to.'

'It's not too far from the village, is it? There'll be plenty of time to go once we've left our belongings at the inn.' Will took a welcome swig of the wine.

'Has no one told you about my home?' Eleanor asked.

Will shook his head, intrigued. 'I know nothing. Tell me,' he prompted but she shook her head.

'It's built of shells?' Will guessed with a laugh.

A slight smile began to flicker about Eleanor's lips.

'It's guarded by sea monsters that rise to do your bidding at dusk?' Will continued. 'It smells of fish?'

'No!' she said with mock indignation. 'You'll see soon enough, then you'll understand.'

'Very well, my lady. Keep your secret for now.' Will grinned, wondering what could possibly be so strange about the dwelling. He held the wine out to her. She lifted it to her lips and drank deeply, tilting her head back. Will stared transfixed at the curve of her creamy throat, barely noticing when she pushed the flask back into his hand.

The sun was low by the time they reached the coast and clouds were starting to gather on the horizon. As the road made a sharp turn to the right, taking them almost to the edge of the land, Will was greeted with a sight that took his breath away. A wide bay of shingle stretched away below them, and beyond that the endless sea, grey as iron and churning with rolling crests of white. It was bitter, unforgiving and the most breathtaking thing Will had ever seen. He pulled Tobias to a stop and raised himself in his saddle to better drink in the sight.

There had barely been any wind as they had ridden there. Now violent gusts blew from the sea, bitingly cold and strong enough to send their cloaks swirling behind them. Will sniffed deeply, inhaling the unfamiliar tang of salt and fish. Eerie cries of seabirds shattered the silence.

From the corner of his eye he noticed Lady Peyton watching him closely. He realised he was staring at the landscape as foolishly as a child.

'Have you never seen the sea before?' Lady Peyton asked in amazement.

Under most circumstances Will would have bluffed rather than admit his inexperience, but now he shook his head, too awestruck to pretend otherwise. 'Only the Bristol Channel. Nothing as wild as this.'

Lady Peyton's eyes crinkled. 'It has that effect, doesn't it? The first time Baldwin brought me here I knew I would be happy, no matter what my marriage would be like.'

Her voice cracked slightly at the mention of her husband. She looked at the ground and without speaking spurred her mare along the steep road towards the sea. Will looked at her thoughtfully, imagining a younger, happier Eleanor Fitzallan gazing on this view and jealousy stabbed him abruptly for the second time that day.

Presently Will began to make out the low-roofed line of buildings that must be the village huddling into the hillside as though trying to shelter from the bleak conditions. A small harbour wall guarded them from the worst of the waves and beyond that an odd-shaped rock stood alone in the sea. It was low and jagged at the edges, but rose up in a mound before becoming almost rectangular in shape.

'What's that?' he asked curiously. 'That rock.'

Lady Peyton lowered her hood and met his eyes, her own suddenly bright but as grey as the waves that were reflected in them. The wind caught loose tendrils of her flaming hair, lifting them with careless fingers to drift around her face. She looked more alive than Will had ever seen her. He swallowed down the lump that unexpectedly filled his throat.

'That's my home,' Eleanor answered, her voice husky. 'That's Rowland's Mount.'

'You live on a rock?' Will asked sceptically.

She rolled her eyes and indicated a causeway of black stone linking it to the land. 'My house is on the mount.'

The sun was sinking behind the rock, casting it into silhouette, and Will squinted, holding a hand to his eyes to try make out the details. Riding closer, he could see where the uneven rocks became smooth stone and that what he had mistaken for a great tooth-shaped rock was in fact a building.

'I understand,' he murmured.

'Understand what?' Lady Peyton asked.

Will waved a hand around. 'This. Why you are reluctant to return to Tawstott for long.'

'Do you see now why I resist marrying again?' Lady Peyton said, her eyes burning. 'Any husband would demand we live on his own estate. I would have to leave for ever.'

'You would choose a house over love?' Will asked.

Lady Peyton laughed bitterly. 'I would choose my home over marriage. I doubt love will be a factor.'

Will opened his mouth to protest that both might be possible, but closed it again as he met Lady Peyton's eyes. For a moment both were silent. Lady Peyton looked away first. She pointed to the horizon where clouds were growing heavier and darker.

'We need to hurry. If a storm comes we don't want to get caught out here,' she said. They spurred the horses on, saying nothing more until they reached the shelter of the village.

There was more to the village than Will had thought from the few buildings he had initially seen. The land curved inwards along a creek with larger dwellings in more sheltered positions towards the back of the narrow streets. The buildings on the shore, Lady Peyton explained, were smokehouses, warehouses and cottages where the fishermen lived. When Will asked who owned them she looked at him as though he were slow witted.

'I do, of course.' Her expression became suddenly fierce. 'And no man is going to take them from me.'

The inn, when they arrived, was small and plainer than Will had been accustomed to in larger towns. The innkeeper showed them to the second floor, speaking in an accent so thick Will could barely understand it.

'I've put tha' man in't room across of yours, my lady. Yous're the only guests so I can vouch there'll not be talk.'

Lady Peyton drew a sharp breath. 'Thank you, Nell. That will be all,' she said hastily, dismissing the woman with a coin.

Will hid a smile. He'd understood that well enough.

When her footsteps became fainter Lady Peyton smiled apologetically at Will, her cheeks still crimson. 'Nell can be…over-familiar, but she has a good heart. She will provide you with food and drink if you wish. I'm going to Rowland's Mount.'

'Now!' Will said in surprise. 'With the storm coming?'

'I can make it back in time. I don't need to collect much.'

'It's going to be dark soon. I promised your father I would keep you safe,' Will said firmly. 'Wait until the morning.' He moved to the middle of the corridor and planted his feet apart, folding his arms.

Eleanor glared at him and Will thought she was about to argue, but instead she opened the door to her room.

'Very well. In that case I shall rest. I am rather fatigued,' she said. 'Goodnight.'

She closed the door before he could answer.

Will shrugged and stowed his belongings in his own room. He looked out of the window, but there was nothing to see other than the back yard filled with crates and barrels. He went back downstairs and wandered through the village until he made his way down to the harbour. Around the low, wooden shacks, the ground was littered with discarded shells and fish carcasses so he carried on past. A wiry-haired old man was sitting before a brazier, grilling a pile of fish, and Will's mouth began to water at the smell. He bought one and stood by the shore, picking the hot, sweet flesh from the bones with his fingers.

'Wind's changed,' the old man remarked. 'Low

un's done wi'. Coming from east now. Storm'll be on us afore moon's high.'

'Yes,' Will answered, nodding politely, only catching half the man's words though the meaning was clear. He looked at the sky. The man was right. The clouds had rolled over, black around the edges. He should get back to the inn before he got a soaking. He said farewell to the old man and as an afterthought bought another fish for Lady Peyton who would no doubt be hungry, too.

There was no answer when he knocked on her door. He knocked again slightly louder.

'Lady Peyton, are you asleep?' he called. 'Eleanor?'

Still no answer. A terrible suspicion began to creep over Will. With Nell's insinuations fresh in his mind he cautiously tried the latch and pushed open the door.

The room was empty.

'Blasted woman,' Will growled. He stormed back down the stairs and found Nell sweeping the front steps.

'Where is Lady Peyton?' he asked.

Nell pointed in the direction of the sea. 'She's gone over. Said if you asked you's t' wait here.'

Will bit back an oath. He had no intention of waiting. He retrieved Tobias from the stable and rode along the shore track until he reached the jetty beside the causeway. Large, black slabs were laid side by side slightly less than half a mile in length. As he urged Tobias on to the causeway the sky echoed with the rumble of thunder. The horse shook its head with alarm. Patiently Will walked the stallion across the stones. Small waves lapped over the edges, trickling away in rivulets, followed by larger waves that surged from one side to the other and covered Will with a fine spray.

By the time he reached the island the wind was whipping around in fierce gusts. Small needles of ice stung Will's face and the sky was black. There was no sign of Lady Peyton so he dismounted and began to lead the horse up the winding path that had to lead to the house. Thunder rolled again and the odd hailstone began to fall.

He met Lady Peyton halfway up. She was leading her mare, a bulging bag across her shoulder, head bowed against the wind and almost did not see him until he called her name. She threw her hood back furiously.

'What are you doing here?' she demanded.

'I could ask you the same question, my lady,' Will replied.

A loud drum roll of thunder made them both jump. The clouds burst and large hailstones beat down upon them thickly, bouncing from the ground and stinging flesh where they hit.

Lady Peyton looked at the black clouds. Another clap of thunder sounded and the sky lit up. She patted the mare and tugged on its bridle.

'No time to argue now,' she said curtly, moving past Will. 'We have to cross back over.'

Will caught hold of her arm. 'Not in this storm,' he said. 'The horses will panic. Wait until it stops.'

Lady Peyton pulled her arm free, but Will caught hold of her again. She rounded on him furiously, her hair lifting and blowing about her face. In her fury she looked as fierce and as magnificent as the storm that raged around them.

'We are not leaving now,' Will insisted. Ignoring her protests, he pulled her to the side of the path where scrubby bushes and rocks provided as much cover as possible. He backed her against the rock face and threw his cloak about both of them. Lady Peyton struggled in Will's arms, her body twisting against him, brushing against parts of Will's anatomy in a manner that did nothing for his composure.

'Will you stop struggling?' he demanded. For ten minutes or more they stood close, Lady Peyton rigid and silent in his arms.

When the storm had finally spent itself and the

hail was reduced to occasional flurries Will released her.

'Now we can go,' he said. Eleanor said nothing. Her eyes were narrowed and her lips pressed together tightly. She lifted her head and marched down the path to the causeway...

Of which there was no sign.

Will stared in dismay at the place where he had crossed and swore loudly. He could just about make out the shape of the rocks as the tide surged across violently. Waves crashed and folded on to the shingle where they stood.

'That's why we needed to go,' Lady Peyton said angrily. 'We can't cross now. We're stranded here until morning.'

## Chapter Fourteen

'Did you plan this on purpose?' Eleanor rounded on William furiously.

'What?' William looked at her, his eyes as grey as the waves that crashed behind him. 'That's a serious accusation, my lady. Do you think me capable of such duplicity?'

'You schemed to accompany me here,' she said. 'Why shouldn't I think you capable of anything?'

He looked outraged. 'You think I might have contrived to strand us here so I could seduce you, I suppose?' William said sardonically.

The heat drained from Eleanor's face. That had been her suspicion exactly, but to hear William speak her thoughts so clearly made her stomach curl with embarrassment. Her heart began to pound with some other sensation she refused to acknowledge. 'I didn't say that!' she answered defensively.

William closed the gap between them in a single stride. He towered above Eleanor. 'You thought it, though. Whatever you believe, I don't need to resort to such trickery when I want a woman's company,' he said contemptuously, 'and I'm not in the habit of forcing myself on unwilling victims.'

Eleanor's stomach did a slow flip at his words. During the storm he had held her with such ease, though she had fought against him fiercely. She had no doubt he could have taken anything he wanted from her if he had chosen to do so and she was unsure how unwilling she would have been. She glanced away quickly in case he saw where her thoughts were leading.

Will sighed and gestured around. 'In any case, the last place I would choose to bed anyone would be a rain-drenched spit of land in winter!'

'Why did you follow me here, then?' Eleanor asked suspiciously.

'Your room was empty,' William said. His brows knotted together as he spoke, as though it was a personal slight. 'I told you to wait until morning before coming here. Why couldn't you obey a simple instruction? If you had done as I said, this would never have happened.'

Eleanor let out a gasp of indignation. 'I am not yours to command!' she said haughtily. She stomped to the water's edge. 'I had plenty of time to get back across safely. This would not have happened if *you* had not ignored me when I said we needed to cross.' She narrowed her eyes as her earlier suspicions reared up once more. 'What were you doing in my room?'

'I wanted to check you were all right,' William said. 'I should have guessed you would have run here as soon as my back was turned, but I thought I could trust you to keep your word.'

'I mean, what did you want?' Eleanor asked again, ignoring the jibe.

William gave a hollow laugh. 'I thought you might be hungry so I brought you a fish. In fact—' He broke off, delved into his saddlebag and produced a greasy roll of crumpled parchment. He held it out to Eleanor who unwrapped it. A solitary mackerel stared back at her through one charred eye, long beyond caring what trouble it had unwittingly caused.

'Well, at least we won't go completely hungry tonight,' Eleanor said with a heavy sigh.

'We could still leave,' William said confidently. 'It isn't too deep for the horses to wade across.' He strode to the shore's edge and peered at the submerged causeway. The dark band of stones could still be seen a foot or thereabouts below the foaming water.

'No, we can't,' Eleanor insisted. 'On a fine summer's day at mid-tide when the sea was calm perhaps we could risk it, but not in this weather.'

William's expression was sceptical and Eleanor's temper flared once more. She stalked to where he stood and gestured furiously at the sea.

'You know nothing about the sea. Men have died trying to cross at full tide,' she raged. 'It may not look deep yet, but by the time we reached halfway the current would have us and we'd be washed off.' She picked up a piece of driftwood and hurled it in frustration across the water in a wide arc. As if to confirm her words, the waves drew back and then surged across the gap that separated them from the mainland, swallowing the wood.

William's blue eyes followed it and he nodded reluctantly. 'Well, then, so it must be,' he said. 'When is the tide low again?'

'In a matter of hours, but by then it will be dark,' Eleanor snapped. 'There are beacons on the mainland and island for if it is absolutely necessary to cross, but with no one to light them they're useless. It's safer to stay until morning and cross at low tide.'

Hail began to fall again and another roll of thunder sounded. The wind blew through Eleanor's heavy wool cloak as though it was the finest silk and she shivered violently, her teeth chattering.

'There's no point in standing here to catch a chill. I'm going back up to the house.'

She stomped back to where the horses stood patiently and picked up the mare's bridle. William had not moved from his position by the shoreline where he faced the mainland.

'As far as I care you can sleep on the shore or in the stable as it's your fault we're here,' Eleanor called to him. 'However, the laws of hospitality dictate I should offer you a place to sleep. If you want a bed for the night, you had better come with me.' She walked up the path, without waiting to see if he would follow.

At the door she drew the key from the pouch at her waist, then hesitated. Little more than half an hour before, she had locked the door, not expecting to return for weeks at least. Now, unexpectedly she was back.

Never before had she been alone with a guest and never before had the guest been a solitary man. William looked at her expectantly as she clutched the key tightly in her hand and she realised how strange her behaviour must look.

'The house is empty...' she began. 'It is cold

and unprepared for visitors. That's why I came like I did.'

William put a hand on her shoulder, sensing her reluctance, and Eleanor inclined her head towards it, his touch reassuring. 'I should stable the horses first, if you show me where,' he said.

Eleanor watched as he disappeared out of sight, then let herself back into the cold main hall. She found a flint and lit as many candles as she could find until the room glowed invitingly. She began to carry them to the private chamber where she preferred to spend her days, but stopped, reluctant to let William into that room.

She ran upstairs to throw open the door to the bedchamber next to hers, the only one furnished warmly enough to bear in such temperatures. The thought of sleeping in such proximity to William sent a shiver through her that similar closeness in the inn had not. Despite Nell's allusion to their privacy, no thoughts of impropriety had crossed Eleanor's mind. Now there was nothing to stop him slipping into her room in the depths of night. And what was to stop her admitting him? Eleanor's blood felt suddenly hot as it coursed through her veins as she pressed her hands against the wall that would separate them. She drew a deep breath.

She returned to the hall, glad the chilled air prevented her cheeks from flushing too obviously. The small supply of logs that remained by the fireplace would not last long, but the room was so cold she could not bear to ration them. She knelt by the hearth and piled them high, striking the flint again and again in an attempt to light the kindling.

'Will you let me do that?' William asked over her shoulder.

She had not heard him enter the room and gave a start as he knelt close beside her. He took the flint from her hand, striking it with a practised motion until the kindling soon caught. He beckoned Eleanor to follow him. On the table he had placed the remaining food from his saddlebag: a crumbled chunk of cheese, a single apple, the mackerel and the flask of wine.

'Not much, I'm afraid,' William said regretfully.

'There may be more in the storerooms. I haven't looked yet,' Eleanor said.

As she spoke she recalled that she was the owner of the house, not he, and that her hospitality was sorely lacking. Eleanor looked at William properly and realised for the first time that his cloak was sodden. He had borne the brunt of the storm in order to keep her dry and must be chilled to the bone. Despite his error with the tide he had been acting with the best intentions and a little of her anger began to melt away.

'Take your cloak off and let it dry out,' she instructed. 'You're soaked through.'

'I will presently,' William replied. 'I noticed there is more wood beside the stable. I cannot vouch for it, but it looked as though it has escaped the worst of the weather. I'll make a trip now while the room warms a little.'

Eleanor took a candle to explore the storerooms, hoping that Goodwife Bradshawe had not emptied them completely. Fortune was on her side and she returned bearing the remnants of a brined ham, a pot of figs preserved in honey and, most welcome, a half-full bottle of brandy. Half-a-dozen logs were stacked against the hearth in front of the fire that was now blazing well. Eleanor put her supplies on the table and looked to see where William was.

He had removed both his cloak and padded surcoat and stood perfectly still at the far end of the room facing away from her, hands linked behind his back. Eleanor's heart caught in her throat and a feeling of nausea washed over her. If allowing William into her house in the first place had unsettled her that was nothing compared to finding him examining the portrait of her late husband.

Side by side the two men could not have appeared more different. William's hair glinted with gold where the candlelight flickered. His plain woollen tunic was damp in places, but clung to the contours of his back and arms, hinting enticingly at the firm muscles that lay beneath. Baldwin with his soft brown eyes and mild expression had seemed gentle and gallant. Now he looked weak and muted compared to the raw masculinity that Will wore like a cloak.

In that moment she hated them both. Hated Baldwin for dying and hated William for possessing all the passion and strength her husband had never possessed even when he had lived.

She crossed the room softly to stand by William. He looked down at her, his eyes full of compassion.

'Do you think about him often?' he asked softly.

'Every day,' Eleanor replied. As the words left her lips shame flooded over her. That was not true. Not recently. She looked guiltily into Baldwin's eyes. For days now he had barely crossed her mind. Even when she had come earlier she had given his portrait no more than a passing glance as she rushed to her bedchamber to find the dresses that were her excuse for coming back.

As for the dreams that had plagued her for three long years, she could not remember the last time she had woken in tears.

'He looks kind,' William said quietly.

Eleanor nodded, swallowing hard. 'He was,' she whispered. 'Kind and gentle and honourable.' *And his smile never sent my head spinning the way yours does*, she thought uncomfortably.

She cast her eyes down, unable to stand the judgement she imagined she saw on Baldwin's face. On balance the smaller chamber would be an easier place to spend the evening. Anything other than sit under Baldwin's gaze.

'This room takes too long to get warm,' she said tersely, taking William's arm and leading him into her sanctuary.

Before long they had established themselves in the smaller chamber and for a time they ate and drank in silence. Candles glowed warmly and William had somehow contrived to transport some of the burning logs to aid the progress of a new fire. They settled at either end of Eleanor's favourite place to sit, a high-backed bench covered with piles of sheepskin.

Outside the wind howled around the side of the building and Eleanor shivered at the sound, pulling a skin closer around her shoulders. William added another log to the fire and thrust the poker into the flames, then poured two measures of brandy. Eleanor watched him with interest. He had been in her house for less than an hour, but already his surroundings seemed to reshape themselves to fit him. To see him occupying the space so easily was unnerving.

When the tip of the poker glowed William plunged it into the cups, causing the brandy to bubble. He handed her a cup and Eleanor held it to her nose, the smoky fumes making her head spin pleasantly. The spirit slipped down easily, simultaneously warming her belly and causing ripples of dizziness in her head. A warm drowsiness settled on her and she gave a contented sigh.

'All things considered, I could not have planned a more pleasant evening if I had all the world's resources at my disposal,' William said, leaning forward to refill Eleanor's cup.

Eleanor's earlier suspicions came back in a rush and she stiffened. She was being unjust, she told herself firmly. William's look of horrified surprise when he saw the causeway had been genuine enough.

'I already told you this was unintentional,' William said in answer to her unspoken mistrust. 'You disapprove of me,' he remarked.

Eleanor looked down, turning the cup in her hands. Jennet's tales of his fickleness sprang to her mind and her heart twisted.

'It isn't my place to approve or not,' she said coolly. The brandy must have loosened her tongue because she added, 'You have no wife. You can behave as you please.'

'No, I have no wife,' William said, his voice hardening as it had done when he first spoke of his betrothal. He refilled his cup and drained it in one swift motion. 'If I find comfort in willing arms, so what? No promises are made and no hearts broken. Least of all mine. You more than anyone should appreciate that.'

'Me?' Eleanor brought her head up sharply to meet his eyes.

He gave her a crooked smile. 'I may guard my heart, but at least I allow myself pleasure. When I asked you to kiss me on the ferry I saw desire in your eyes, but you're too scared to risk your heart.'

Cold sweat broke out along Eleanor's spine. She pushed herself from her seat. 'You're wrong! That's not why I wouldn't kiss you.' She took a long drink of brandy, hoping he did not see the way her hand trembled. 'The request was improper. You were a complete stranger.'

William raised an eyebrow. 'You know me now. Kiss me now.'

His eyes glinted temptingly. Images of his lips on hers, his hands on her body ran through Eleanor's mind. Obeying him would be so easy. Stopping at a kiss almost impossible. The fear she had just denied coursed through her, hammering the temptation into submission. She stumbled to the window and stared into the blackness.

'Your smiles and words may work on tavern girls and milkmaids, but they will not work on me. You are arrogant and rude. You are no gentleman and the way you look at me...'

She crossed her arms protectively, bowing her head. 'You look at me as though I am no lady,' she cried.

'I see the woman as well as the lady,' William answered, his voice deep and low.

A fresh surge of longing coursed through Eleanor's body. She leaned her hands on the windowsill as a soft moan escaped her lips.

William moved to stand behind her. She could feel the heat from his body and smell the brandy on his breath. She wondered if it would taste as sweet on his lips. He brushed the hair back behind her ear and Eleanor closed her eyes, leaning her cheek into the palm of his hand.

Will's other hand slipped to her waist. 'It isn't wrong to feel,' he whispered into her ear. 'Listen to what your heart is telling you. Don't you miss a man's lips on yours, his arms around you in the night? Three years without a husband in your marriage bed must feel like eternity!'

His words drenched Eleanor like a pail of water over a drunkard and she stiffened. She twisted from William's arms and pushed him away.

'Baldwin died at our wedding feast,' she said through trembling lips. 'Think about what that means!'

William's eyes were full of confusion, then understanding began to dawn in them.

Eleanor nodded. 'I had no marriage bed. My marriage was never consummated.'

A blush began deep between her breasts, creeping hot across her chest and throat. 'You didn't know!' Eleanor whispered hoarsely, but before William could reply she pushed past him. She fled to the safety of her chamber and slammed the door. The room was freezing, but shame at what she had revealed warmed her better than a dozen burning logs ever could. With trembling fingers she pulled at the ribbons on her surcoat and let it fall to the floor. Her dress followed and she threw herself into bed.

She wanted to weep, but now she was alone no tears came. She stared unseeing at the shadows until her eyes would remain open no longer and she slipped into sleep.

## Chapter Fifteen

If Edmund Fitzallan had walked through the door at that moment Will would have throttled Eleanor's brother without remorse.

Edmund must have known the true nature of Eleanor's marriage. No wonder he had been so firm about setting the limit of the wager at a kiss. Even the most dissolute brother would not play the bawd with his sister's virginity!

The anguish and shame in Lady Peyton's voice as she blurted out her revelation had twisted in his chest like a knife. How could he continue the wager knowing what he now did? He should put an end to it as soon as he returned to Tawstott.

Angrily he seized the brandy from the table. He reached for a cup, then snorted and took a swig straight from the bottle, glaring into the flames. The fire was burning intensely and the air was stifling. He paced the room fretfully, then stormed into the chilly outer hall, bottle in hand.

Even that was not enough to cool his temper. He threw open the door and stomped down to the shore, relishing the icy gusts that blew about him. The storm had abated though the wind surged strongly and the moon appeared and vanished behind the heavy clouds. He sat on the damp shingle and watched the waves churn around, deep in thought.

He shivered and took another draught of brandy to warm him. It was good quality, far beyond what his purse would buy, something that befitted a knight such as Sir Baldwin or Martin of Allencote.

Just as Eleanor Peyton did.

Why had he ever thought a woman of her status and beauty would look at him? He had no wealth or lands, nothing that she could ever need. His only hope of gaining anything approaching the scale of wealth he would need was through his investments and to do that he needed money. His indecision regarding the wager vanished. He burned to kiss Eleanor, so what would be the sense in making himself poorer in the process? He would just have to take more care than usual to ensure Eleanor did not get hurt.

The sleet had become heavier so Will scrambled

to his feet and went back to the house, only to find the door had blown wide open. He pulled it closed and took one of the candlesticks from the table, leaving the brandy bottle in its place, and made his way up the stairs. One door was firmly shut, but the one beyond it stood open and he guessed it was the room intended for him.

By candlelight Will stripped down to his braies, hung his wet tunic and breeches on the back of a chair to dry, then climbed into the low bed. He drifted in and out of sleep, half-waking occasionally to notice that the moon had moved further across the window.

Then he heard the cry.

He wondered at first if he had dreamed it, or mistaken the call of a seabird, but the sound came again. A low moan cut off abruptly before returning as a high sob of anguish.

Will sat bolt upright, his body tensed. He'd left the door open earlier when he walked to the shore. Had there been someone else on the island who had intruded while he was on the beach?

The sound came again, unmistakable this time: a female voice, calling out in distress.

Eleanor!

Will sprang from the bed. His hand moved to where his sword should be, but this was not his room and the weapon was safely at the inn with the rest of his belongings. Spitting out an oath, he seized the candlestick and crept into the passageway, moonlight streaming across the floor to guide him. Lady Peyton's door was closed and no one was in sight. Raising his makeshift weapon high, Will burst through into the room.

The door slammed back against the wall with a crash that echoed throughout the building. The room was empty save the occupant of the bed who jerked upright, eyes widening and hands rushing to her mouth as she screamed in terror.

'It's me, my lady,' he said urgently.

'Will?' She was on her knees now, looking around in confusion. Her eyes rested on the candlestick in Will's hand. He bent to place it on the floor.

'I heard you cry out,' he explained quickly. 'I thought you were in danger.'

She shook her head, the tangle of her hair shifting as though each copper strand was alive.

'A nightmare,' she whispered hoarsely. 'The same dream that…I…'

Her voice died away with a strangled sob and she buried her face in her hands. Her entire body convulsed violently.

Will was on the bed before he had time to consider the wisdom of his action. He held her to him protectively, enfolding her tightly in an embrace until her sobs began to subside.

'A dream,' he soothed. 'It was only a dream.'

Eleanor began to shake again. Her hands slipped around his waist, her fingernails searing lines of fire on to his bare skin.

At her touch Will became acutely conscious of how little he was wearing. He had rushed through without thinking and was clothed in nothing apart from his linen braies. Her shift clung to the curves of her frame and every muscle in his body stiffened as he felt the heat radiating from Eleanor's body. He drew her head on to his chest and buried a hand in her hair, glad of the darkness and hoping she was not aware of how little lay between them.

'He dies and I can't prevent it.' Eleanor wept. 'I couldn't then and I can't in my dreams. Over and over. Only this time—'

She broke off and peered up at Will in confusion, as though seeing him clearly for the first time. Her lips were inches from his.

'The eyes...' she murmured and her mouth twisted in distress. She shuddered, a powerful tremor that ran the length of her body and did nothing for Will's self-possession. Damp tendrils of hair stuck to her forehead and cheeks.

Will smoothed them back, tracing the line of her cheekbone with a thumb.

'Eleanor,' he whispered comfortingly. He rolled the name around his tongue. It felt strange to be saying it out loud, but he had abandoned all sense of propriety when he had thrown himself on to her bed. 'Eleanor, you cannot blame yourself for what happened.'

'I know, but it feels so real. I cannot bear it.'

She trembled again and her body sagged. Will clasped her tighter, stroking a comforting hand down the curve of her back. She leaned into him. The sensation of her breasts pushing against Will's bare chest sent waves of desire cresting over him. Will realised how cold he was even as he was thankful for the effect the temperature had on cooling his ardour. Eleanor must be freezing. He drew the heavy feather bolster snugly around her.

'I'll be back soon,' he said. Shivering, he walked swiftly to his own room, pulled on his still-damp tunic and breeches and went downstairs. He found the brandy bottle and lit a candle. In the dim light his eyes fell on the portrait of Sir Baldwin.

There was no passion in those eyes. This noble knight would have courted his bride cautiously, no doubt waiting patiently for their first legal coupling. Had those weak lips ever done more than kiss his betrothed's hand, a chaste brush of the cheek at the very most? It was little wonder the prospect of another marriage held so few attractions for Eleanor and little wonder Will's attempts at seduction had so disconcerted her.

Eleanor had described him as kind, as though that was the only attribute that mattered in a husband. Perhaps, for a noblewoman with no choice over whose wife she became, it was. Edmund had said Eleanor needed reminding she was a woman, but she had never discovered it in the first place!

He returned to the bedchamber. In the vastness of the bed Eleanor was small and fragile. Will wondered how many nights she had lain here and cried alone for that aloof figure in the portrait. She sat with the covers pulled up about her waist and her hands clasped in her lap, watching him expectantly. Her eyes were black smudges against skin the colour of cream. Will dragged his eyes from the alluring contours the candlelight revealed and concealed with each flicker.

He held out the bottle to her. 'Drink this. We've both had more than enough to make our heads ache tomorrow, but you need something to warm you.'

Instead of taking it, Eleanor caught him by the wrist. Taken aback, Will settled the candle on the chest beside the bed. He allowed her to draw him on to the bed until he sat alongside her. They were close, but not touching, and the layers of sheets and bolster were as effective a boundary as any wall, but Will's pulse began to race faster than in the presence of any woman he had bedded.

He held the bottle out again. Eleanor put it to her lips and drank deeply. Candlelight shadows moved across her skin, daring Will's lips to catch them. As innocent as he now knew her to be, could she really not suspect what effect this proximity was having on him?

'Thank you for coming to me,' she said, a weary smile on her lips as she passed the bottle back.

'I promised I would defend you,' Will said gravely.

When she looked at him next her eyes were solemn and wide. 'Tell me about the nightmares,' he prompted.

'I did not want to marry Baldwin, but I accepted my duty. When he died—after the shock had passed—I felt relief that I was free to live as I chose.' Eleanor twisted the bolster between her hands, her eyes downcast. 'I think the nightmares are my punishment for that.'

Anger and pity flared in Will's heart. He twisted around and took her by the shoulders. 'Don't think that,' he said forcefully. 'The past is what it is. If you close yourself away, you may as well have died when he did.'

Eleanor reached a trembling hand to Will's chest. Her eyes were heavy-lidded and full of barely suppressed longing mixed with apprehension. As she parted her lips Will tensed. He had imagined this moment many times, but not like this.

As he pulled away Eleanor's hands slid around his neck. 'Stay with me, Will,' she whispered beseechingly into his ear.

Will closed his eyes and gritted his teeth. No man should have to turn down such an entreaty, but as much as he would regret leaving now, it would be nothing to the guilt he would feel if he did not go. He took her hands and laid them on her lap.

'You don't mean that,' he said softly. 'Not truly. Not in the way a man wants to hear it.'

'Go then,' she said in a voice so heart-rending that Will almost changed his mind. She began to turn away, but Will took hold of her arms and pulled her back round to face him once more.

'No, Eleanor. I won't allow any shame or sadness. Believe me, I want what you are offering more than I can say, but not under these circumstances.' He stared deeply into her eyes, willing her to understand what he meant. 'Anything you did now you would regret and I won't let you make that mistake.'

Eleanor nodded. She smiled faintly. Impulsively Will bent and planted a kiss on her forehead, then left the room before his resolve weakened.

Back in his bedchamber he stood at the window, gazing out into the night. Eleanor wanted him as much as he wanted her; he knew it with absolute certainty now. He had believed he had nothing to offer Eleanor, but he had been wrong. He would kiss her as Baldwin never had. He would show her the passion that lay within her and the power she could wield over any man she flashed those wide emerald eyes at. Whichever noble claimed her next would not be able to get away with treating her as coldly as Baldwin would have.

'Let that be my wedding gift to you, my lady,' he muttered under his breath, wondering if he did, how he would ever find peace again.

They crossed over the causeway as soon as they were able, riding silently side by side, slightly uncomfortable in each other's presence. As Will had predicted, Eleanor's head ached from the brandy, but the dull throb at the base of her neck was nothing to the knives of shame that ripped her stomach whenever she looked in his direction.

Will had made no mention of what had passed between them, only talked politely of practicalities, stowing Eleanor's bundle of dresses safely in her saddlebag and tidying away the remnants of their meal. Eleanor's breath caught in her throat at his unexpected sensitivity. If he had made a mockery of her clumsy attempt at seduction or reproached her for it, she was certain she would have taken Baldwin's sword from the wall and run herself through rather than face him again.

As they reached the mainland Will spurred his horse into a gallop, his cloak streaming behind him and rode ahead to the inn. A shiver ran through Eleanor's body at the memory of his flesh beneath her fingers and his taut muscles iron hard against her as he enclosed her within his embrace. Thank goodness he had shown more strength than she last night. She inhaled the cold, fresh air and let out a long sigh. Better deny utterly that it happened rather than court insanity by wishing herself back into his arms.

By the time Eleanor reached the inn Will had collected their belongings and was waiting outside. There was no sign of Nell.

'I paid her well,' Will said. 'She seemed happy to take more than the agreed amount for the inconvenience of guarding two empty rooms.'

Eleanor smiled nervously. Nell could be relied upon for discretion, but to talk of last night sent her thoughts spiralling into inappropriate places. 'I have to arrange the oyster delivery. You can wait here if you like,' she offered. 'I won't be long.'

'I'll come,' he replied firmly. 'I walked to the harbour yesterday and some of the men looked unruly.'

These rough fishermen and oyster farmers were Eleanor's own serfs, long loyal to Baldwin, and would do her no harm, but she was strangely reluctant to mention her husband's name to Will after last night. Instead she jiggled the reins and led the way down the narrow street.

Eleanor and Will picked their way between beached boats and piles of nets until they came to the low storehouse at the end of the harbour where the bailiff was waiting. Will followed her inside the dim building, standing protectively close as she conducted her business.

Negotiations over, Eleanor lifted the lid on one of the crates and gazed longingly at the rough shells.

'Try one, milady,' the bailiff suggested, handing her a knife.

With a practised hand Eleanor twisted the short, wide blade and levered one open, sucking it from the shell. Until the briny liquor hit her tongue she had not realised how ravenous she was. She chewed with a deep sigh of appreciation. She licked her lips and caught Will's eye. He was watching her keenly, a look of hunger in his eyes as though he was tasting the sweet flesh himself. She reached for another.

'Here—have this one,' she said, shucking it open with hands that felt unexpectedly clumsy.

He regarded the offering suspiciously.

'You have eaten oysters, haven't you?' Eleanor asked.

'Of course,' Will said. 'Steamed or baked, though.'

Eleanor grinned at his reluctance. 'I thought you were a sophisticated man of the city,' she teased.

Will returned her grin. 'I'm a sophisticated man of an *inland* city.' He took the oyster and tossed it back, defiantly swallowing it whole.

'That's not how to do it,' Eleanor scolded. She held another out to him. 'Eat it slowly, savour the taste.'

Will inclined his head until he was level with hers, closed his hand over Eleanor's, his thumb brushing the soft hollow of her wrist. His eyes never left hers as he guided the shell to his lips. He tilted his head back to tease the creamy flesh past his lips with a sensuous slowness that caused Eleanor's pulse to race. His eyes gleamed as he chewed. He ran his tongue slowly around his lips.

'You're right,' he said. His lips curled into tantalising smile. 'But I find most experiences are better savoured than rushed.'

Eleanor blushed and drew her hand away. She made her farewells to the bailiff, issued some final instructions and they returned to their horses.

As they climbed the hill Eleanor looked back over her shoulder at Rowland's Mount. The trip had not been at all how she had planned it. True, she had escaped her mother's demands for a new marriage, but as to forgetting about Will Rudhale she had failed completely. The less she thought on that matter the better it would be. The house would keep her secrets, but would she ever be able to return without thinking of what might have happened between them? No time to wonder now, however. It was time to return to Tawstott and her fate.

# Chapter Sixteen

They galloped through Tawstott Town gate as the first peal of the curfew bell sounded, coming to a stop in the marketplace. The last few remaining traders and merchants bustled about, shutting up workshops and loading carts, seemingly oblivious to the weary, mud-soaked pair on horseback.

Panting hard, Eleanor pulled on the reins and slowed the mare to a trot. She slipped from the saddle and stretched, arching her back until the throbbing in her shoulders began to lessen. Since the ferry the wind had been against them and swollen clouds had threatened to burst at any moment. As it was, a fine drizzle hung in the air, soaking cloaks and boots.

They had ridden hard and Eleanor had been pushed almost to the limit of her stamina. They had little more than a mile to travel. At Tawstott Mote a warm fire would be waiting, a soft mattress and dry clothes. There would also be a reckoning with her mother, suitors and duties. Nausea and melancholy began to churn deep in her belly.

A discreet cough tugged her attention. Will was looking at her expectantly. Eleanor realised she had not heard anything he had been saying and smiled apologetically.

Now she was no longer on horseback tiredness washed over Eleanor and her body was as heavy as if it were made of stone. She yawned and leaned against a wall, pulling her cloak tightly around her body and closing her eyes.

'Eleanor, what are you doing?' Will asked anxiously.

'Just resting,' Eleanor said, another yawn escaping. 'Let's stop for a moment.'

'It's too cold and damp and the streets will be empty soon,' Will said firmly. 'We're almost home.'

'Why shouldn't we rest here? I am in no hurry to return,' Eleanor said, bitterness creeping into her voice. A sob of tiredness welled up in her throat. She bowed her head, her hood falling forward to mask her face.

She sensed Will move close in front of her and draw the hood back. His hands were warm as he lifted her chin. The memory of him pulling her from the terror of her nightmare into his strong arms rose again, sending heat pulsing along the length of her limbs. She knew she could tell him anything and he would not condemn her.

'I don't want to go back.' She sighed. 'Everything that awaits me...'

She broke off, unable to finish, but she would never have finished the sentence in any case.

'Better find a darker alley if you're going to sard your whore against a wall,' a rasping voice jeered behind Will.

Will spun on his heel, pushing Eleanor behind him protectively. She looked past him to where two taggle-bearded men in roughspun tunics stood leering at them. The taller swigged from a bottle and belched loudly.

'Stay still,' Will muttered to Eleanor. He stepped forward smoothly, covering the ground between him and the men in two easy strides.

'Apologise to the lady before I have the tongue from your mouth,' he ordered harshly.

The speaker nudged his companion in the ribs. 'He should have kept her hood up. If she sees that face, she'll charge double,' he smirked. 'I'm prettier, why not try my pole instead?' he called to Eleanor with an obscene gesture.

Will spat out an oath. Eleanor's hand fumbled

for the dagger at her girdle. Before she had it free Will had knocked the speaker to the ground with a powerful blow and drawn his sword at the man's throat. The second ruffian dropped his bottle with a whimper and fled without a backward glance.

Will reached down and hauled the snivelling man to his feet by the hair. He dragged him bodily to where Eleanor stood and hurled him to his knees where he begged forgiveness and babbled entreaties over and over.

'Say the word, my lady, and I'll run him through,' Will said harshly, pressing the point of the sword into the man's neck. His eyes were iron hard with controlled fury.

Eleanor shook her head weakly. Will's face softened. He reached out a hand as if to caress her, then stopped and instead sheathed his sword. He gave the man a firm push with his boot that sent him sprawling into the dirt.

'You're fortunate the lady is more merciful than you deserve,' Will said, his voice dripping with loathing. 'Crawl home, you drink-addled cur.'

The man scrambled to his feet and loped off down an alley.

Eleanor was still gripping her dagger in a trembling hand. Gently Will took it from her. 'Why do you have this?' he scolded mildly. He slipped it back into the scabbard at her girdle. 'I told you I would protect you.'

His fingers brushed lightly against her waist. A ripple of exhilaration travelled down her spine.

'You could have been hurt,' Eleanor whispered. 'I'm sorry. It was my fault we stopped. If I hadn't insisted...' She raised her eyes to meet his. Blue eyes. She gave a cry of shock and clutched Will's arm as the blood drained from her face.

Will studied her with concern. 'Well, I certainly can't take you back to Tawstott in such a state!' he said lightly. 'You're so pale that your father will have me flogged for ill-treating you!'

He lashed the mare's reins to Tobias's bridle and mounted the stallion. Before Eleanor had time to protest he bent down and lifted her effortlessly on to the saddle in front of him, one arm about her waist to stop her slipping off. She stiffened at the unexpected closeness, but feeling the warmth radiating from him allowed her body to relax.

As Will slowly walked the horses down the darkened street Eleanor fought to control the beating of her heart. Her nightmare had been different last night, but until she had looked into Will's eyes just then she had not understood why. Now she understood that the eyes of the dying man had not been Baldwin's. They had belonged to Will and the thought of his death filled her with a terror deeper than she could bear.

Will slipped into a narrow alley and stopped before a low door. Music and voices drifted from within. He dismounted and helped Eleanor down.

'Where are we?' she asked uncertainly.

'You don't want to go back yet and until you are happier I don't intend to take you,' Will said as he looped the reins around a rail. He opened the door and gestured for Eleanor to pass through. She found herself inside a tavern, the air thick with wood smoke. Will slipped an arm through hers and guided her past couples dancing to a piper's tune to a low, long bench by the fireplace. He nudged the occupants along with a few muttered explanations and helped Eleanor to sit.

'We'll have ale, please, Molly,' he called out.

Eleanor watched the dancers spinning with arms about each other and her foot began to beat in time with the rhythm.

'Would a dance raise your spirits or are you too weary?' Will asked.

She shook her head, though the idea of being in Will's arms once again sent her stomach fluttering. 'I told you before, I don't dance.'

'You told me you don't wear colours, yet I see you in blue,' he said, gesturing to her gown. 'You told me a lot of things that you don't do and I'm not sure I believe you any longer.'

A young skinny woman with a mass of curly hair brought a jug and two cups and deposited them on the table.

'There'll be a penny for Matty if you can send him to the Mote to tell Sir Edgar that we're here,' Will said. 'We'll be along as soon as Lady Peyton has recovered from the journey.'

Molly smiled warmly at Will and cast a suspicious eye at Eleanor, who returned the look boldly. She shifted closer to Will on the bench until their shoulders touched. Molly walked away with a toss of her curls, hips swaying seductively. Eleanor slid a sidelong glance at Will to see if the woman's efforts had hit their target, but his head was bowed and he was busy pouring the ale. She wondered how many other women Will had brought here. His betrothed surely must have been among them. He turned to hand her a cup and caught her studying him. Eleanor looked away guiltily.

'Does my face disgust you?' Will asked.

His voice was guarded, but after the drunkard's jibe that was understandable. He lifted his head better to display the scarred side, pushing back the hair that usually covered it. Eleanor regarded him closely. The scars were thin, pale tracks that were barely noticeable from a distance. Even as close as he was now sitting, her eyes slipped over them, she was so used to the sight. When he smiled or his eyes fell on her with such intensity she forgot them altogether.

'Do you think me so petty that such a thing would trouble me?' she asked indignantly.

Will shrugged. 'It matters to some' was his reply. There was no self-pity in his voice; he simply stated it as a fact. Shame twisted her guts.

'Will…what I called you yesterday, I was unfair. You are neither rude nor arrogant. I'm sorry.'

He smiled at her, handsome in the firelight, and Eleanor wondered why any woman could think him ugly.

'We both said rash things last night,' he mused.

Eleanor's cheeks flamed and she took a cooling drink of ale.

After a while, Will sprang to his feet, holding a hand out. 'You look more like your fair self again. I really must return you home.'

'Not my home,' Eleanor pointed out, slipping her hand into his. They stood face-to-face. His fingers tightened briefly on hers and a pang of sadness stabbed Eleanor. 'I don't know when I shall return there.' *Or who with*, she thought.

She rode the final miles back to Tawstott Mote in silence, keeping her eyes on the road until the lights of the house came into view.

Sir Edgar and Lady Fitzallan were both waiting in Sir Edgar's library. Eleanor's eyes widened in surprise at seeing her parents sitting together.

Sir Edgar welcomed Eleanor back with a warm embrace. 'You're much delayed. Was there trouble on the road?' he asked, his brow wrinkling.

'Nothing that should concern you, Father,' Eleanor said hastily. 'Master Rudhale kept me perfectly safe.'

'Safe from what?' Lady Fitzallan asked sharply, rising from her seat.

Eleanor dug her nails into her palms, heart sinking at her blunder. 'From everything...I mean, from nothing...' she stammered. She moved to Will's side. He gave her a smile that made Eleanor's hair stand on end.

'I received a message from a tavern runabout that you had stopped in town,' Sir Edgar said.

Lady Fitzallan turned her cold eyes on Will.

'You took my daughter drinking like some low-born wench?'

Will put his hands together and assumed a respectful expression. Only the set of his jaw told Eleanor how well he was hiding his temper. 'Your ladyship, the weather was bad and Lady Peyton was exhausted. I would not have her fatigue herself when there was somewhere to shelter.'

'You should have taken a carriage and behaved properly,' Lady Fitzallan said to Eleanor. 'If I had known your plan before you left, I would have forbidden it absolutely.'

'*I* allowed it,' Sir Edgar said. His voice was low but firm and his wife sat down once more.

'You also allowed our daughter to assist Master Rudhale like a common servant,' Lady Fitzallan said firmly, fixing her husband with a glare. 'Well, no more. The preparations are almost completed. Master Rudhale can manage perfectly well now so there is no reason for Eleanor to be in his company any longer.'

Eleanor's stomach gave a lurch. Her eyes flashed from her mother to Will and she opened her mouth to protest, but Lady Fitzallan's glare quashed her rebellion. There was no reason for her mother's words to cause distress. She had left Tawstott to escape his company after all.

She bowed her head. 'As you wish, Mother.'

'Thank you for bringing Eleanor back safely, William,' Sir Edgar said warmly. 'You must be tired, too. You may leave us.'

Will nodded to Sir Edgar. He swept a low graceful bow to Lady Fitzallan and Eleanor, his face void of any emotion. Eleanor swallowed and inclined her head, not trusting herself to speak. Will's eyes narrowed and he strode past her to the furthest door, close enough that the tail of his cloak swept against her skirts.

'Master Rudhale, wait!'

He paused at the door and Eleanor ran to him. His eyes burned into her.

'I should give you my thanks also,' she declared loudly. 'Thank you for what you did tonight, Will.' She lowered her voice so only he could hear. 'And last night. You were a good friend to me.'

Will's lips became a thin line and the flesh around his eyes tightened. 'I am your humble servant. Goodnight, my lady,' he said stiffly. He left the room without a backward glance.

Eleanor watched him go in confusion. She had known the closeness they had shared would have no place in Tawstott. She must be Lady Peyton again and he Master Rudhale, but this sudden coldness was like a slap to the face. She bit back her misery and curtsied to her parents.

'Will you excuse me also? I am too weary for any more talk tonight.'

That night sleep refused to come. Eleanor closed her eyes and was transported back to her chamber. Will was beside her in her bed, his lips on her throat, and his hands on her body, caressing her in ways that had little to do with comforting. She threw herself on to her front, burying her face in the pillow with a moan of frustration. Last night she had come so close to surrendering to him, craving something she only half-believed could exist. To think such thoughts made her no better than the whore the drunkard had mistaken her for!

It would be better for both of them to never speak again. Anything else could only end in misery.

Will found Edmund in the Great Hall playing knucklebones with Rob and two ushers. The young noble slammed the jacks on to the table, knocking a wine jug over in the process, and opened his arms to Will.

'The traveller returns,' he slurred, beaming. 'Have you come to collect your winnings?'

Will frowned, pointedly looking at the other men, and Edmund closed his mouth with exaggerated care. Will cocked his head towards Edmund's companions.

'Leave us,' he said pleasantly. The three men stood. 'Not you, Rob.'

'Well, tell all.' Edmund grinned. 'Clever of you to convince my sister to take you along.'

'I'm not here for money,' Will said curtly.

'You mean even with two days alone you couldn't kiss her?' Edmund laughed.

'Oh, I could. And plenty more besides,' Will said darkly. He watched disdainfully as Edmund considered the information and had the satisfaction of seeing his eyes widen in panic.

'Tell me you didn't bed her,' Edmund said in alarm.

'Of course I didn't!' Will replied. He glared at Edmund. 'You didn't tell me she was a virgin!'

Edmund reached for his cup, raising his eyebrows. 'Is she? I always wondered after the abrupt end to her marriage. Does it make a difference?'

Will leaned forward and slammed his hand on to the table, scattering jacks and dice. Edmund gaped at his outburst.

'It makes all the difference,' Will growled.

'I understand why you're angry,' Edmund said reasonably. 'It makes the challenge harder after all. Do you want to raise the stakes?'

'The challenge is not the point,' Will said. 'A worldly woman is one thing, but toying with an innocent maiden is another. The capacity to hurt the lady is greater, to say nothing to the damage to her honour.'

'It's a kiss, Will, nothing more! Eleanor won't get hurt, I'm sure you're skilled enough to see to that.' Edmund grinned. 'And virgin or not, she's still a widow. She must have been kissed! No husband would expect her to come to his bed completely unworldly, not even Baldwin.'

Will took a long, slow breath and bunched his fists. The matter of Eleanor's heart was one best left well alone and the thought of a future husband pierced his own like a dagger.

'I dislike being deceived,' he muttered. The words sounded hollow in his ears, but Edmund seemingly did not notice as he lurched to his feet and spread his arms wide to embrace Will.

'The deception wasn't intentional, but I apologise,' Edmund said. 'I have full confidence that you will succeed.'

Will received his friend's drunken embrace, then

left the hall. Rob caught up with him in the passageway.

'There's more bothering you than Edmund's idiocy,' he said shrewdly. 'Are you sure it's Lady Peyton's heart you're concerned with?'

'Who else's? Don't think mine is being squeezed,' Will said with an unconvincing laugh. 'The wager stands and I *will* win it.'

He climbed the staircase to his room. As he passed Eleanor's chamber he stopped. No sounds came from within. Was she sleeping peacefully or was her night plagued by nightmares once again? There would be no one to hold her tonight if she awoke weeping.

*A good friend!*

He rubbed his eyes wearily. Eleanor meant it kindly, but her words had stung him more than any insult. He had barely kept his composure long enough to leave the room. What sort of friend would deceive her so? Moreover, how would friendship ever satisfy him when he was increasingly wanting so much more?

# Chapter Seventeen

Red-and-gold banners whirled and waved, buffeted by the wind that transformed them to a string of flames dancing along the road from Tawstott Town.

Eleanor sat in the window seat of the solar and watched Duke Roland's procession draw closer to Tawstott Mote. She drummed her fingers irritably against the windowsill, trying to block out the sound of Anne's lute. Anne fumbled a note and began the tune for the seventh time.

'That is enough, Anne!' Lady Fitzallan stood and brushed down her skirts. 'Eleanor, how much longer do you think before they are here?'

Eleanor turned her head back to the window, wondering how days so short could last so long. She had spent only two days in the company of her mother and sister, but it had felt like a month. Lady Fitzallan, pleased with Eleanor's obedience, had

made no reference to the words that had passed
between them previously. Anne had obviously not
forgiven Eleanor's interference with Will and ac-
knowledged her presence with barely concealed
animosity.

The banners were closer now. Eleanor could
make out the guards on horseback flanking the
gilded carriage drawn by four stately horses. Four
men rode chargers behind, their coloured pennants
flapping back and forth so that Eleanor could not
make out the symbols they bore.

'Very soon, I would say,' she answered.

'We should assemble to greet them,' her mother
replied. She looked her daughters up and down
with her cool green eyes. She sniffed, reached
out and straightened the fur at the shoulder of
Anne's surcoat, then with a nod of satisfaction,
swept from the room. Eleanor watched her depart, feeling like a child discovered with her hair
full of twigs. Anne's expression was much as she
imagined her own to be and Eleanor risked a conspiratorial smile.

'I'll wager a plate of honey cake that Mother will
have a dozen "headaches" before the visit is over.'

Anne frowned, but her lips twitched with
amusement. Eleanor patted a hand on the cush-

ion beside her. Anne joined her at the window and peered out.

'I can see the knights, but I can't make out their faces. Just think, our husbands might be riding towards us right now,' she said wistfully. Her face lit up and Eleanor did not have the heart to share her own views on the subject. She swallowed down the sense of dread and forced a smile.

'I suppose they might.' She picked up the cup that stood on the window ledge and was surprised to feel her hand shake as she raised it to her lips. 'I truly hope you find your husband, if you think it will make you happy.'

Anne squeezed her hand, friends once more.

'We'd better go,' Eleanor said. 'If Mother is going to behave as though we were seven years old, I wouldn't put it past her to whip our legs if we're late!'

She linked arms with her sister and they made their way to the Great Hall. The tables were laden with plates and dishes in readiness for the arrival of the guests. The scent of roasting meat wafted enticingly through the room, though this would be a modest feast in comparison to the one that would take place in two days' time. Serving maids and pages stood to attention, waiting, and checking the final preparations had been taken care of was Will.

He had his back to them, unaware of their presence. Unusually his fair hair was pulled tightly back into a cord at the nape of his neck. He was dressed in a black jerkin, trimmed and edged with Sir Edgar's green and orange that fitted his form closely. Eleanor watched him with an unbearable sense of yearning. Since their unexpectedly formal farewell Eleanor had not seen Will. She had known that he would be present to greet the duke and his retinue, but to come across him without warning set her heart thumping unbearably.

He walked between the tables, speaking to the servants and making small adjustments here and there. He moved at a leisurely pace with an assured calmness. Confidence radiated from him and had it not been for the liveried uniform he wore Eleanor could have believed he was master of the house himself.

Anne's hand tightened on Eleanor's arm. She glanced down at her sister to see that Anne was watching Will, too. Anne's eyes were hard and she scuffed her foot on the stone floor.

'He didn't love me, did he,' she whispered, her voice hard.

It was a statement rather than a question. Eleanor's heart tightened in pity. She put her arm about Anne's shoulder and gave the girl a sympathetic look. 'I'm sorry you were upset by his words, but whatever his faults I don't believe he willingly hurt you.'

'Have you fallen for his charms completely?' Anne asked incredulously.

'No!' Eleanor said, quicker than she intended. 'That is, I don't defend him for no reason. I don't think he realised you cared so deeply for him.'

'I hoped he would come to care for me in time, but when I saw how he looked at you I knew he never would,' Anne said bitterly. 'Whether you intended it or not, it's you he loves, not me.'

Eleanor looked back at the steward who had walked to the high table on the dais. He still had his back to them as he spoke to Sir Edgar's cup-bearer.

'He wants me. I'm not too blind to see that. But love?' A lump filled in her throat as she thought of Jennet's tales of him running from any attachment. The closeness they had shared on Rowland's Mount had vanished as soon as they returned to Tawstott. 'I don't know if Will has any intention to love anyone,' she said quietly.

'In that case I pity the woman who falls in love with him,' Anne said darkly. Her brow knotted together. 'Don't let it be you, Eleanor, or he'll break your heart, too.' She tossed her hair back and ran through the Great Hall, vanishing in a flurry of skirts.

Eleanor watched her go with a mixture of sadness and relief. To see such hardness in Anne's young eyes was heart-rending, but better her anger was transformed to sadness than she spent her days wishing for someone she could not have. 'Let her at least find happiness this week,' she murmured to herself.

She followed Anne's path and as she passed by the dais Will looked around and saw her. His mouth widened into a smile so unlike the cold expression when he had last said goodbye that Eleanor's step faltered.

'Lady Peyton,' he called softly.

He cocked his head and beckoned her with a raise of an eyebrow and a twitch of his lips. Eleanor's instinct was to run, but Will held her eye and she stood frozen to the spot. When she did not move, he walked to her.

'What have you been doing these past two days? Eating sweetmeats and petting lapdogs like a noble lady while I toiled alone, I'll bet,' Will said, his voice light and full of humour.

'Not at all,' Eleanor said indignantly. 'I have

spent most of my time in the solar, but I haven't been entirely idle. I've been weaving garlands for the feast.' She gestured to the greenery that ornamented the tables; red holly berries and white mistletoe wound around yew twigs and holly branches.

'This is your work?' Will said, raising his eyebrows sceptically.

'Do you doubt me?' Eleanor asked.

Will unexpectedly took hold of her hand and held it palm up. At his touch Eleanor's skin fluttered as though moths had landed on her palm.

'What are you doing?' she asked, startled at his boldness.

'Checking for proof of your claims,' Will answered sternly.

He grinned to show he was joking and Eleanor felt a laugh bubble up inside her. She did not think she had smiled at all in the past two days and until then had not realised how much she had missed Will's presence. The days had never dragged when she had him to argue or joke with.

'Why, yes, I see where the prickles have left their marks,' Will said, brushing his thumb across the red pinpricks that covered Eleanor's palms and fingers. 'You are telling the truth. And I thought you had abandoned all your intentions to aid me.'

He was teasing, but even so his point was barbed and it stung.

'The choice was not mine as well you know,' Eleanor protested. 'I would much rather have continued as before.'

'You would rather have been counting wine barrels and hams than embroidering and weaving?' Will asked.

Eleanor lowered her eyes, reluctant to admit she had missed Will's company. Anne's warning echoed in her ears. It would be a foolish woman who gave her heart to such a man, and Eleanor feared she was more than halfway to being that fool. 'I dislike my time being unoccupied,' she said defensively. 'Naturally I regretted the end of our association.'

'It was the activity you missed, of course,' Will said as he replaced Eleanor's hand by her side.

For two nights she had forced herself not to think about what she had wanted so much. Now seeing him again her limbs weakened with a need to touch him once more. The simple touch of his fingers on her flesh had sent waves of desire through her entire being and resisting the urge to seize his hands once more and guide them to her waist was physically painful. In her mind his arms wound around her body, his fingers nestling in her hair, his breath warm against her neck. She gazed up at him through her eyelashes to find him watching her keenly. Could it be that he was fighting the same urges she was working so hard to deny? She shivered with longing and drew a deep breath to calm herself.

'I must go. The duke is almost here and I cannot be absent when he arrives,' she mumbled.

'May I escort you?' Will asked. He held out an arm, but Eleanor shook her head. Her eyes flickered to the doors that led to the Outer Hall where Lady Fitzallan would doubtless be waiting in disapproval.

'Thank you, Will, but I had better go alone.'

'Of course. You would not invite Lady Fitzallan's disapproval on to your head by being in my company,' he said archly. 'You're much too obedient a daughter for that.'

Eleanor's cheeks coloured. 'That's unfair!'

'Is it? She told you to stop working with me. You stopped. Do you intend to comply with your mother's commands in all matters?' Will asked darkly.

Eleanor tucked a loose strand of hair back under her pearl-trimmed cap and gave Will a faint smile. 'Better to make concessions now and fight the battles it matters to win.'

She left him and walked through the house to

the courtyard. A cold blast of air hit her that fortunately cooled her cheeks and cleared her head.
Eleanor joined Sir Edgar and the rest of the family under the shelter of the great stone archway
of the main door, taking her place between Edmund and Anne, ignoring the disapproving look
her mother threw her.

Will slipped past her and took his place at the
head of the line of liveried servants that stood
along one side of the courtyard. He smiled at her,
then his eyes moved to Edmund and his expression changed, the eyes hardening and the smile
vanishing. There was no time for Eleanor to wonder why as the heralds blew a long, clear note and
the courtyard rapidly filled with carriages, horses
and men.

Duke Roland descended with some difficulty
from his carriage, leaning heavily on his duchess's arm. Sir Edgar stepped forward to greet him
on bended knee. The knights assembled behind
him as Sir Edgar's family came before the duke
to offer their fealty.

'Lady Peyton, you are more beautiful than ever,'
the duchess said when it was Eleanor's turn to
curtsy. She gestured to the red-and-gold crest on
the carriage door. 'If only I had an unwed son I

would marry you to him at once. Your hair would complement our colours perfectly.'

Eleanor blushed and dropped her curtsy deeper. 'Your Grace is too kind.'

The duke himself lifted her hand and helped her to rise. 'Nonsense. My wife speaks the truth. The last time we met was when you were newly widowed.' His voice boomed through the courtyard. 'I would say that widowhood agrees with you, only I think it improper for a young woman to remain unmarried. You should hasten to remedy the situation. I insist on it.'

Hot waves of mortification washed over her at such a public declaration, but she had no chance to dwell on Duke Roland's words as other visitors were waiting in line to greet her.

With practised grace she played her role perfectly as though she was indeed delighted each guest was there. She was sure no one watching would be able to say she was not. There was only one present who would perhaps see through her smiles and she dared not allow herself to think of him. She kept her gaze from where Will stood and turned her attention back to the row of knights. She wondered which of the men were the prospective husbands her mother had spoken of. She studied each face keenly as they bowed to her. They were broad and slender, dark and fair, and none of them made her heart race in the slightest.

Will watched with admiration as Eleanor stood elegant and dignified while the various men fawned over her in greeting. To all outside appearances she had recovered her composure almost seamlessly after the duke's vulgar comment, but Will was not taken in. He tried to catch her eye to offer her some sort of comfort, but she did not turn in his direction.

He was called forth by Sir Edgar to meet their honoured guest and by the time Will had finished kneeling before the duke and his entourage, Eleanor had long since departed, borne away by Lady Fitzallan and the duchess.

Their paths did not cross again until the evening banquet was drawing to a close and Will finally paused long enough to observe her. Eleanor sat at one end of the dais, a knight on each side and another at the end of the table. None of them could tear their eyes from her.

Will did not blame them. She was dressed in her simple grey gown with a cap pulling her hair back to emphasise her heart-shaped face. With the candlelight turning her hair to flame Eleanor would command the attention of any man with blood in his veins.

He watched carefully to see if Eleanor showed any signs of interest in a particular man, but her expression did not change as she spoke to each in turn. A servant passed him, bearing a flagon of wine. Will relieved him of it and crossed the room.

'My lords, Lady Peyton, would you care for more wine?'

Eleanor held her cup out and Will took it in his hand to steady it. Their fingers brushed and she smiled at him.

'I would like to compliment you on how smoothly your plans were carried out, Lady Peyton,' he said. Eleanor's smile deepened, a glimmer of pride appearing in her eyes.

'You assisted in the preparations?' asked the knight to Eleanor's left, a handsome fellow with dark eyes and glossy chestnut curls. 'How unusual.'

Will crossed the man off his private list of potential husbands as Eleanor's eyes narrowed and she smiled with deceptive sweetness.

'Not at all. I have run my own affairs for years. Besides, I found Master Rudhale an excellent associate. It was taxing, however, and I am rather tired.' Eleanor stood and inclined her head to the men. 'Will you forgive me if I retire for the night?'

She curtsied to the duke and her parents, then wove her way through the hall, bestowing smiles and words on those she passed. Will realised she was not heading towards her chamber. He removed the empty wine bottles and took them to the pantry. He slipped out of the side door and doubled back, then followed her.

Eleanor was standing in the courtyard staring up at the pale moon. She smiled to herself at the sound of Will's footsteps.

'Did you know I'd be here?' she asked quietly.

'I saw you leave,' he said. 'Was the evening very taxing?'

'Not at all,' Eleanor replied with a mischievous smile that set Will's heart throbbing. 'I'm sure I'll have many more days listening to exploits in the lists or mêlée so I would rather escape when I have an excuse.'

Will hid a smirk at hearing the evening so disparagingly dismissed. 'Were none of these fine knights to your taste?'

'After one evening how could I tell that?' she asked.

'Don't you believe it possible to know instantly?' Will asked. He took a step closer.

Her eyes flickered, long pale lashes that almost brushed her cheeks. 'I have so little experience, but I suppose it might be.' She tilted her head to one side and regarded him gravely. 'Then again, some people take time to become agreeable.'

A spark of anticipation ignited within Will. He moved closer to Eleanor. When she did not retreat he reached a hand to hers. The flame burned hotter, searing Will's chest from within as he drew her towards him. Will closed his eyes, his heart thundering rhythmically in his ears.

He opened them again as he became aware that the rhythm had become the sound of hoofbeats crossing the moat. A white horse burst through the archway and Eleanor and Will sprang apart.

The rider wheeled his mount around and lowered the hood of his cloak. He let out a cry of joyful disbelief.

'My lady, how astounding to meet you again,' said Martin of Allencote.

# Chapter Eighteen

The blond knight dismounted. He advanced towards Eleanor who was hastily smoothing her hair back under her cap. He dropped to one knee at Eleanor's feet, bowed his head and reached for her hand.

'Once again I find myself at your service. Please tell me you remember me!'

'Of course, Sir Martin! How could I forget after the circumstances we met under?' she said with a gracious smile.

Will's jaw clenched involuntarily. For the second time Martin of Allencote had intruded into a situation where he was far from welcome. Will moved into the shadows, widening the gap between himself and Eleanor, but Allencote paid him no heed.

'What are you doing here, my lady?' Allencote asked in wonder.

Eleanor gestured around the courtyard. 'This is my father's house.'

'So you must be Lady Peyton!' Allencote's face broke into a rapturous smile. 'My liege lord has spoken many times of the beauty of Baron Fitzallan's daughter. I could never have suspected that our paths might first cross in such a manner!'

Will looked at Eleanor to see what effect the man's effusiveness was having on her. Her cheeks had taken on a pink hue at his flattery. Allencote was still holding her hand and she seemed in no hurry to reclaim it. The knight rose in a graceful motion that struck Will as more suited to an acrobat than a nobleman.

'We share a bond of kinship already that renders my previous service to you even sweeter,' Allencote said, his voice echoing confidently around the courtyard. 'Your husband's father and mine were cousins. We are related by marriage.'

What other bond did the knight hope to share? The hairs on the back of Will's neck prickled. He stepped forward to Eleanor's side.

'I am pleased to meet you, Cousin. You will recognise Master Rudhale, my father's steward,' Eleanor said, casting a smile at him that made Will's chest tighten.

Allencote finally appeared to notice him. He

lifted his head and shot Will a dismissive look down a long, straight nose. Will's temper quickened.

'I must apologise. I don't know your name,' he said politely. 'One moment, please.' He drew a fold of parchment from the pouch at his waist and peered at it. From the corner of his eye he could see Eleanor scowl and he dropped his pretence.

'Sir Martin of Allencote,' he said, dropping a knee. 'I bid you welcome, sir. Let me find someone to take care of your horse and baggage.'

He strode back inside the house, hurriedly woke the pageboy who was dozing in the Outer Hall and sent him with a message to the stables. When he returned to the courtyard Eleanor and Allencote were standing close. Allencote was talking, Eleanor listening, her face raised to his. Neither of them noticed his presence.

Eleanor glanced at Will as he approached them, then smiled back at Allencote. 'I shall accompany Sir Martin to meet my father before I retire.'

Will smiled through gritted teeth. 'As you wish, my lady.'

Eleanor led the way to the Great Hall on Allencote's arm. Will picked up the pannier that Allencote had removed from the saddle and followed behind.

Duke Roland and his entourage greeted Allencote's arrival joyously.

'My apologies for not joining you immediately, but family matters forced me to detour,' Allencote explained, kneeling before his liege.

'Of course. How is your father?' Duke Roland asked.

Allencote's face darkened. 'His body is strong, but his mind is failing. He did not recognise me, sire, but the physicians believe he may yet live for years.'

'I pray he does so,' Duke Roland replied.

'As do I,' Allencote said gravely. He took a seat on the dais and swiftly drank a goblet of wine. Will clapped his hands and a servant appeared bearing a tray laden with venison stew and bread. He placed it before Allencote, who elegantly washed his hands in the silver ewer before selecting a small hunk of bread and dipping it into the gravy.

'Sir Edgar, you honour me greatly with your hospitality,' he said between mouthfuls. 'My thanks, steward, you run a fine household.'

'Very true. Perhaps I should entice Master Rudhale to work for me,' Duke Roland said with a laugh.

'Or I shall,' a swarthy noble called out. 'My own

seneschal will not last the year out, I swear. I have twice the estate Sir Edgar has, Master Rudhale.'

'I beg of you not to tempt him so, my Lord Etherington,' Sir Edgar said with a laugh. 'If I am not careful, I will be left with an empty house.'

'Such is the lot of the host,' Allencote said. 'I'm sure we could all find someone here to bear away with us.' His eyes flickered to Eleanor, who was sitting quietly at Edmund's side. A faint hint of rose bloomed in her cheek and she lowered her head. She made no response, but was clearly not insensible to Allencote's meaning.

Will returned the ewer to the pantry, seeing it safely cleaned and locked away. He instructed more wine to be taken to the Great Hall and dealt with the trivial matters that had arisen over the course of the evening. As soon as he was able he left the room to return to the Great Hall.

He left the pantry to find Eleanor was waiting in the passageway.

'Why did you pretend not to know who Allencote was?' she asked before Will had time to greet her.

'He did not introduce himself to me when we met.' His lip curled at the memory. 'Why would he, though? A servant would be beneath the notice of a nobleman. I did not want him to think you had been discussing him behind his back with a mere servant,' Will said scathingly.

'You're being foolish,' Eleanor snapped. She put her hands on her hips and tossed her head angrily. Her hair rippled with copper flames and her eyes flashed alluringly. Will had to resist pulling her into his arms. Now his reward would most likely be a slap to the face instead of a kiss.

'I told you before, don't call me a fool,' Will warned.

'Then don't be one!' Eleanor cried.

Will's temper rose as her words stung him. 'The man threatened to kill me when last we met. You can't expect me to greet his reappearance with a joyful heart?'

'You know why he did that.' Eleanor sighed.

Will stared at her, unable to believe she was taking Allencote's part. He remembered the way she had smiled at the knight before and his stomach twisted.

'Fortunately you were there to welcome him so warmly. I am sure you were able to amuse him admirably while you waited for me to return,' Will said, feeling his stomach lurch at the thought of them alone together. 'Though I see *he* did not give you his fine cloak to keep you warm like others might have.'

Eleanor's face paled. 'That was petty,' she snapped. Her eyes filled with hurt and Will wished he could bite back the words, but she spun on her heel and stormed away.

He returned to the pantry and poured a cup of ale, then sat on a low stool by the fire, staring into the flames miserably, their angry words eating into his guts. His last quarrel with Amy sprang suddenly to mind: bitter recriminations he had not thought of in years, her eyes filled with revulsion and his rage that had formed over the years into a protective casing that he had only recently found the key to.

He had known Eleanor would almost certainly marry one of these nobles, however much she protested her reluctance. Now Allencote had burst into her life, a dashing figure with his finery and flattery, making no secret of his admiration.

Watching Eleanor smiling and blushing at Allencote's unreserved admiration had felt like daggers twisting in Will's guts. For the first time since starting his wager he began to doubt he would succeed and he wondered darkly whether it would matter anyway. Even with twice his stake to invest he would never have the sort of wealth a man like Allencote had been born to. What woman could remain unmoved by such attentions and from a man as handsome and noble as Allencote? And how could Will—lowly and disfigured—hope to compete?

He drained his cup and pushed himself to his feet with a grimace. He had no time for leisure. He had work to do. Back in the Great Hall the numbers had diminished, but the candles burned low before Will could finally set the skivvies to work and retire to bed. He climbed the stairs wearily, his body craving rest. As he slipped along the passageway to his temporary accommodation in Edmund's room voices caught his attention. Candlelight flickered beneath a door.

'I need more time.'

Will paused outside the door. He could not be sure, but he thought the voice was Allencote's.

'Two months is the most I can do. I have my debts to pay, too, and yours are mounting' came the reply.

'If only Father would stop clinging on. A fraction of his wealth would see the matter settled, but Mother refuses to settle any—'

The second voice interrupted. 'Where you get it isn't my concern. I'll take it in land if necessary. You have your manor.'

The floor creaked and a shadow passed across the door. Will hurried past. As he undressed and settled on to the low cot he mused on what he had just heard. If he had understood correctly, Allencote's finances were not so great as one might suppose from his fine horse and clothing. He was still mulling it over as he fell asleep.

Wherever Eleanor went, Martin of Allencote would also be there. His talk was amusing and his words complimentary, but Eleanor wished he would at least make the pretence of interest in any of the other women present. He chose her as a partner in the games of cards and found the seat closest to her when tumblers entertained the household in the evening. She could have tolerated his constant attention if it was not for Will's presence. He had made no attempt to speak to her beyond the courtesies he showed to all the ladies, but Eleanor saw him watching whenever Sir Martin spoke to her.

The tumblers finished and Will walked to Eleanor's table, his face solemn and his eyes intensely fixed on hers. With a curt smile she took the plate of figs he offered. He had behaved like a fool and she was most certainly not going to break the silence first.

'A charming man,' the duchess murmured as

she watched him walk to the next table. 'Very well looking.'

'Half so at any rate,' Sir Martin joked. 'He would make a one-eyed woman an excellent husband.'

Will's shoulders stiffened and Eleanor glared at Sir Martin, horrified at the thought Will had heard his words. Sir Martin's laughter died away at her expression.

'One could overlook his disfigurement if he was richer,' the duchess said.

'Perhaps,' Lady Fitzallan replied. 'Though he would have to be rich indeed. It's a shame he has no prospects.'

Eleanor's cheeks flamed as she looked in Will's direction. Angry as she was with him she could not let such slurs go unchallenged.

'The wine you are drinking is William's and he does have prospects,' she said smoothly. She turned her attention to Sir Martin. 'And as her ladyship so rightly says, an excellent wife would see beyond his scars,' she said with a warm smile at the duchess.

When Duke Roland's retinue rode out to the hills the next morning Eleanor was unsurprised to find Sir Martin draw his horse alongside her, slowing to a trot. She inclined her head stiffly and adjusted the sleeve of her dress, disinclined to talk to him.

'I offended you with my jest yesterday. I apologise,' Sir Martin said. 'Your loyalty towards your father's servants is commendable.'

She looked him squarely in the eye. It had been no jest. Sir Martin's words had been deliberately cruel.

'It has nothing to do with loyalty. I would not hear him disparaged for something beyond his control. William Rudhale is a good man,' she said fiercely.

'A good man who I found with his sword against your breast?' Sir Martin said contemptuously. 'When I encountered you being mistreated in such a way it was all I could do not to run the blackguard through on the spot.'

'I was not being mistreated. William was teaching me to defend myself,' Eleanor explained. Goosebumps broke out down her arms at the memory of Will's eyes full of determination and passion boring into her along the length of his sword. 'I lost the fight.'

'A gentleman would never let a lady lose. If, that is, he indulged her in such an unseemly activity in the first place.'

He sounded so pompous that Eleanor had to suppress the urge to ride on and leave him behind. 'He would if he wanted the lady to understand where she had made the mistake,' she countered.

Sir Martin gave a laugh that stopped at his mouth. When Will was amused his eyes shone with glee it was impossible to suppress.

'Very well, then I shall take your word that he is not a rogue,' Sir Martin announced. 'Let us pick a happier subject. Will you tell me about Rowland's Mount? I have only the vaguest memories of visiting when I was a child and Baldwin's father was still living.'

He made Eleanor describe the house in detail, pressing her for more and more information about her businesses, the village and warehouses until the subject was quite exhausted.

'I would like to return one day,' Sir Martin said. 'I doubt Baldwin could have left it in any better hands than yours.'

Despite her best intentions Eleanor blushed at his flattery.

'It must be hard to bear such demands alone,' Sir Martin continued, his voice deepening with concern. 'You must wish for someone to take the burden from you at times.'

'So most men believe,' Eleanor said serenely.

She snapped the reins and spurred her mare to

a gallop. Sir Martin responded by giving her a salute, digging his spurs into his charger's flanks and galloping ahead to join the other knights.

Eleanor watched him go, still irritated by his assumption that she must need someone to take care of her, that she was someone to be sheltered and supported.

In all the time they had worked together, Will had never treated her as anything less than an equal partner at work. Not once had he suggested she might not be capable of managing her own affairs. He would never expect her to forfeit the independence she guarded so carefully.

Their quarrel seemed unimportant now and she spent the rest of the morning wishing the ride was over so she could return to the house. She longed to speak to Will, but with one night left until the feast he was occupied whenever she encountered him and she lacked the courage to approach him in front anyone else.

After a day spent trying to evade one man and locate the other Eleanor was exhausted by the time evening arrived. The Great Hall was noisy and hot and the thought of being in company was unappealing. Craving solitude, she wandered wearily into the Outer Hall and settled on to the low bench by the door, closing her eyes. She heard a soft footfall and glanced up to see a tall figure in silhouette. Blond hair framed his face by the light of a candle. Her heart leapt and she leaned forward eagerly before she realised it was not Will, but Sir Martin.

'I'm glad to find you, Lady Peyton,' he said, lowering the candle. 'I have looked for you since returning from the ride, but no one could find you. Even your Master Rudhale did not know where you might be.'

'You asked William?' Eleanor frowned, imagining the response.

Sir Martin sat beside her on the bench and faced her.

'My duke told me I should marry. He said I might find a bride here.' Unexpectedly he grasped her hand and Eleanor stiffened. 'I could never have hoped that the beautiful woman I encountered on my journey would be the same one who could give me the greatest happiness in life. Marry me, Lady Peyton!'

'How can you propose such a thing?' Eleanor exclaimed. 'We know nothing of each other!'

'Forgive my rashness, but I must seize the opportunity while you are still free. I know you have been married already, but I don't care that you are no maiden.' Fervour shone in Sir Martin's eyes. Eleanor tried to pull her hand away, but his grip was firm. 'Let me be the one to bear the responsibilities you have borne for so many years.'

'No!' Eleanor said firmly. She took a deep breath and wriggled her hand free. 'I don't love you.' She was not sure that she even liked him.

'Is that all that concerns you? Love will come. Give me the chance to show you how loving I can be.' He seized her hand again and raised it to his lips. His mouth was warm and slightly moist. Unconsciously Eleanor wrinkled her nose. She pulled her hand free and stood, wiping it surreptitiously on her skirt.

'I'm sorry, Sir Martin, I cannot—will not—marry you.'

He frowned. 'You don't have to make a decision immediately. There is another week before I leave. I will ask you again. You may change your mind yet.'

'I'm sorry. I won't,' Eleanor said and walked away.

She made it back to her room before her legs gave out and she slumped into her chair. Sir Martin had made no secret that Eleanor attracted him, but the proposal had taken her completely unawares and Sir Martin had barely given her time to consider his offer. She had done the right thing though, of that she was certain. Unexpectedly tears pricked her eyes and she blinked them away rapidly. Despite his handsome face, Sir Martin's touch did not move her in the slightest.

Not as Will's did.

# Chapter Nineteen

'You refused him!'

Lady Fitzallan drew herself to her full height. Her face reddened and her forehead wrinkled in anger.

The summons to Sir Edgar's library had come before breakfast. Sir Martin must have gone straight to her parents after Eleanor had rejected him last night. She had hoped that would be the end of it, but on reflection she had been naïve to assume he would keep the matter to himself when he would find such a ready ally in Lady Fitzallan.

Her mother had never looked so furious. Eleanor looked back defiantly at Lady Fitzallan, though her hands trembled as she clasped them together tightly.

'I did.' Her voice sounded firm and she derived some small satisfaction from that.

Sir Edgar looked over from his seat at his table,

half-hidden by piles of boxes and scrolls. 'Sir Martin visited me before asking you, as is right and proper. He believed his proposal would be met with success.'

'I don't know why he thought that,' Eleanor protested. 'I have given him no such hopes.'

Lady Fitzallan curled her lip. 'He thought that because he was aware that Eleanor had been instructed to accept an offer should she be so fortunate as to receive one.' She walked around her daughter and stood behind her. She put her hands on Eleanor's shoulders. 'Because I had made it clear to him that you knew what was expected of you.'

'He asked me after one day,' Eleanor said. 'We know nothing about each other. Even you waited a month before you gave me to Baldwin!'

Lady Fitzallan's fingers tightened. 'Sir Martin is well connected and wealthy. His father has estates far greater than yours that he will inherit one day. You will *never* make a better match than this.'

Eleanor twisted from her mother's grip and spun to face her. 'It is a poor match if I don't want it,' she cried.

Selfish! Obstinate! Wilful! Her eyes on the flames, Eleanor let the tirade wash over her.

'You think nothing of your family,' Lady Fitzallan said, her voice like a whip. 'Think what such a connection would do for Edmund. Think of the suitors Anne might meet through your marriage.'

'Is that my only worth?' Eleanor snapped back bitterly. 'To aid their progress?'

'That is enough,' Sir Edgar said firmly. He walked round the table to stand beside his wife. 'Tell me why you are set against this man, Eleanor.'

Eleanor hugged herself tightly. 'I don't love him. Oh, I know it is too soon for that, but when he touches me, when I look at him—'

She broke off as a longing so intense rushed through her, so powerful it almost dropped her to her knees as she thought of the man whose touch promised to send her into ecstasy. She clutched her stomach tighter and raised her head, her eyes threatening to overspill at the least provocation. 'I feel nothing and I know I never will.'

'Accept Sir Martin,' Lady Fitzallan commanded. 'He's handsome and well built and in all likelihood the passion will follow. Love and poverty are all very well, but love and wealth are better.'

Eleanor lifted her chin. 'And if it was a choice of one or the other?' she asked.

'You don't have other men making offers as far

as I am aware so you don't have that dilemma,' Lady Fitzallan replied haughtily.

Eleanor's heart lurched. Her mother's words struck deeper than she could have imagined. The heat began to rise to her face and a welcome draught whipped around her neck as someone opened the door behind her.

'But if I did?' she asked. 'I married for wealth and position once. If I wanted to marry for love alone, would you permit that or is money all that counts?'

Why was she even asking? That circumstance would never arise. The only times Will had ever spoken of marriage was to deny it held any attraction for him. She swallowed down a knot of pain.

The sound of the door closing softly made her turn. Will stood there, his arms full of scrolls. They had barely spoken since their quarrel and the thought that he had heard her words made Eleanor cringe.

'I can come back later,' he said.

'Yes,' she answered, just as her father replied with a 'no'.

Will crossed the room and began placing the scrolls into boxes.

'Of course money matters. You aren't living in a book of poetry, Eleanor. Anyone with a brain in their head would say the same,' Lady Fitzallan continued serenely. She gestured to Will. 'Even Master Rudhale would agree, I'm sure.'

Will looked up from his task. His mouth twisted bitterly as his eyes met Eleanor's, pools of blue ice in the pale morning sunlight.

'So many swear they will choose love over prosperity, but most hearts will be swayed when put to the test,' he said shortly.

Eleanor's eyes began to smart. Had he learned so little about her that he could suspect such a thing of her? *I would*, she wanted to cry.

Lady Fitzallan nodded, victorious. 'Go back to your room, my dear,' she told Eleanor in a voice that was iron coated in honey. 'I won't expect your attendance in the solar today. Contemplate what we have talked about. Perhaps the feast and dance tonight will help you to see things clearer. The decision is not irreversible.'

She guided Eleanor to the door with a firm hand. Eleanor's last view of Will was his of his broad back, his arms raised as he lifted a box to the high shelf: the only arms she ever wanted about her and the ones that never would be.

Eleanor sank under the water, closing her eyes and holding her breath. She wondered idly whether drowning was an easy death. Right now it held some attractions certainly. When the throb in her lungs outweighed that in her heart she sat up. It was not really an option, even if the alternative was a slow death that took a lifetime of coldness to achieve.

Jennet was staring at her anxiously. Eleanor lay back, her head resting against the edge of the deep oak tub as Jennet rinsed the suds from her hair and combed it through until it gleamed.

'Leave me, please. Come back when the candle has half-burned away,' Eleanor instructed. Soon she would be summoned to the feast, to be on display once again when all she wanted was to hide here.

She smoothed the soap bag across her body, the touch of her hands on her breasts sending ripples of longing through her. The sudden throb between her legs was so intense it was painful. She whipped her hand away and moaned in frustration.

She had spent the day considering Sir Martin's offer as Lady Fitzallan had instructed and each time she reached the same conclusion. She did not love him and did not want to spend her life with him. She wanted no one except Will. She could never have him, but the need to satiate her yearning for his touch was almost irresistible.

One kiss. That was all she craved. She could take the memory and bury it deep inside her like a jewel, keep it safe to be brought out whenever she needed it. If she could only have that, then perhaps she could be the obedient daughter she had been reared to be and accept Sir Martin's offer.

Nothing more needed to be done. The beeswax candles glowed on each table, chandelier and wall sconce, their scent mingling with bundles of dried lavender. The tables were laid with Sir Edgar's finest plate, enamelled silver glinting in the firelight. Fresh rushes had been laid on the floor and the soft music of lute and harp drifted from the gallery above.

Will looked round with satisfaction and smiled to himself. He pictured Eleanor's expression when she saw the Great Hall and raised his cup to his lips in silent tribute to her. By his side Edmund continued to talk though Will had stopped listening. He could have done without Edmund bragging about his latest bedroom conquest in his ear.

*Love or wealth.*

Will had been thinking all day about Eleanor and Lady Fitzallan's argument when he had interrupted them and had a dreadful suspicion they were discussing Allencote. The knight had been seeking Eleanor out the previous evening and Will had rarely seen them apart over the last two days. Had he told her of his debts and did she want to marry him despite her parent's wishes? He found it hard to believe she had fallen for Allencote so quickly, but could think of no other explanation for her words.

'You're playing a risky game, Will,' Edmund said.

Will started at hearing his name.

'It's a lot of money to lose and she won't unbend by midnight. Admit defeat and I'll cut the stake by three groats,' Edmund said magnanimously.

The wager. Will ran a hand through his hair as, not for the first time, his conscience stabbed. If Eleanor was reckless in choosing love over wealth, he was guilty of doing the opposite, continuing to chase his stake when Eleanor had long since filled his heart more than the thought of riches filled his mind. He had seen enough to know he had awakened the feelings Edmund believed Eleanor had buried, but if she was planning to bestow them on Allencote, money was all Will could hope to gain from the wager. That and a memory to console himself with.

He frowned at Edmund's words. 'It isn't midnight yet. I'll still win,' he said confidently.

'Win what? What stake?' Anne Fitzallan's head appeared over her brother's shoulder. She peered at the men curiously. Edmund pulled her around into a hug and she laughed with delight.

'William is about to make me a richer man.' Edmund grinned.

Anne narrowed her eyes suspiciously. Will glared at Edmund. 'It's nothing of note,' he cut in quickly, 'simply a silly game.' Changing the subject, he asked, 'Are you looking forward to the feast?'

Anne twirled around, displaying her flowing skirt. 'Yes, I am. The Earl of Etherington's squire has asked me for the first dance. I think he likes me.'

Will smiled. 'I'm happy for you. The lad's of good family and the earl is a fair master.'

Anne danced away. It was fortunate her attachment had not been long-lasting, Will mused. He doubted his own heart would mend as quickly.

A fanfare sounded and the Master of the Chamber swung the great double doors open. Guests began to file into the room and take their allotted places, colourfully and extravagantly clothed. Allencote appeared, looking handsome and confident in a burgundy surcoat with broadly slashed sleeves and cuffs. Will glanced down at his own attire: a plain black surcoat and breeches, the discreet orange-and-green collar and cuffs the only outward indication of his position. Let others dress themselves like peacocks to display their greatness. Will had no need.

Eleanor walked through the doorway and Will forgot everything.

She wore green. Pale silk under a mantle of heavy, emerald velvet laced with gold braid from beneath her high breasts to her slender waist. Her hair had been twisted atop her head and encased in a net of gold so that her braids flamed between the metal. The gown left her shoulders bare and the elegant expanse of creamy flesh sent Will's heart thudding into his stomach.

Half-a-dozen men leapt to their feet as they saw Eleanor, but Will was quicker. He tore his gaze from the curve of her throat and collarbone and strode to her. He bowed before her, then lifted his head. His eyes travelled slowly up her body until he met her gaze, determined to leave her in no doubt of the effect she was having upon him. She looked uncertain until Will gave her a discreet wink. She smiled back and the world brightened, as though a hundred more candles had begun to burn.

'Let me escort you to your seat, Lady Peyton,'

Will said formally. As she took his outstretched arm he whispered in an undertone, 'You're the most beautiful woman in the room. It was worth the hailstorm to see you in that dress.'

Eleanor said nothing, but a blush crept across her cheeks and her fingers tightened on his arm. Will led her to her seat, reluctantly relinquishing her to the company of the Sheriff of Tawstott. He could barely keep his eyes from her for the rest of the feast.

When the final dishes had been removed the tables were cleared for the dancing to begin. The musicians tuned their instruments and an expectant hush fell over the hall.

Allencote began to thread his way through the crowd towards her and Will crossed the room to her side. The two men reached her at the same time. Eleanor looked from one to the other apprehensively.

'Will you dance the first measure with me, Lady Peyton?' Allencote asked, a shade before Will could ask the same question.

Eleanor's eyes flickered briefly to Will's. He held her gaze boldly though his stomach curled with anxiety. It was out of his hands now. If she chose Allencote, he had lost everything.

She smiled apologetically at Allencote. 'I'm sorry, Sir Martin, but I owe a dance to Master Rudhale.' Her expression radiated innocence as she looked back to Will. 'I lost a wager, you see.'

She stepped towards Will who somehow mastered his emotions, preventing himself from giving a yell of victory.

'You won the wager,' he murmured. He took her by the hand and led her to the centre of the room. The music began, a slow, stately heartbeat accompanied by the lilt of a solitary pipe. Will's own heart raced twice as fast.

Eleanor smiled demurely. 'I had another book,' she admitted as she circled him gracefully.

Will lifted her high, hands circling her waist. 'What made you decide to admit it now?'

'It was a dishonest way to win. Besides, the wager seems unimportant now,' Eleanor said.

They parted, wove between the rows, their eyes never parting. They united once more, closer than was strictly necessary for the dance. Palms raised, they faced each other, the touch of Eleanor's hands sending bolts of lightning through Will. 'Unimportant how?' he asked.

Her eyes shone as she laced her fingers through his and they circled to the quickening beat. 'I didn't know you then,' Eleanor whispered. 'Now I find I want to dance with you after all.'

Will put a hand around her waist. It wasn't a proper step, but he didn't care. He spun her round and pulled her close, his hands spreading wide to caress her back. 'I'll dance with you as many times as you'll permit,' he said.

To monopolise Sir Edgar's daughter for the entire evening would be to risk gossip, but Will and Eleanor met as often as propriety would allow. They rarely spoke but there was no need. Hands met, shoulders and hips brushed, and glances told of all the desire they could no longer deny.

When the musicians ceased playing and were replaced by a troupe of jugglers Will sought Eleanor out and drew her to one side. 'Will you walk with me?' he asked quietly.

Surreptitiously they slipped from the Great Hall. Every fibre of Will's body was alive with anticipation as they hurried to the courtyard, but as they reached the dimly lit archway he stopped short.

He could have won the wager three times over yet had halted at every turn. It wasn't that he didn't *want* to kiss Eleanor—far from it. He wanted it so intensely it hurt almost physically.

He couldn't do it.

If he forfeited the wager, he would lose his stake. It would be the end of his chance to invest in Master Fortin's ship. If he did not, he would never be able to live with himself.

Eleanor's words came back to him: *a dishonest way to win.*

He dropped Eleanor's hand. Her eyes widened with hurt.

'Wait here,' Will entreated. 'I will come back, I swear, but there's something I must do.'

He ran back into the Great Hall and cocked his head urgently at Rob. Together they found Edmund in the corner playing dice.

Will flung a pouch of coins on the table.

'I forfeit,' he said tersely.

Edmund smirked and pulled the bag towards him.

'I told you she'd never look at you,' he called, but Will was already leaving.

He expected to find an empty courtyard, but to his relief, Eleanor was still standing where he had left her.

'I wasn't sure…' she began uncertainly.

Will shook his head firmly. 'I told you I would return.'

Her eyes were wide with apprehension, but she

tilted her face upwards towards him expectantly. Will's fingers curled into the hollow at the nape of her neck as he drew her lips within reach of his. He slipped his other arm around her waist and pulled her close.

From the town the sound of a bell heralded midnight and Will smiled. Finally, after waiting for so long, he kissed her.

Eleanor stiffened in his arms. Had he misjudged her willingness? He started to pull away, but her hands came about his neck, drawing him to her and finding his lips once more with hers. This time her lips were softer and yielding to the motion of his. He tightened his embrace, fearful that she would leave, but she only pressed closer against him, her fingers featherlight against his neck. Their rhythm slowed to a sensuous pulse and Will's mind emptied of all thoughts.

Around them snow began to fall.

## Chapter Twenty

Will's lips moved with a slow, determined intensity that took Eleanor's breath away. A soft moan escaped her lips and he pulled away gently. Their eyes locked. Smiling, Will brushed a thumb across Eleanor's cheek. She reached up and twisted her fingers into the blond tangles that fell across his eyes, brushing them back from his face. Will tensed as her fingers slid over his scar. Eleanor turned his cheek to face her, stood on tiptoe and kissed him gently along the faint line. Will gave a sound that could have been a laugh or sob. He turned his head to trap her lips in his.

Wordlessly, they came together again. This time it was different, fiercer and more urgent. She leaned against Will, the whole length of their bodies touching. One hand cradled her head, his other arm iron hard around her back. Even if she had wanted to she could not have broken free—but she had no such wish.

Will ran his tongue along Eleanor's lips, teasing them apart. Her head swam at this fresh sensation and she drew a ragged breath.

'We have to stop,' she gasped breathlessly. She lifted her face to the sky, soft flakes of snow cooling her burning cheeks.

'Do you mean that?' Will whispered huskily into her ear. His voice was a growl and the sound reached inside Eleanor and caused a throb of desire to course through every part of her. The thought that this would be the only time such a thing could ever happen was too much to bear.

'No. Yes! I don't know. It's too much!' Already the need to feel his mouth on hers again was intense, like a drunkard craving wine. The soft bristles of Will's beard prickled against her neck, raising goosebumps on her flesh, and she moaned in delight. 'We can't stay here,' she murmured even as her lips sought his out once more. 'We'll be missed.'

'Not for a while,' Will replied. He kissed her jaw, his lips travelling to her mouth, catching her bottom lip between his and tugging gently. Eleanor responded hungrily even as she knew she should push him away. It was only when she was limp in his arms and all thoughts of returning to the feast had been banished from her mind that he finally released her lips.

The entrance door slammed open and footsteps sounded loudly. Voices filled the air as revellers spilled out of the hall. Eleanor stiffened.

'We can't be found together,' she whispered in alarm. Will nodded. He slipped into an alcove, concealing himself in the shadows while Eleanor took an uncertain step towards the house. After the warmth of his embrace the snow flurries were bitingly cold.

'Lady Peyton, there you are!'

Eleanor's heart sank. She had barely enough time to adjust her clothing before Sir Martin was by her side.

'Once more I find you out here like a wraith in the night. You are alone? Not in the company of your steward this time?' He sounded suspicious. 'I've been searching for you.'

Eleanor's chest tightened at the mention of Will. She circled quickly around Sir Martin, so he had to turn his back to the figure in the shadows.

'Now you've found me and I am alone, of course! Why would I be with Master Rudhale?' she said with a bright laugh, hoping she sounded convincingly indifferent. Will's black tunic concealed him effectively and anyone who did not know he was there would have glanced over him, but the thought of his discovery made Eleanor's stomach churn.

Sir Martin held out an arm. 'Allow me to escort you back inside.'

Reluctantly Eleanor placed her hand on Sir Martin's arm. He placed his free hand over hers, clutching it tightly.

'Have you reconsidered my offer?' he asked as they walked back.

'Please, don't ask me that now,' Eleanor entreated, her heart twisting. She could not even bear to think of Allencote after what she had just experienced. It took all her resolve not to turn and seek out Will's eyes one final time, but if she did she would never be able to leave him. She had barely begun to discover the pleasures to be had in his arms. Now it was too late and she never would.

Will stepped from the shadows and watched them depart, jealous bile rising in his gut. Allencote again! The man had unerring timing in frustrating Will's plans. He tried telling himself the interruption was for the best. A few minutes more and Will was certain he would have carried

Eleanor to somewhere they would not have been interrupted and...

And what? He'd already taken liberties enough by kissing her, but to do everything else he had in mind was beyond impossible. He found himself hardening as he imagined Eleanor's hands on his flesh, her body eager and welcoming. He leant back against the wall and stared at the whirling whiteness around him.

He would have paid a great deal to have heard what Eleanor and Allencote were discussing as they returned to the house. Eleanor's laugh of pleasure at Allencote's arrival had driven a fist into his ribs. Could he have misjudged her feelings towards himself so greatly? After five years of guarding his heart from all assailants, perhaps he was no longer capable of telling true passion from false.

The thought of Allencote in Eleanor's bed had doused his passion as the cold air had failed to. He pushed himself to his feet and returned to the Great Hall determined to watch, but only from a distance. To venture too near Eleanor would cause him more pain than it would cure.

The music was wilder than it had been before they had left. He spotted Eleanor dancing as part of a large circle, Allencote at her side, gripping her

hand tightly. The circle broke and laughing couples spun away, arms about each other's waists.
Eleanor's eyes fell on Will and her step faltered
before Allencote dragged her back into the crowd
and out of Will's sight.

Will sat on the end of a bench and poured himself a goblet of wine. Eleanor danced into view
again, her eyes fixed on him. Despite the lump in
his throat Will forced himself to smile at her. The
music ended and she took a seat beside Allencote
at the fireplace. Will had always known she was
not for him, so why did the sight of them together
cause him such misery? He supposed he should
feel victorious that he had stolen a kiss from her
without Allencote's knowledge, but he simply felt
hollow. He had taken what he had wanted for so
long and given Eleanor something she, too, had
craved. That should have been enough to satisfy
him.

*May it make you happy, my lady*, he thought as
he slipped away from the table, *for it has almost
killed me.*

Eleanor stretched her arms high above her head,
running her fingers over the smooth carved knots
on the wooden headboard. She wriggled back
under the covers and smiled sleepily. Her dreams

had been full of Will, his kisses and caresses more intimate than she had thought possible and a flush of heat flooded through her as she recalled them. She closed her eyes tighter as though they were a net that could prevent the memories escaping.

Beside her Anne rolled over with a snort. Eleanor frowned, wishing she had lodged Anne somewhere else when she had planned the sleeping arrangements. Thank goodness her sister had been asleep last night; Eleanor had been able to slip into bed in peace while her mind replayed the night's events.

'Wasn't last night wonderful?' Anne asked, throwing an arm around Eleanor's waist and squeezing tightly. She sat up, parting the curtains around the bed.

The harsh daylight that intruded brought Eleanor to her senses with the brutality of a slap. She had kissed Will with the full knowledge that she would hold no interest for him after he had what he wanted. Far from trying to claim her for another dance, he had not even spoken to her once he had returned to the house. Eleanor closed her eyes and nodded silently, unable to prevent tears from leaking between her lids.

'Why are you crying?' Anne asked.

Eleanor quickly wiped a hand across her face.

'It's nothing. I'm tired still and last night was more taxing than I had anticipated.'

'You must have spent half the time wishing Baldwin had been there,' Anne said sympathetically.

'I suppose so,' Eleanor replied guiltily. Baldwin had not been in her thoughts for days.

'At least you had Sir Martin to keep you company, to say nothing of William. Neither of them could keep their eyes from you. I bet he never even had time for Edmund's silly wager.'

'Wager?' Eleanor asked distractedly, Anne's words barely registering.

'Oh, something Will had to do before midnight, I don't know what,' Anne said with a shrug. 'Some silly game, he said. Did you see me dancing with Thomas, the Earl's squire? He must like me because we danced till…'

'Hush, please!' Eleanor snapped. Anne's face fell. 'I'm sorry, only I have too much to think about and my head aches. I don't want to hear about games or dancing.'

She climbed out of bed and rinsed her face in the ewer of cold water, then threw her fur-trimmed surcoat over her nightshift.

'I'm going to stay here today. If anyone asks, tell them I'm indisposed,' she told Anne. She waited patiently while Anne dressed, doing her best to block out the excited chatter of her sister and the maids.

Finally she was left in peace, if the emotions that assailed her could be described as such. Sharp blasts of a hunting horn signalled that the party had departed for their daily ride. Eleanor gazed around the chamber. Within another fortnight she would be gone. She wished she could hide here until the time came to leave as the thought of seeing Will's eyes devoid of interest almost sent her packing her belongings and running from the house.

How could she have been so foolish to imagine one kiss could ever suffice? It would have been better to remain ignorant than to understand what was beyond reach for ever.

She sat on the bed, curled her feet under her and unwound her thick plaits, brushing the tangles away until a gentle tapping at the door made her jump. Wearily she opened it to find out who was intruding.

Will.

Eleanor's hand trembled as it dropped from the frame. She started at him dumbly through the gap before she found her voice.

'What are you doing here?'

'Anne told me you were unwell. I was worried so brought you something to eat.' Will indicated the tray he held. 'You'll have to let me in, though.'

Eleanor opened the door wider and retreated to the window, heart thumping. Will kicked the door shut with his heel and placed the tray on the table. His eyes flickered the length of her body. Eleanor glanced nervously to the door. She pulled the edges of her surcoat closer. After the intimacy of the previous night she was acutely conscious of what the delicate lace and linen might reveal. 'You shouldn't be here...' she began.

'I know, but I wanted to see you,' Will said huskily. His brow knotted into a frown and his broad shoulders stiffened. Hurt flickered momentarily in his eyes. 'Of course, if you have no wish to see *me* I shall leave.'

'I do! It's only, I didn't think...' Eleanor's neck grew warm at the memories. 'After last night I did not expect to see you again.'

Will moved beside her. She caught the intoxicating scent of his skin and her muscles contracted with a longing so intense it was bordering on painful.

'Last night ended far too soon,' Will said, his voice full of temptation.

Eleanor's heart gave a violent throb at his words.

She nodded in agreement, thinking a lifetime would be too soon. Will took her face between his hands and raised it until they were looking deep into each other's eyes. He ran his fingers through the length of her hair. He gathered it together, coiling it around his fist like a rope. His other hand strayed to her waist, tugging her towards him.

Eleanor needed no beckoning. She gave a gentle sigh as she slipped her arms about Will's neck, her lips parting in anticipation. Will's tongue dove between her lips and she clutched him tighter, her breasts pushing against his chest. She gave a low moan of pleasure. Will pulled back and fixed her with an intense gaze. 'Don't marry Allencote,' he commanded. 'You might think you love him, but you barely know him.'

'What makes *you* think I love him?' Eleanor asked incredulously.

'Yesterday I heard you talk about choosing love over money,' Will said.

'I wasn't talking about him!' Eleanor cried. She blushed and lowered her eyes. 'Do you think I would have kissed you if I loved him? He asked me and I said no.' The thought of Sir Martin laying his lips on her, of touching her as Will had done, made her skin crawl. 'I don't want to marry him, but I think I will have no choice,' she whispered.

Will took her hands. 'Eleanor, you're a widow with an independent income. You could live your days in celibacy or take a dozen lovers and no one could prevent you.'

Shocked, Eleanor pulled away. 'Is that what you think I should do?'

Will grinned wickedly and drew her into his arms once more. 'Not a dozen. One, perhaps,' he whispered, his lips brushing her ear.

'You? I've heard enough gossip about you. You stay until you're tired of someone, then you leave,' Eleanor said. She put a hand to his chest to ward him off, ignoring the ripples of excitement that ran down her fingers.

'I will never tire of you, Eleanor,' Will said passionately, taking her hand to his lips and kissing the palm softly.

Eleanor bowed her head, willing herself to believe him. Defying convention in such a manner was impossible, but a *frisson* of excitement coursed through her at the idea. She reached her arms about Will's neck, pulling his mouth on to hers. Through the thin fabric of her shift she could feel the heat between them and the rise and fall of his chest brushing against her breasts. Her fingernails scraped across his back and he growled, deep and animalistic.

The ground fell away as Will lifted her into his arms. He held Eleanor's gaze as he carried her across the room and they sank on to the bed. Will's body covered hers as his lips teased the hollow behind her ear, murmuring endearments. His fingers stroked her waist, then further down to map the curve of her thigh. Eleanor's breath came in short, sharp gasps, the anticipation causing her head to spin. She tightened her arms about his neck, pulling his mouth on to hers.

His fingers danced across the delicate fabric of Eleanor's shift, causing ripples of exhilaration that pulsed along the length of every limb. His mouth roamed across her jaw and down her exposed throat as he kissed her bare flesh. His kiss became fiercer, his touch harder. Eleanor tilted her head back as Will's lips travelled further down teasingly until they brushed the swell of her breasts. She whimpered as waves of pleasure crested over her.

Now she truly understood what she had been offering him that night on Rowland's Mount, and what control he must have had to refuse, because she knew that option was far behind her now.

She was barely aware of the door opening until she heard the sharp cry of disgust. Anne stood in the doorway, her mouth a wide circle of surprise as she whipped her head between them. She sat bolt upright as Will sprang to his feet.

'How could you? You knew how I felt about him.' Anne's voice was a knife of accusation.

'Anne, it isn't what it seems. We haven't done anything—' Eleanor began.

'How long have you been lying to me?'

'I haven't lied.' Eleanor struggled to her feet. She ran to Anne and took her hands, but the girl tore them away. 'It was only last night, I swear. We kissed, nothing more.'

Anne's face reddened. 'Last night?' She narrowed her eyes and glared at Will. 'Before midnight?' she demanded.

Will strode towards her. 'Anne, don't,' he said, a note of warning in his tone.

'Don't what?' Eleanor asked in confusion. She rounded on Will. 'What is she talking about?'

'That was the wager, wasn't it?' Anne said. She rounded on Eleanor, her face scornful. 'Did you think he cared for you? Whatever he did was for one of Edmund's games.'

The words threatened to choke Eleanor, but she forced them out. 'Is she telling the truth?'

Will's face twisted into a mask of misery. It was all the admission she needed.

'Let me explain,' Will said, moving towards her, arms outstretched as if to embrace her.

The sight of him made her stomach revolt. She stumbled backwards, arms around her body, squeezing tightly as though she could stop the pain from bursting forth. 'I don't want your explanations! I trusted you. I told you things I've never shared with anyone and all the time you were lying to me! Get out of my sight,' she whispered.

When he didn't move Eleanor picked the wine flask and hurled it at him.

'I said get out!' she screamed.

Will sidestepped it neatly and it smashed against the doorframe. On legs that would barely hold her weight she walked to him, summoning all the dignity she could muster.

'Leave now before I have you thrown out of Tawstott.'

Will said nothing, only set his jaw and left the chamber without a backwards glance. Anne threw a look of pity at Eleanor and followed him.

Eleanor's self-possession crumbled. She drew a ragged breath as hot tears flowed down her cheeks. She sank to the floor, sobbing as blackness closed over her, and she knew nothing more.

# Chapter Twenty-One

Muffled sobs came through the door, ripping Will's heart to shreds.

'Did you intend that revelation to hurt me or your sister?' He fixed Anne with a grim stare.

'No one! I didn't think,' Anne said forlornly. She looked as grief-stricken as he felt. 'What you and Edmund were discussing yesterday suddenly made sense.' Her face reddened. 'You have no right to be angry at me. How could you toy with her like that, Will? If you really cared for Eleanor I could have borne that, but it was just a joke to you.'

Will leaned back against the wall, shaking his head. He opened his mouth to contradict her, but from inside the chamber Eleanor's sobbing stopped abruptly, replaced by an ominous silence. The blood drained from Will's face as he and Anne both reached for the door handle.

Eleanor lay on the floor, her copper tresses obscuring her face like a mourning veil. With a cry of horror Anne fell to her knees.

'She's dead!'

Will reeled. Fighting his rising panic, he knelt by Eleanor's side. The rise and fall of her ribcage was so slight that Will had to resist laying his head on her breast to make sure he was not mistaken.

'She's in a faint,' he announced with relief.

With infinite care Will lifted her into his arms. The heat of desire rose in him at the touch of her body. That his body should react in such a manner while Eleanor was insensible felt akin to a violation. He forced himself to forget the intimacy they had shared only a short time ago and laid her down on the bed. Knowing he would never again touch her, he could scarcely bear to let go.

Eleanor's eyes flickered and she sighed. Colour started to return to her ashen cheeks. She looked serene, though Will could only guess at the turmoil she would feel when she awoke.

His fault! He took one lingering look, then firmly took hold of Anne's elbow and led her from the chamber.

'Where are we going?' Anne protested.

Will stopped at the door and grimaced. 'She'll recover soon, but do you think she will want to

see either of us when she wakes?' he said heavily.
Anne shook her head, tears springing to her eyes.

He closed the door softly and stood with his
back to it, folding his arms and gritting his teeth.

'What are you doing?' Anne asked. 'You said
she wouldn't want to speak to you.'

Would Anne believe him if he told her there was
nowhere else he wanted to be? 'I know, but that
doesn't matter, I'm staying anyway.' He planted
his feet firmly apart and prepared to wait.

Will could not say how long he had stood outside Eleanor's room, but the corridor grew dim and
cold. He shifted his weight, hoping to find a more
comfortable position. A bleak voice told him the
discomfort was his penance, but the aches in his
body were nothing compared to that in his heart.

He desperately wanted to know what Eleanor
was doing. Was she angry or sad, or filled with
loathing for him? Which emotion would be worse
to see on her face?

Every possible variation of recrimination and
self-loathing circled his mind. There was nothing
Eleanor could call him, no accusation she could
make that he had not already judged himself with.
He leaned back against the door, listening keenly
for any sound from within.

Before long the maidservants would come to light the lamps and Sir Edgar and his guests would return. He was fortunate most of the household had gone on the ride and the servants were all occupied. He could not be found lingering outside Eleanor's room. That would be to invite scandal. However much he wished to stay Will had no intention of adding to the pain he had already caused Eleanor. When voices echoed up the stairs he walked away.

For a good while he succeeded in immersing himself in his work. No one would have guessed the pain in his heart from looking at him, but he was heartily glad when he could escape to the kitchens to oversee preparations for the feast. He was halfway out there when Sir Edgar approached him.

'I haven't commended you for your labours over the past weeks,' the baron said warmly.

Will bowed his head. 'Thank you, my lord. The efforts were not mine alone, however.' Honesty compelled him to acknowledge Eleanor's role even though he could not bring himself to speak her name.

Sir Edgar saved him the trouble. 'Eleanor. Of course.' His face became serious. 'That is another matter I wished to speak to you about.'

Will's heart lurched. Had Eleanor already told her father of his duplicity? He steeled himself for his immediate dismissal. Sir Edgar spoke in a low voice.

'You wouldn't realise, but she has changed so much. I haven't seen her so happy for years and that is your doing. I owe you a debt I can never repay.'

Sir Edgar's words seared a brand across Will's already lacerated conscience. Accusations would have been a blessing in comparison. Will muttered his thanks and excused himself before his composure fractured completely.

He made his way to the pantry and sank on to a stool. He glanced up to find Rob standing over him holding a bottle of wine, but shook his head.

'I've been looking all over for you,' Rob said. 'Duke Roland was pleased with the peregrine. He said she's the finest bird he's seen in years and gave me ten groats. With the ten from you last night, Eliza and I will be able to marry sooner than we expected.'

Will mumbled congratulations.

'That was tactless of me,' Rob said. 'You're still downhearted about the loss of the money. I'm sorry, I know what you had planned.'

As if the money mattered at all! A sudden urge

to confide struck Will and he leaned back, his smile vanishing.

'Eleanor knows about the wager,' he said bleakly.

'Is that the reason you failed?' Rob asked. He sucked his teeth. 'That's bad fortune. I was sure you would succeed. Edmund was still crowing about it this morning.'

Will grimaced. He might as well share the whole story now. 'I didn't fail,' he admitted quietly.

'But you forfeited the stake,' Rob said.

'It felt dishonourable, so I paid you, *then* I kissed her,' Will explained. His stomach twisted with a disconcerting mixture of lust and guilt at the memory. 'I kissed her last night and it was better than anything I could have imagined. I went to see her this morning and Anne found us together. She'd overheard me discussing the wager with Edmund and told Eleanor, who reacted as you would imagine.'

Rob winced and patted Will's shoulder. 'It's bad luck about the money, but you'll find another infatuation before long. You always do.'

'Not this time,' Will muttered quietly.

'Don't tell me you've lost your heart?' Rob laughed.

'Lost or found, it makes no difference now. She looked at me with such disgust. What happened between me and Amy is nothing in comparison.' His chest tightened as he remembered the betrayal in Eleanor's eyes.

The expression of sympathy in Rob's eyes was almost too much for Will to bear. 'You said you were done with love after Amy,' Rob pointed out.

'I intended to be. It's bad enough I fell for her, but I think she cares for me in return. This wasn't supposed to happen.' Will sighed. He closed his eyes and touched a hand to his scar, the memory of Eleanor's lips there causing his eyes to sting. Already he missed the laughter they had shared and the closeness that had grown between them. He could not bear to give that up any more than he would willingly stop breathing. Pushing himself to his feet, he looked at his brother.

'I need to see Eleanor again.'

'Do you think she'll forgive you?' Rob asked.

'I don't know, but I'd regret it for ever if I didn't try.' With a confidence he didn't feel Will forced a grin. 'I won her once—maybe I can do it again.'

Eleanor woke disorientated and nauseous. The last thing she remembered was sinking to the floor as she had allowed her shock to claim her. How she came to be in her bed she could not say. A soft tapping came at the door followed by Will's low voice speaking her name.

A stab of sadness shot through her. She rolled on to her front and stifled a sob. She tried to block out her memories and cast the images from her mind, but they refused to be banished. It was all a lie though. Will's sensuous gazes, his smiles and confidences had been nothing more than a charade. She closed her eyes and ignored the sound of Will's voice. Finally it came no more and she slept.

When she awoke it was dark and the room was cold, the fire reduced to a handful of barely glowing embers. She glanced at the folded green gown and smiled bitterly. Colours belonged to another time and another Eleanor. There would be no such foolishness again. Shivering, Eleanor dressed in her drab grey dress.

There was a knock at the door, firmer than earlier, but Eleanor knew who it would be. Anger boiled in her stomach. Her urge was to ignore it again, but she drew herself tall. She would not be able to hide away for the rest of her time here and she would not be able to avoid Will while she remained. The knock came again, slightly louder. She stormed to the door and flung it open.

Will stood, hand raised mid-knock. He looked

startled at the absence of door, but Eleanor watched
as his expression changed to relief. His eyes lit
with their customary gleam and his lips softened into a smile. Eleanor's heart fluttered with
the anticipation she had come to anticipate in his
company. She commanded it firmly to stop such
foolishness and stared at him coldly.

'Why are you here?' she asked icily.

Will reached a hand to her. He stopped and withdrew it. 'I was concerned about you. I found you
in a faint earlier.'

That explained how she came to be in her bed.
A shiver ran down Eleanor's spine at the thought
of Will's arms about her. He had held her so protectively, his strength flowing into her when he
had pulled her from the nightmare on Rowland's
Mount. Had he been as gentle this time when he
no longer needed to pretend?

'I need to speak to you,' Will said. He looked
along the corridor. 'May I come in?'

'To justify your actions?' Eleanor folded her
arms across her chest, a barrier that Will noticed
because his eyes flicked down. Pain crossed his
face briefly and Eleanor felt a gleam of satisfaction.

'I have no justification. I deserve your anger,'
Will said. 'I want to apologise.'

Eleanor shrugged and walked back inside, not looking to see if Will followed. She heard the door shut.

'How much did you wager?'

The question clearly was not one he was expecting because his eyebrows shot up. 'Why does it matter? It was unforgivable to do it at all.'

'I knew when I let you kiss me that it was just a game to you, but I thought you at least liked me. Now I find you were just doing it for *money*! So tell me how much!' she demanded.

'Ten groats apiece,' Will admitted quietly.

She looked at him in disgust. 'Is that all you thought I was worth?'

Will's face was a picture of anguish. 'There isn't the money in all the land to measure your worth to me.'

'Don't lie! Nothing you said or did was real, was it?'

Will moved towards her swiftly and took hold of her hand before she could prevent it. She struggled as he pressed it against his chest, but he held it immovable. His heart pounded against her palm.

'Everything I felt was real,' he said fervently. 'It wasn't supposed to be, but it was. You must believe me.'

'Why should I believe you?' she asked harshly.

'Because I l—'

'No!' Eleanor cried, cutting him off. Cold sweat pooled in the small of her back and she felt bile rise in her throat. 'Whatever you were about to say, don't! I won't let you insult me in such a way.'

'I don't intend to insult you,' Will said. He took her face between his hands and she did not resist. 'I can never atone for the deception, or the grief I've caused, but I care for you more deeply than I thought possible.'

'I thought you were my friend. I should have known better!' Eleanor cried. 'You're untrustworthy, Will. Just like Edmund. I was stupid enough to hope it would be different with me, but you're faithless and fickle.'

'You don't know what you're talking about.'

'And why not? Why am I wrong? You leave every woman you tarry with. You left your betrothed and you'd leave me too!' Her fury overflowed and she rounded on him, punctuating each word with a slap to Will's chest. 'Tell. Me. Why. I'm. Wrong.'

He took each blow as though it was a feather's touch.

'Because I didn't leave Amy,' he shouted. His eyes burned into Eleanor. 'I didn't end the betrothal. She left me.'

Eleanor's hands dropped to her sides. No explanation could have been more astounding.

'What did you do?' she asked suspiciously.

Will rubbed his eyes, looking suddenly weary. 'The fault must have been mine naturally?' He gave a wry smile. He walked to the window and stared out. 'I deserve that, I suppose, but in truth I did nothing more than receive an injury.'

Eleanor walked to stand beside him. He raised an eyebrow questioningly and she nodded to prompt him.

'This,' he said, brushing his hair behind his ears to reveal his scar.

Despite her anger Eleanor reached a hand to Will's face, tracing a finger along the faint lines. 'But why?' she asked softly.

'Amy wanted the prestige and income of a falconer's wife. When I decided to end my apprenticeship we quarrelled. She said she could bear an ugly husband or a poor one, but not both.'

He spoke without self-pity. Eleanor's blood rose at the injustice, the words so similar to the duchess's verdict. She felt a burst of anger against the woman who had so ill treated Will.

'Did Amy not want you even when you came back a richer man?'

'Perhaps we may have reconciled, but I was too

proud and hurt to ask. Besides, by then I had met your brother who introduced me to the fun that could be had with willing women who wanted nothing more than a few hours of company. I decided I was never again going to allow a woman to command my heart.' He looked into Eleanor's eyes, holding her gaze until her head spun. 'And I didn't for five years.'

His meaning was clear and Eleanor's heart pounded. His gaze was almost irresistible. Eleanor shook her head as though waking from a dream.

'So you decided to spend your life hurting others in revenge for her mistreatment of you?'

'No!' Will exclaimed. 'No woman I have seduced has been unwilling, and none were hurt. I was always careful that the attachment, if any, was slight on both sides.' He ran his hands over his face, then rubbed his eyes wearily and looked at her with anguish. 'You were the first who cared and whom I cared for in return.'

'Do you think that excuses what you did?' she asked curtly.

'No.'

Will looked as grief-stricken as Eleanor felt. She knew that if she stayed in his presence much longer her resolve would crumble to dust.

'I'm sorry, Will. I understand, but I cannot forgive you. Goodbye.'

On legs of glass she left the room without a backwards glance and made her way downstairs, taking deep breaths to try to regain her composure. She had been absent from the company for too long and it would be remarked upon. Naturally, the last person she wanted to see was the first she encountered as she entered the Great Hall. Sir Martin broke off from his conversation with the Earl of Etherington. He rushed to Eleanor, then walked her to an alcove and drew a stool for her.

'I searched for you this morning. When I heard you were indisposed my heart cracked as though I was the one who was ill. Are you recovered?'

Eleanor nodded dumbly, doubting she would ever recover from what had just happened.

'Lady Peyton, I am sorry to press you, but I must know. Have you thought any more of my offer?' Sir Martin said.

'Your offer?' Eleanor stared at Sir Martin blankly.

Sir Martin took her hands, trapping them between his own. 'Tell me you have reached a decision,' Sir Martin urged.

'This is too sudden,' Eleanor whispered, her voice dull. She withdrew her hands.

'It may be sudden, but what sense is there in waiting when I know I want you? Just think what it means for you,' Sir Martin said with a smile. 'Baldwin's lands passing to me: to a blood relative instead of a stranger.'

His intensity was overwhelming, his words persuasive.

'I want you for my wife,' he continued. 'My hopes of happiness depend upon your answer.'

Happiness! What hope of happiness did Eleanor have now? Will owned her heart and always would, but below the passion she had craved there had been an acid that had burned any such hopes away. The prospect of years alone stretched out ahead of her. She dug her nails into her palms as fresh pain overwhelmed her and raised her head to meet Sir Martin's eyes.

'Sir Martin, I don't love you. I have no hope or expectation that I will ever love anyone.' Her voice trembled as she spoke. 'If you can accept that, I will be your wife.'

## Chapter Twenty-Two

It took all Will's strength to regain his composure by the time he reached the Great Hall. He had not intended to reveal the truth about his failed betrothal and it had stirred painful emotions that, coupled with his encounter with Eleanor, threatened to tip him into a misery he might never escape from.

The Great Hall seemed louder than usual. Will's eyes roamed the room searching for Eleanor and found her sitting with Allencote in an alcove beside the fire. Had the knight sought her out or had she gone straight to him for comfort? Will's heart ached at the thought. He watched them from a distance, studying Eleanor's face for signs of her disposition. She was perched rigidly on the edge of a low stool, her face white and her eyes deeply ringed with shadows. Allencote was speaking and

Will's temper rose as the knight prattled on, seemingly unaware of his companion's discomposure.

Eleanor glanced around and caught Will's eye, then frowned and looked away rapidly, distress twisting her mouth. Weariness washed over Will. He craved rest from the pain in his heart. He wanted more than anything to take Eleanor in his arms and steal her away to somewhere private. To hold her close until the misery that consumed them both diminished and sleep with her in his arms as he should have done that night on Rowland's Mount. To make her understand that what he felt for her was no jest.

Allencote was still talking. All around them people were drinking, but Eleanor held no cup. He thought back to the table in her room where the tray he had brought that morning had remained untouched. There was no evidence that she had eaten or drunk since arriving and she must be near faint with hunger by now.

If he could not comfort her, he could at least offer sustenance. He filled two goblets of spiced wine and began to thread his way through the crowd to where she sat, but guests and householders accosted him, commanding his attention. He dealt with every matter efficiently, glad that one thing remained normal in his life. Finally he retrieved the wine and moved towards the alcove, but Eleanor and Allencote were no longer there. A swirl of grey amidst the coloured gowns caught his eye and he saw them heading towards the doorway, Allencote's hand in the small of Eleanor's back. As they passed through the door Eleanor glanced back at the hall, her face solemn. Allencote muttered in her ear and she followed with uncharacteristic meekness. Sensing something was afoot, Will put the goblets on a table and followed without a second thought.

A few paces ahead of him Eleanor stopped suddenly between the narrow staircase and the corridor that led to Sir Edgar's library. She caught Allencote by the arm. Will stepped behind the stairs out of sight, ready to intervene if necessary.

'What's wrong?' Allencote's tone was sharp.

Will's fists clenched in response.

'Do we have to do this tonight?' Eleanor asked quietly.

'Why wait? Let me speak to your father now,' Allencote urged. 'With his agreement we could be wed within the week. Duke Roland will approve and the matter can be settled immediately.'

A lump formed in Will's throat. He willed himself to have misunderstood, but knew he had not.

So soon! She must have gone straight to Allencote after leaving him.

'There's no need for such haste, is there?' Eleanor asked.

A shadow passed across the floor in front of Will. Allencote paced back and forth. 'Haste, you call it. I call it eagerness. If you are to be my wife, I want no delays. There is nothing that could prevent us, is there?'

Through the banisters Will saw Eleanor shake her head reluctantly.

'No, but the thought of marriage after so long is strange to me. Please, wait until tomorrow when I am more accustomed to the idea.'

Allencote laughed indulgently. 'Very well, if your modesty demands it I will submit this time. A kiss will suffice to seal our bargain.'

Eleanor's arms hung limply at her sides as she received Allencote's kiss. Her back was straight and she showed no signs of the passion Will remembered all too well. Allencote pulled her closer to him, murmuring appreciatively. He either did not notice Eleanor's reluctance or did not care.

His guts twisted at the thought that his actions had driven Eleanor to this. Creeping stealthily back a few paces, Will banged the door loudly and began to walk on heavy feet towards the couple, whistling. Affecting surprise, he bowed.

'Lady Peyton, good evening. I was hoping to speak with you, but our paths have not crossed tonight. There is a matter I have to consult you on.'

Allencote had moved away from Eleanor at the sound of approaching feet. Relief crossed Eleanor's face before the now familiar hatred blazed in her eyes.

'There are people I must speak with, too, so I will leave you to your arrangements,' Allencote said, taking Eleanor's hand and kissing it. 'Until tomorrow, my lady.' He gave a smug curl of the lips that Will met with an even stare, then headed back to the Great Hall without a backwards glance.

'What are you doing here?' Eleanor snapped. 'Haven't I made it clear I don't wish to talk to you?'

'I must speak to you about something.'

Eleanor frowned. Will's eyes were bright and full of hurt.

'How much did you hear just now?' she asked suspiciously.

Will's lips twitched with distaste. 'Enough. And I saw enough, too, to convince me you're making a mistake if you intend to marry Allencote.'

Eleanor's eyes began to sting. Sir Martin's kiss had been forceful, almost bordering on rough, yet at the same time somehow dispassionate. The only sensation she had felt had been slight distaste. Being kissed by him was nothing like Will's tender caresses and the contrast in the way her body had responded instinctively to the man who now stood before her was so acute it was cruel.

'You look sad for someone who has so recently become betrothed,' Will remarked. 'Such a quick decision must be alarming, of course.'

'Leave me alone,' Eleanor cried. Her eyes filled and she pushed past Will. She dragged open the heavy door, stumbling out into the falling snow, the flakes burning cold where they met hot tears on her cheeks. She wondered how she even had any tears left, but still they came.

She had reached the archway before Will caught up with her. She caught the spicy earthiness of his scent on the cloak he draped silently around her shoulders. She wiped an angry hand across her face, hating the feelings that threatened to overpower her at a gesture so simple.

'Why did you follow me?' she demanded.

'Haven't you realised yet that when I see you upset I'll always follow you?' Will said intently. He gave a hollow laugh that rang with pain. 'Besides, someone has to bring you a cloak as you never remember your own.'

'If you think I'll forgive you because you brought me a cloak, you're wrong,' Eleanor said disdainfully.

Will looked at her reproachfully. The snow fell fast about them, glinting in the brightness of the moon like ice needles. He must be half-frozen, yet stood firm.

'You don't love Allencote,' he stated.

Eleanor crossed her arms tightly about herself as though that could stop her heart twisting. 'Does that matter?' she asked bitterly.

'It should,' Will said firmly. 'Does he know?'

Eleanor nodded, the lump in her throat too enormous to allow speech.

'And yet he still wants to marry you.' Will frowned. 'Does *he* love *you*? Have you asked him?'

When she had accepted him Sir Martin's eyes had lit up, but not with the desire Eleanor had seen in Will's. A hunger, and something more: triumph, perhaps? He had not minded when she said she did not love him. A doubt began to gnaw her mind, but she banished it and fixed Will with a cold stare.

'Marriages for women like me are seldom based

on love,' she replied bitterly. 'He must have some regard for me else he would not have asked.'

'Are you really so naïve?' Will rolled his eyes in frustration. 'I don't intend to belittle your appeal. You know how highly I regard you, but there are any number of reasons why Allencote might wish to marry you and most of them are not honourable.'

'Don't you speak to me of honour! Not everyone is as deceitful as you, Will,' Eleanor sneered. 'You don't want me to marry him and you'd say anything to stop me.'

Will's face twisted with pain. 'Of course I don't want you to marry him. Watching him kissing you just now almost drove me to my knees.'

Eleanor stared at him furiously. 'Why am I even discussing this with you after what you did?'

'Because we understand each other. Because you know I'm right. If I thought you would be happy I would say nothing, even though it would kill me. You won't be, though, and you know it too. I will not stand by and witness that.'

Will took hold of her hand, enclosing it in his. 'You have years ahead of you, Eleanor, too many to spend with someone you don't love. If you realise you've made the wrong choice, there's no guarantee you'll be fortunate enough to get widowed again!'

'How dare you mock me!'

The blood rose to Eleanor's cheeks. She drew her arm back and delivered a slap to Will's cheek. The whip-crack rang out across the silence of the courtyard. Will jerked his head to the side. Eleanor stared at her stinging palm, her eyes widening in shock. A stark mark stood out on his face, his white scar a fine line down the centre of the red. His eyes flashed angrily as he raised a hand to his face and rubbed his cheek, but when he spoke his voice was rueful.

'I deserved that.'

'Yes, you did! You dare talk of honour when you used me in a game? You lied to me and humiliated me.'

'I did, and if it was within my power to undo that wrong I would. You're angry with me and you have every right to be, but you're not soft-headed,' Will snapped. 'Barely a week ago you intended to marry no one and barely an hour after we spoke I find you betrothed. If you marry that man because of what happened between us, you'll regret it for the rest of your life. Don't punish me, or yourself in that way.'

'I'm not marrying Sir Martin to punish anyone.

I was always…' Eleanor tailed off, her heart twisting at the realisation she had let slip her intention. Silence hung in the falling snow.

'You were always going to marry him, weren't you?' Will said eventually, his voice flat.

Eleanor twisted away in dismay, her cheeks colouring. She could feel Will's eyes on her and she risked a sideways look. His mouth was twisted into a grimace.

'It seems I'm not the only one capable of deception,' Will said tightly. 'You kissed me knowing full well you were going to give yourself to another!'

'I didn't intend to. You tricked me into kissing you,' Eleanor blustered. Her heart began to beat faster. She glanced towards the house, wishing she could run from his questions. How far would she have to go before he stopped following her?

Will lifted his jaw. 'No, I didn't. My motive may have been questionable, but I used no trickery. You came to my arms willingly. More than once, in fact! You can deny it all you like, but you wanted me as much as I wanted you.'

Eleanor closed her eyes, not bothering to fight the memory of Will's hands on her body, his lips exploring her exposed flesh. The sensations flooded her senses so clearly the longing was almost painful.

'Yes, I wanted you,' she whispered. 'I wanted to know what it felt like before...'

'Before what, Eleanor?' Will's voice was colder than she had ever heard him be. 'What were you intending to do, store the memories and conjure me while your rich lord bedded you?'

'That isn't why I did it!' she protested. 'It wasn't for money, or to bolster my reputation with my friends. There is no comparison between what we did.'

She raised her head and met Will's eyes. Blue, bright and searching her face keenly with an intensity that knocked her sideways.

'No comparison? Money or memories—which is the more valuable currency, I wonder? Would twenty groats have bought me more lasting satisfaction than what you took for yourself?'

Eleanor's heart hammered with mortification at the thought Will could think her capable of such deception, but with a sickening realisation she saw he had spoken the truth. Her actions had been no better than his.

'You have no right to be angry with me,' she protested.

'Don't I? I have been consumed with guilt at

the thought of what I had induced you to do to and now I find that far from being swept up in a moment of passion you had already planned your path. Did it matter that it was me or would anybody have sufficed in my place?'

'No!'

Will raised his eyebrows in disbelief. Eleanor turned her back, swallowing down tears. 'It could only ever have been you. I wanted something I'd never had, or expected to have again. I wanted to know what it was like to care for someone.' Her voice cracked and she forced the words out. 'And be cared for in return. I thought you did, but I was wrong.'

Before she had finished speaking Will's arms were about her, wrapping tightly around her and holding her close. He rested his head against her neck, murmuring her name passionately. Even with the thick cloak between them his body was warm and comfortingly powerful.

'I care more than you can imagine. If you believe nothing else I tell you, believe that,' Will murmured fiercely, his voice husky and intoxicating. 'Tell me how to atone and I will do it, whatever it takes.'

He reached for her hand and held it tightly, lacing his fingers through hers. His touch sent a shiver along her arm and she lowered her head to prevent Will seeing the emotions on her face. He had always been able to read her heart. He sounded so convincing and had appeared genuinely hurt at her admission. Eleanor leaned back against him, remembering how she had craved his touch before she had learned the truth.

All it would take would be a turn of her head to bring his lips within her reach. Longing sent her head spinning. Pride fought back. If he knew how close she was to forgiving him, he would surely begin his attempts again and Eleanor knew she would never be able to withstand him. She had to leave. Now, before she gave in to what her heart screamed she wanted.

Eleanor sighed weakly and wriggled free from Will's embrace. 'I will not change my mind. I have agreed to marry Sir Martin and that is the end of it.'

'It doesn't have to be,' Will insisted.

Eleanor raised her eyebrows. 'You of all people are advocating ending a betrothal!'

'A betrothal as ill conceived as this one?' Will said, his lip twisting. 'Without question.'

Eleanor unclasped his cloak from around her neck and held it at arm's length, stepping backwards out of his reach. When he made no move to take it she dropped it on the ground and walked back to the house, tears blinding her once more.

Walking through the Great Hall Eleanor saw betrayal or coercion at every turn. Anne and Lady Fitzallan sat with the duchess in front of the vast fireplace. Their presence held no attraction for her.

Edmund had taken in with the group of knights and squires who sat drinking and dicing at the far end of the room. Her temper flared as she thought of his part in her misery. That was a reckoning she had yet to have! Her brother hailed someone as Eleanor passed and she glanced around in time to see Will return the greeting with a curt nod of the head, but continue on his way, face grim.

Sir Martin was sharing a bottle of wine with the Earl of Etherington, heads close together and deep in discussion. As soon as Eleanor saw him the suspicions Will had planted in her mind reared up. She tried to dismiss them as jealousy or some other game she had not discovered yet, but they would not be quieted. If she never asked she would wonder for ever. Brushing the last droplets of melted snow from her dress, Eleanor took a deep breath and approached him.

'...in your hands within the month!' Sir Martin

said. He glared up at the interrupter before seemingly recognising Eleanor.

'Lady Peyton, my apologies, I was lost in thought! Did you sort out your matters with Master Rudhale?' Sir Martin asked.

Eleanor blinked before recalling Will's pretext for interrupting them.

'Oh, yes. He merely wanted to ask about the oysters for tomorrow's meal.'

Sir Martin smiled. 'I look forward to finding out if they live up to their reputation. I hope to visit Rowland's Mount before too long.'

'May I speak with you alone?' Eleanor asked.

The earl gave her an appraising look, but took the bottle and moved to a nearby table. Sir Martin reached for Eleanor's hand to pull her beside him on to the bench, but she stood firm.

'Why do you want to marry me?'

Sir Martin grinned at her boldly. 'Why would I not?'

'That isn't an answer,' Eleanor said. 'We know nothing of each other. How do you know we'll be happy?'

Sir Martin's smile vanished and he stood abruptly, causing Eleanor to step backwards. 'Are you regretting your decision?'

Eleanor hesitated. The regret was becoming

greater with each passing moment. 'I just want to know why when I have told you I don't love you,' she said.

'I could beguile you with soft words and poetry, but let me be unsentimental for a moment, Lady Peyton. Society expects people in our positions to marry, so if it is to each other then so much the better.'

'Is that the only reason: a convenient set of circumstances?'

Sir Martin's lips pursed. 'That is the least of it! Do you doubt I already feel affection for you? I find you beautiful and I hope I'm not too unsightly as to be disagreeable. Once our lives and lands are joined I have no doubt we'll be happy,' he said, patting her hand. 'I shall speak to your father tomorrow as planned. Once you are my wife you need think of nothing more than which gown to wear and how to dress your hair if you wish.'

Eleanor exhaled angrily. 'I hope I haven't given the impression I intend to be so idle!'

'Of course not!' Sir Martin waved a careless hand. 'You will be chatelaine of my estate after all. I don't imagine you will spend all your days sewing in your chambers, though there will be children, I hope, to occupy you before long.'

Involuntarily Eleanor's jaw tightened. 'We can

discuss that another time. Goodnight, Sir Martin,' she said, lifting her hand for him to kiss and indicating the conversation was over.

She walked away deep in thought. Sir Martin had been frank, but she sensed he wasn't telling her the whole truth. Will was standing against the far wall, his eyes boring into her and an expression of deep concern on his face. He nodded his head and walked away. Was there anyone here who had not hurt or deceived her in some way? She would have gladly walked out of the building and never gone back.

Perhaps she should.

She stopped walking abruptly as the notion overwhelmed her.

Who would be able to prevent her from leaving? Her father would frown and her mother would be furious, but what of it? Since returning to Tawstott she had lapsed into the habits of childhood, being treated—and behaving—like a girl, with no control. Look where that had got her. A betrothal she didn't want and a heart broken as soon as she had given it.

She could never be happy with Sir Martin until she was gone from Will's presence and it was that which tipped the balance. She had run from him once before—the memory of the resulting night set her heart thumping and caused her cheeks to redden even now—but it would be different this time. She would go alone and she did not plan to return.

## Chapter Twenty-Three

Eleanor half-ran to Sir Edgar's study. She hammered on the door and entered before she lost her nerve. Her father looked up from his book in surprise.

Eleanor dropped a curtsy. 'Father, I wish to return home. I intend to leave in the morning.'

'I'm sorry, Eleanor, I cannot sanction your leaving now.' Sir Edgar put his book down and gave her a hard stare.

'I came to tell you as a courtesy, but will you stop me by force?' Eleanor asked. 'Am I a prisoner here now?'

'Don't be so hysterical, Eleanor,' Sir Edgar said mildly. 'Tell me what has caused this.'

He listened as Eleanor told him of her betrothal, frowning unexpectedly at the mention of Sir Martin's name.

'You don't approve?' Eleanor asked in surprise.

'When we last spoke of him you were set against the idea,' Sir Edgar said. 'I had not noticed any signs of fondness between you. Are you certain you want to marry him?'

Eleanor's lip trembled and she shook her head violently. 'No, I'm not at all.' She collapsed on to the low chair by the fire and put her head in her hands.

Sir Edgar patted her head comfortingly. 'And if you leave will that help you decide? How will you explain your departure to Sir Martin?'

Eleanor leaned back in the chair, weariness crushing her. She could not remember the last time she had eaten. She shrugged. 'I'll tell him I want to prepare my home to welcome him. I don't see how he can object to that. If I decide I no longer wish to continue the betrothal, it will be easier from a distance.'

'Do you require an escort?' Sir Edgar asked. 'I don't think I can spare William if I am losing you, too.'

'No!' Eleanor's head shot up. She lowered her voice. 'No. Master Rudhale will not be required.'

'Ah!' In one quiet word Sir Edgar's tone brimmed with understanding and pity. Eleanor tightened her arms about her chest and looked bleakly at her father. Sir Edgar poured Eleanor a cup of wine and sat opposite her.

'I will not prevent you if you truly wish to go, but it saddens my heart,' Sir Edgar said. 'You spent years grieving for your husband. Your mother and I wanted you to find a husband who would make you happy. We did not intend this to be the outcome.'

Eleanor smiled wryly. It was too cruel that the loss of Will should cut her far deeper than the death of her husband. But she had never loved Baldwin.

'Neither did I,' she admitted.

She sipped the wine gratefully. It was the same variety Will had brought with him and the rich spiciness transported her back to their first meeting in this room. Furious at his behaviour on the ferry and unsettled by the effect his gaze had on her, even then she had been unable to tear her eyes from him. Little wonder he had seen her as an easy target for his games.

Now she barely recognised herself as that woman who lived in mourning and shook in fear at the smile from a man. For weeks Will had been gently nudging her back to life. Slowly, one by one, he had broken the links of the shackles she had barely known she wore. Had that been part of his plan all along, or was it an unintentional irony that she should realise her power and leave him? She would never know, but for that, if nothing else, she would always be grateful to him.

The snow had stopped falling and early morning sun streamed into a courtyard that was almost deserted, save for the servants loading Eleanor's carriage. Sir Edgar had bid Eleanor a fond goodbye and even Lady Fitzallan, placated by the promise of an impending marriage, had spoken kindly to her daughter.

Engulfed in her cloak and with her hood drawn over her face Eleanor stood in the doorway, watching as her chest was loaded on to her carriage and Jennet sleepily arranged piles of furs on the seats.

Sir Martin stood at Eleanor's side. Though he had not taken news of her departure in good spirits he had accepted Eleanor's story of wanting to prepare for his arrival at Rowland's Mount.

'I will follow you in two days, Lady Peyton,' he declared. 'I will be counting the hours until we are together again.'

Eleanor studied him. He was handsome and not devoid of manners. She hoped marriage would be bearable once she had become accustomed to his company. And when she had had time to banish the memory of Will from her mind. He moved towards her as though he planned to kiss her, so she held out a hand. He looked taken aback, but lifted it to his lips, then hurried back inside out of the cold.

As she left the building a flash of colour in the corner of the courtyard caught Eleanor's eye. A figure wrapped in a familiar wine-coloured cloak passed beneath the archway. He cast a baleful look in her direction, then turned back the way he had come. Eleanor's stomach lurched. This could not be how they would part after all they had shared! She ran to him.

'Were you not going to bid me farewell?' she whispered hoarsely.

Will's eyes were circled with dark shadows. He looked as though he had barely slept. 'I did not believe you would welcome my presence,' he said stiffly.

Eleanor forced herself not to weep at the formality in his voice. Will shot a look of undisguised dislike towards where Sir Martin had been standing. 'You asked him, didn't you? Was his answer satisfactory?'

Eleanor's brow creased and she twisted her hands together. The urge to confide in Will was too hard to ignore. 'I don't know. Something feels wrong, but I can't say what.'

Will gave her arm a reassuring squeeze. 'I will find out. If he plans to use you badly, I will discover it, I swear.'

'And then what?' Eleanor asked. Alarmed at how his touch still set her heart racing, her voice was brusquer than she intended. 'Will you expect my forgiveness for what you did to me?'

Will withdrew his hand and looked at her reproachfully. 'No. Hard though it may be for you to believe, I'm not doing it for my benefit. I'll expect you to use the information in whatever way makes your life happiest. Farewell, Eleanor.'

He strode away without looking back.

Eleanor walked to her carriage to find Edmund leaning against it talking to her driver and throwing wide grins to Jennet who sat inside the coach. Eleanor glared at her brother. The last person she wanted to see was Will's collaborator in her misery.

'Stop looking at my maid like that, she isn't going to be one of your conquests!' she snapped. 'What are you doing here anyway?'

Edmund looked taken aback at her venom. 'Why are you angry with me? I've come to say goodbye to you,' he protested. 'And what do you mean "conquests"?'

'You know exactly what I mean. Anne told me of your game. Of the wager you and Will made about me. Did you even think how that would hurt or were you just concerned with your fun?' She swept past him and climbed into the carriage, slamming the door. 'You're a pathetic child, Edmund.'

Edmund's face fell. 'It was only a spot of merriment. I don't know why you're so angry anyway, it isn't as though you kissed him,' he said, reaching in to pat her arm comfortingly.

The carriage rocked on its chains as the driver climbed to his seat. Eleanor gripped the window frame tightly.

'What makes you say that?'

'Ten groats, of course!' Edmund frowned in confusion. 'Will forfeited the bet. It was hard enough to persuade him in the first place. He must have known all along you were beyond his reach.'

A cold sweat ran down Eleanor's back. She looked frantically around the courtyard, but Will was nowhere to be seen. She gripped the window frame tightly. 'When did he forfeit?' she called urgently to Edmund.

Edmund raised his hands in a foolish shrug and

Eleanor's fingers twitched with the effort of not slapping some sense into him. 'You expect me to remember that? It was two days ago.'

'Try,' Eleanor muttered darkly.

Edmund raised his voice to answer as the carriage began to move. 'The wager was set to end at midnight, so some time before then, I suppose.'

Eleanor slumped back into her seat as the carriage jolted down the road. What Edmund said didn't make any sense. If Will had forfeited before he kissed her, then he hadn't done it for the money. And if money wasn't the reason, then what was? The implications were almost too momentous to think about. Well, now she had all the time she liked as the carriage carried her away from Tawstott and away from Will.

Eleanor was gone and Will's world was darker and smaller. His final promise to Eleanor burned fiercely in his mind. He stuck as close to Allencote as he dared without drawing attention to himself, but saw nothing that would explain his misgivings. Watching Allencote returning to the house deep in conversation with the Earl of Etherington, Will felt certain the answer was to be found there.

'Mayhap you're imagining it,' Rob told him. 'You're hardly impartial after all.'

'I'm not,' Will insisted. 'Someone knows and somehow I'll find out.'

The answer came the following evening as he walked along the upstairs corridor noting which chests should be sent to which cart. Raised voices were coming from Allencote's chamber.

'I had your word you would secure it, but now she's left.'

'You have my seal on the document, that should be assurance enough for now. She has agreed. But once she's my wife the point is moot anyway. And she *will* become my wife.'

His tone sent a chill down Will's back as he wondered how Allencote would ensure Eleanor's cooperation.

The door opened and Lord Etherington strolled out, a folded parchment in his hand. Will pressed himself against the wall, heart beating rapidly. Allencote owed money, Will already knew that. No wonder he was so eager to marry Eleanor when a handsome dowry would settle his debts, but Eleanor would want more proof than an overheard conversation.

He found Edmund in his chamber, a half-clothed

serving girl in his lap and a jug of ale to hand. Edmund protested as Will dismissed the girl, then listened as Will explained his suspicions.

'What business is it of ours to intrude into Eleanor's matters? She hates interference,' Edmund answered.

Rage boiled inside Will. He rounded on Edmund, backing him against the wall. 'It's thanks to our treatment of her that Eleanor is marrying Allencote in the first place,' he hissed. 'We owe it to her.'

Edmund looked contrite. 'How do you think I can help?' he asked. 'Sir Martin won't share his plans with me.'

'If you won't ask Allencote, then find out from Lord Etherington himself. I don't care how, but find out!' Will left the room before Edmund could reply.

The next morning Allencote departed for Rowland's Mount. Will watched him go bitterly, his hopes dying. He waited until the distant hoofbeats died away, then turned to the house and almost collided with Edmund who was running at full speed through the courtyard.

He clutched at Will's arm. His breath was heavy with wine and his clothing dishevelled, but his expression was more serious than Will could remember ever seeing.

'It took almost all night and a lot of wine to coax it out of Lord Etherington, but I've found out,' he said grimly. He pulled Will to where the Earl of Etherington stood.

'My Lord, please tell Master Rudhale what you told me,' Edmund asked.

The earl looked puzzled, but finally spoke. 'I am owed considerable payment for some personal matters. Sir Martin proposes that I take part of his new estate upon his marriage.'

Will's scalp prickled. Here was his answer.

'Which part?' he asked. The earl produced the parchment Will had seen the previous night. The note promised the transfer of the property known as Rowland's Mount from Sir Martin to Lord Etherington. He swore. It wasn't Eleanor's money Allencote wanted; it was her home.

'Sir Martin has assured me Lady Peyton has consented,' the earl said.

'Eleanor would never give up that piece of rock!' Edmund exclaimed. 'She loves it too much.'

'My lord, may I take this?' Will asked. 'I fear Sir Martin will have to find other means of repaying you. Lady Peyton does not know his intention and Edmund is right. She will never to agree to that.'

'If this is true, then someone should warn Lady Peyton,' the earl said, frowning. 'Sir Martin can be very persuasive and is not above coercion when the need arises.'

Edmund blanched.

Will tucked the parchment inside his jerkin. 'Then we have to prevent him having the opportunity.'

'And how will you do that?' the earl asked in surprise.

Will was already heading towards Sir Edgar's library. He called back determinedly, 'The only way I can. I'm going to Rowland's Mount.'

'What I don't understand,' Sir Edgar said, turning the parchment over in his hands, 'is how you came to play a part this matter.'

'Lady Peyton had misgivings about her marriage. I promised I would discover anything that would help her make up her mind.'

'And it seems you have. I agree with you, Eleanor would never have allowed such a thing. I am sure she will be most interested to read this. Well done, William, I shall find a messenger as soon as I can.'

'Let me go, please,' Will said.

'Why you?' Sir Edgar asked.

Until this moment Will had not considered how he would explain his involvement in Eleanor's affairs. Now standing in front of her father, Will felt his stomach clench as guilt at what he had done struck him afresh.

'I am fond of Eleanor.'

'Fond of her?' Sir Edgar watched him closely, staring at Will through green eyes so like his daughter's. For all his seeming absentmindedness he shared Eleanor's astuteness.

'I love her,' Will admitted. His mouth softened into a smile as he said aloud what he had been trying to deny for so long. 'I love her...but I have wronged her.'

'What did you do?' Sir Edgar's voice was barely a whisper.

Shame crept over Will as he related the tale of the wager, of their kiss and Eleanor's discovery.

'If there is any way I can save Lady Peyton from a life with someone who plans to wrong her further, then I will do it,' he finished. He bowed his head, waiting for Sir Edgar's judgement. Nothing happened. He looked up. Sir Edgar's face was stern, his lips a thin white line.

'I couldn't understand why Eleanor agreed to marry Sir Martin in such haste, but now I see. She always did make rash decisions when her heart or pride was injured. It doesn't surprise me that Edmund is involved in such a scheme, but I admit I thought better of you.'

Will ran his hands through his hair, his stomach twisting with guilt. His throat filled with a lump large enough to choke him.

Sir Edgar folded his arms and sat back in his chair. 'We *will* speak of what you've told me, make no mistake about that, but I think the final verdict will rest with Eleanor.' He handed the fold of parchment back to Will who stored it safely in his pouch, relief coursing through him.

'The wrong is yours to right, William. I suggest you leave as soon as possible.'

Will rode hard, pushing Tobias faster and faster until the horse's mouth was flecked with foam and his flanks glistened. On the deck of the ferry he paced like a caged animal.

'How long since a knight came this way?' he asked.

'Tall man, aye? Came with his attendants, but that were before the sun was over the trees,' the ferryman said. 'You'll be lucky to catch him.'

'We'll see,' Will muttered, mounting Tobias. He dug his heels in and cracked the reins as soon as the craft neared the far bank and cleared the water smoothly without a backwards glance. Visions of his first encounter with Eleanor seared themselves across Will's memory. What a fool he'd been to play such a game with her, but then he had been so slow to recognise her worth. He might as well have kicked rubies around the courtyard for sport!

The first sight of Rowland's Mount made Will's breath catch in his throat. He dismounted. Small lights glowed among the low buildings of the village. Beyond that Eleanor's house lay shrouded in near darkness, only a single light to be seen. Will leaned against Tobias's broad neck as a fresh realisation of what he'd lost threatened to overpower him. Why was the house so dark? Was Allencote already there and what form would his coercion take? He swallowed down his nausea and spurred Tobias into a gallop.

The last toll of the curfew bell died away as Will rode through the village and along the rough road to Rowland's Mount. Icy spray spattered his face and the tang of the salt assaulted his senses. The tide had changed towards shore, waves in turn lapping gently, then crashing on to the shingle in no pattern Will could discern.

Nearing Rowland's Mount, he saw what had not been clear before. The light shone from the room where he and Eleanor had shared their meagre supper and where she had blurted out the true circumstances of her marriage. The thought of her now secluding herself away at Allencote's mercy tore at his heart. Will dismounted and strode to the shoreline.

He swore loudly at what he saw. The water had already begun to cover the causeway. The stones were still visible just below the surface: a black pathway darker than the sea that streamed across it, leaving foamy puddles where it receded. Eleanor said it would be too hazardous to cross, but when the tide retreated Will could see the slabs clearly. The sky was clear and the moon almost full otherwise he would not even have contemplated crossing, but the journey would take no more than ten minutes. Even in the fading light there could be no danger.

He rode down to the causeway. As foam swirled around Tobias's hooves the horse stopped, ears back. Will tapped his heels to urge the animal forward, but it gave a toss of the head and whinnied in alarm. He dismounted and tried to lead him across, but Tobias pulled back. Heaving a sigh, Will walked the animal back to shore. He unravelled a rope and tethered Tobias beneath the shelter of a clump of trees.

'You'll be fine here until morning,' he said reassuringly. He unbuckled his cloak and threw it across the horse's back for warmth. With sleet dripping uncomfortably down his neck he walked down the jetty between the shingle and once more walked on to the causeway.

# Chapter Twenty-Four

A dozen paces were enough to convince Will he had been unwise. Even in the short time it had taken him to tether his horse the tide had risen and was already calf-deep. The current tugged and Will clenched his toes as though that would offer him some stability through his thick-soled boots. Sense told him he should turn back, but the thought of Eleanor with Allencote was too much to resist. He ignored the voice of warning and carried on.

Before he had gone much further the sea was surging around his knees, filling his already sodden boots. It was harder to walk now. He took smaller steps, feeling his way cautiously across the causeway, but the water was rising and if he did not hurry he would lose all sight of the stones beneath his feet. Will shivered as a violent gust of wind buffeted him. He focused on the light in

Eleanor's window and headed towards it, his purpose spurring him on.

The granite was treacherous underfoot and almost invisible in the water that swirled like inky glass. A wave crested out of nowhere, knocking Will sideways. One foot plunged into nothing. Flailing his arms to try to keep his balance, he slipped sideways, landing heavily on his hands and knees. Panic filled him. How had he come to be at the edge of the rocks when he was so certain he was in the centre? Another wave crashed over the causeway and over Will, drenching him. He gasped at the shock of the cold and another wave filled his mouth with saltwater. He coughed and pushed himself to his feet once more as the current tried to take him with it. Blood pounding in his ears, he drew a ragged breath and took another step.

Eleanor had warned him what happened to people who tried to cross when the tide was high, but he had not fully believed her. Now he understood.

He was going to die.

He pictured himself washed out to sea, his body undiscovered and unmourned. He cried out in rage and despair and his voice echoed across the bay. Not loud enough to attract help, but the sound gave him hope where before there had been none.

He fumbled at his waist until his fingers closed around his hunting horn and gave three long blasts. He took another step, keeping his eyes fixed on Eleanor's light.

Three more blasts, shorter this time, as Will's breath would not come easily through his shivers. One more step. One more blast. Pain racked his ribs.

And without warning there she was. The light from the room was obliterated as Eleanor stood silhouetted in the window frame, red hair like flames. The most beautiful thing Will had ever seen.

He gave another blast of his horn as tears filled his eyes. If he died, he would hold this final vision of her as long as he had breath in his body. He gave another blast that sent his head reeling. His hand dropped to his side and, ignoring the burning in his lungs, he cried her name with all the strength left in him.

Eleanor had been sitting with a book by the fire, not even seeing the words on the page. She had dismissed most of the servants, keeping only Goodwife Bradshawe and Jennet on the island. Tomorrow Sir Martin would come from the village and she would have to accept or end their betrothal. Will had promised to discover what he could, but there had been no word. Either there was nothing to discover or he had played her false yet again.

The sound of a horn broke the silence, cutting through her despondent thoughts. She gave a start as three more discordant bursts followed. Someone was in distress!

Running to the window, she stared into the darkness as another note rang out. Surprise transformed to horror as she realised that the hunched shadow standing where the causeway should be was the figure of a man. As she watched he raised the horn to his lips and blew once more.

Will!

So faintly she half-thought she had imagined it, she heard a cry blown on the wind. She gripped the windowsill in terror as she watched Will battling forward through the waves. He would never make it across unless he had something to guide him. Three years ago she had watched Baldwin die before her eyes and had been unable to prevent his death, but the seas themselves would burn before she would let any harm befall Will.

'I'm coming,' she screamed, though she had no hope of her voice reaching him.

The beacons had not been needed in all the

time she had lived on Rowland's Mount, but they were still in place. She ran from the window and grabbed the large lamp from the table then hurried back, forcing the window wide open.

She reached for the chain to pull the beacon up. The iron cage held no lantern so Eleanor took a knife from the table and slashed at her skirt until she had three broad strips of cloth. She stuffed one inside the cage and plunged the lamp wick into it. Almost instantly the material caught. Hot oil spilled across her hand, burning her palm, and tears sprang to her eyes, but she pushed the pain away. Weeping with relief, she let the chain down and ran from the room, lamp and cloth in hand, shouting for her servants to aid her.

The second beacon was at a bend in the path to the shore. Again Eleanor lit the cloth and ran on to the beach to light the final beacon. When aligned they provided a true guide across the causeway. There was barely any light and they would not last for long, but hopefully long enough.

She ran to the edge of the water and cupped her hands around her mouth.

'Keep the lights in line,' she shouted. 'Walk straight towards them. Come to me.' Over and over she screamed her instruction until her voice was hoarse. She paced back and forth, her eyes never leaving Will as he waded through the thigh-high waves towards her.

It could barely have been minutes, but it felt like a lifetime before Will made it to the island and fell to his knees, both hands gripping handfuls of shingle. Eleanor threw herself down beside him. His arms came around her, clutching her tightly to his chest as though the sea was still threatening to part them. For a while they knelt, motionless in each other's arms, but now the danger was passed Eleanor's fear was replaced by cold fury. She pushed herself away roughly.

'What were you thinking?' she ranted. 'You nearly died!'

'It's thanks to you I didn't. I owe you my life, my lady.' Will heaved himself to his feet, pulling Eleanor with him and looked around urgently. 'Where is Allencote?'

'Sir Martin is lodging at the inn. He arrived at dusk and sent word that he would come tomorrow at the low tide.' Eleanor's legs shook once more and she glared at Will. 'He isn't foolish enough to risk his life crossing the causeway,' she said furiously.

Will's body sagged with visible relief. 'So you are unharmed!'

'Why would I be harmed?' Eleanor asked in confusion.

Will fumbled in the pouch at his waist. 'I have proof of Allencote's ill dealings. Once you are married he intends to use Rowland's Mount to pay debts owed. Lord Etherington said he was intending to persuade you by any means.'

He passed her a sodden fold of parchment. Eleanor unfolded it with trembling fingers and stared at it. She turned it over, then back again.

'You risked your life to bring me this.'

Will moved towards her, so close Eleanor could feel his breath on her cheek.

'I'd risk everything for you,' he answered huskily. He looked down at her, the intensity of his gaze making Eleanor's head reel. So many questions bubbled up inside her, but at that moment rapid footsteps echoed down the path. Goodwife Bradshawe and Jennet appeared, lanterns in their hands.

'This is what you hope will make me end my betrothal?' she said quietly as the servants rushed across the shingle.

'It's what you need. If it still isn't enough to make you doubt Allencote's intentions, then question him when he comes tomorrow. If you still want to marry him, then at least do so knowing what you stand to lose.' Will's expression became fierce, his eyes piercing Eleanor's heart.

'I need to think,' she said quietly. 'Clearly you can't return to the mainland so you must stay here for the night. I'll make my decision in the morning.' She turned away and walked up to the house, Will following in her path.

It was only when they reached the warmth of the house that the result of Will's exertions became clear. His face was ashen and his eyes circled with shadows, his hair plastered back making him look more disreputable than ever. Eleanor stared at him in shock as she saw him fully in the lamplight. He needed warmth and rest. The questions she had intended to ask would have to wait.

Eleanor's bedchamber was the only one with a fire lit so she insisted he take it despite his protests. Neither of them spoke, but as Goodwife Bradshawe bustled about inside the chamber, adding logs to the fire and furs to the bed, their eyes met, saying words unspoken since she had discovered his deception. Eleanor bit her lip as memories of the night they had spent here threatened to overwhelm her. She began to pull the door closed, but Will took hold of it.

'Wake me in the morning,' he said. 'Don't admit Allencote without me there.'

Eleanor nodded and closed the door between them with a trembling hand. She leaned her forehead against the door, fingertips lightly brushing the wood as though she was touching Will himself.

She made her way downstairs and wrapped herself in furs on her favourite bench in front of the fire. She unfolded the parchment and studied it once more, her stomach churning. The ink had run, obliterating any words it had once contained. Only dark smears remained.

Eleanor pulled her knees up and hugged them, thinking about Sir Martin's interest in her estate, the questions he had asked about her business and his eagerness to visit her home. She remembered the triumph she had seen in his eyes when she accepted his proposal, and the alarm when he thought she was wavering.

Then she thought of Will. The man who had deceived her, broken her heart and driven her into Allencote's arms. The man who had risked his life tonight to ensure her safety despite the deceit she had committed herself. Her belly curled in shame. Will hadn't been the only one who had acted badly. She closed her eyes and rested her head wearily on her knees. Tomorrow would decide everything. She would deal with Sir Martin first and then she would deal with Will.

\* \* \*

Eleanor awoke, confused why she felt so uncomfortable until she realised that she had fallen asleep by the fire, head resting on the bench. She peered from the window. The pale sun had risen and the faint slabs of granite were starting to appear beneath the waves. A figure on horseback was trotting from the village, causing Eleanor's stomach to lurch.

She ran to her chamber and raised her hand to knock, but then hesitated. There was no sound from within. Will had been exhausted and half-frozen. What need would there be to wake him? His warnings about Sir Martin were simply exaggeration. She withdrew her hand and returned downstairs where Jennet helped make her as presentable as possible.

She walked alone to the causeway, eyes cold and head erect, watching her betrothed cross. She curtsied as Sir Martin dismounted and stepped off the causeway.

'Welcome, my lord.' She waved an arm and smiled. 'Do you like what you see here? What say you that we live here after we marry?'

Sir Martin's expression was blank. 'Perhaps, for a while. Though I have an estate of my own that I can't leave for too long.'

'Then in the summer.' Eleanor smiled. 'We could return every summer?'

Sir Martin's lips curved into a smile. 'We can discuss such details after we are wed.'

Eleanor stalked to him. 'Or perhaps we can come as guests of Lord Etherington, as he will be the owner,' she hissed through clenched teeth.

'What are you talking about?' Sir Martin said, his eyes wide with innocence. 'What has the earl to do with matters?'

Eleanor took the parchment from the pouch at her waist, folding it carefully so only the seal was visible. She held it out of Sir Martin's reach. 'You signed this and it was not yours to give. I do not give my consent,' Eleanor said firmly.

'I don't need your consent. Once we're married I can do as I please with what becomes rightfully mine,' Sir Martin said, his eyes hardening.

'I am declining your offer of marriage.'

Sir Martin seized hold of her arm, his fingers iron hard. 'You will not refuse me. If you don't marry me, I'm ruined,' he snarled. 'I'll consummate the marriage here and now if necessary.'

Eleanor screamed in shock and tried to twist from his grasp.

'Stop that. You agreed to marriage and invited me into your home when we're completely alone,

Eleanor. Oh, don't pretend otherwise,' he said as she opened her mouth to protest. 'Your message yesterday said as much. Only a couple of women with you. Who would believe you weren't willing? If anyone asks...'

He never completed the sentence because at that moment a figure hurtled down the path and, with a roar of anger, threw himself bodily at Sir Martin, knocking him sideways.

Eleanor took in the sight of him. He wore no jerkin, merely a shirt, flapping loose and unlaced at the neck. His hair fell in knots as though he had only just awoken.

'I told you to wake me!' Will yelled, rounding on her. 'Thankfully your maid knows how to obey an instruction!'

'You! What are you doing here?' Sir Martin spat. His hand moved to his sword, but Will took a step towards him, drawing Baldwin's weapon which was buckled at his waist.

'I wouldn't,' Will said quietly, his voice laced with menace.

Sir Martin's face changed to scarlet as he glared at Will. 'I should have run you through when I had the chance,' he snarled.

Will looked at the knight contemptuously. 'That was the least of your mistakes,' he said.

'My father will hear soon enough of your actions this morning,' Eleanor said. She marched to the causeway and stood on the shoreline. 'I shall travel back to Tawstott today. I'm sure Duke Roland will also be interested to hear my story. Now, get off my island before I have you thrown into the sea.'

Sir Martin looked at the parchment in her hand once more. His face crumbled. 'I had no choice,' he said bleakly. 'I cannot lose my estate and until my father dies I have no means of drawing on funds.'

Eleanor said nothing. Sir Martin swore and gave Will a look of undiluted hatred, then clambered on to his horse and galloped off.

Eleanor put a shaking hand to her face and drew a jagged breath, her head spinning with relief. She felt Will's arms slide around her, holding her tightly.

'It's over,' he whispered.

Eleanor felt his soft kiss on the top of her head and her eyes filled with tears as the emotions she had determined to bury rose to the surface. How could she even have contemplated life with Sir Martin when Will was within her reach?

'I need to show you something,' she said. She held the parchment out to Will so he could see for himself.

Will's eyes widened. He ran his hands through his hair.

'I believed you before I heard a word from Sir Martin,' she said softly, dropping the ruined scrap to the ground.

Will was watching her carefully, his gaze intent. 'You did?'

Eleanor's lips twitched. 'Even you wouldn't do something so reckless unless you were telling the truth.'

Will smiled wearily. He gazed back at the mainland. For a moment Eleanor feared he was about to walk back across the causeway himself.

'Before I left Tawstott, Edmund told me you had forfeited the wager. Is that true?'

Will looked away, his face unreadable. He nodded slowly.

Even until this point she had doubted Edmund's words. 'It was your stake in the ship!' she whispered, shocked at his confirmation. 'That was your chance to make your fortune and you gave it up.'

Will looked contritely at Eleanor. 'It doesn't matter. A fortune made on such terms would not have been worth having.'

'But I hated you,' Eleanor whispered, her eyes filling with tears. 'If I had known that…'

'You still would have hated me and you'd have

been right to do so,' Will said. 'I should never have accepted the wager. I should have ended it when I suspected you had begun to care for me. And when I realised how strongly I care for you. When I kissed you I wanted it to be for me alone.'

'I should never have hated you. My pride was hurt, but if you were wrong, so was I. You were right, I kissed you willingly. I used you just as much as you used me,' Eleanor said, her voice quavering.

'I think we can both agree we did not show our best characters to each other!' Will said gently.

He reached a hand tentatively to her face, smoothing his thumb across her cheekbones. She covered it with her own, his touch sending tremors across her skin. He took her hands and placed them over his heart.

'I love you, Eleanor. I'm not rich and at this moment I have no hope of becoming so, but I will work and strive, until one day I might be worthy of you. Will you wait for me?'

Eleanor's heart had been to race at his words. Now it stopped completely. 'I don't want to wait,' she said, shaking her head.

Will's face crumpled and his whole body sagged. 'If I was a rich man I would go down on my knees here and now and beg for your hand, but I have nothing. What could I offer you?'

'Will, don't you understand me at all?' she said in exasperation. She squeezed his hands tightly. 'I don't want to wait. I meant what I said before. It could only ever have been you I kissed. I want you now, as you are! I married a rich husband once. I have all the wealth I need, but what I never had was love.'

Will's smile widened as comprehension dawned. He slid a hand behind Eleanor's head and tilted her face towards him.

'That I can give you in an unending supply,' he said huskily. His eyes were so full of love and desire. A familiar sensation of longing twisted Eleanor's belly into knots and sent a throb of desire through her body.

Will's face grew serious. 'You asked me once if I sought Amy out once I was richer and I said no. The truth was I didn't love her enough to humble myself, but I keep returning to you, over and over. I will never stop doing so and I will never cease loving you until the day I die.'

His lips found hers, drawing her into a kiss stronger than the current of any sea. She pulled him closer, matching his ferocity equally. For a long time there was nothing else in the world but the kiss. Eventually Will drew his lips away. He wrapped his arms tightly around Eleanor, pinning her to him as though he feared she would vanish.

'I came so close to kissing you when we were here,' Will said. 'Walking out of your room that night was the hardest thing I've ever done.'

Eleanor's scalp prickled at the memory of Will on her bed. She had barely known what she wanted then, assaulted by confusing sensations and half-understood emotions that scared her as much as they had tempted. Now she knew that the feelings his kisses stirred inside her were only the beginning of what she had to discover. She smiled shyly at him. Will laughed quietly as though he had read her thoughts.

He pulled her closer and craned his head to kiss her with a touch as soft as a snowflake. Eleanor met his lips eagerly, sliding a hand to his cheek. His kiss was slow and tender at first, but as Eleanor matched his eagerness it became faster and more urgent, pulling Eleanor into a dizzying whirlpool of passion.

Unheeded by both of them the parchment floated away on the tide.

# *Epilogue*

Their course of action was settled.

They had left at midday, riding side by side. When dusk fell they had secured rooms at a small tavern, where they talked into the night about what might greet them at Tawstott if Sir Martin carried out his threats, vowing that whatever happened they would face it together.

Their arrival at Tawstott the following day was met with surprise. Sir Martin had not returned. Eleanor recounted her tale to everyone assembled, with a distinct emphasis on Will's courage in revealing the truth to her.

Duke Roland's face was a mask of outrage. 'Sir Edgar, I can assure you Sir Martin will receive my particular attention as soon as he is found.'

He regarded Will carefully. 'Master Rudhale, your loyalty is to be commended. If I had some means of rewarding you other than this paltry offering, I would give it.' He passed Will a small pouch. 'Sir Edgar tells me we have you to thank for the remarkable wine we have been drinking. Do me the honour of sending me a barrel when your ship next returns to England.'

He inclined his head and led his entourage away, leaving Eleanor and Will staring in astonishment at the small gold coins in the pouch.

After that there was only one thing left to be done. Requesting a private audience, Eleanor and Will stood before Sir Edgar and Lady Fitzallan as Will formally asked for their daughter's hand. Lady Fitzallan began to protest, but her husband silenced her with a wave of his hand.

'Have you forgotten what sort of man the suitor you championed revealed himself to be?'

Lady Fitzallan snorted contemptuously, but Sir Edgar looked at his wife. 'Jocelyn, in case you have forgotten, there are more needs than financial that a husband must satisfy,' he said, raising an eyebrow. 'Eleanor would not be the first woman to forgo wealth for passion, would she?'

To Eleanor's astonishment her mother blushed like a maiden. She asked the question she had never dared before. 'You are an earl's daughter, but you married a baron. Why?'

Lady Fitzallan gave her husband one of her rarely seen smiles. 'Because a quick-tongued young knight spun me such tales of his plans for the future that my head was turned.'

'And because I danced you away from richer men at the old duke's spring tournament, don't forget that,' Sir Edgar said, taking hold of his wife's hand.

Eleanor looked away at the unexpected sight of her parents' affection. She caught Will's eye and he winked. She knew they had won.

Sir Edgar took Eleanor by the arm and led her to the fire. He spoke quietly so that only Eleanor could hear. 'When you left Tawstott you were determined not to even speak of William. Now you intend to marry him? I can't say I am surprised, but do you truly mean this?'

'I do,' Eleanor said. She glanced at Will, who was busy pouring a goblet of wine for Lady Fitzallan. Tears sprang to her eyes, but now they were of joy. 'I mean it with all my heart.'

'In that case I have only one regret,' Sir Edgar grumbled as he led his daughter back to Will and Lady Fitzallan. He looked sternly at Will, but couldn't hide his smile. 'And that is to be losing an excellent steward after such a short time!'

* * *

Affairs took on their own momentum.

Duke Roland extended his visit for another fortnight, much to Sir Edgar's dismay and Lady Fitzallan's delight: even the thought of so humble a
son-in-law could not diminish the prestige of having a duke in attendance at the marriage.

The organisation naturally fell to Will and Eleanor who laughed and bickered their way through
the arrangements, delighting in each other's company and recalling with fondness the previous
tasks that had thrown them together.

The evening before their marriage Eleanor was
gathering greenery when Will found her in the
gardens.

He gave the private smile she had come to realise he reserved for her alone. 'I thought I would
find you somewhere quiet.'

'It's too busy in the house.' Eleanor slipped her
arms about his waist and leaned her head against
his chest. Simply being in his arms gave her
strength. 'I'll be glad when tomorrow is over and
we can leave!'

'Don't wish it away too quickly.' Will laughed.
'Tomorrow will pass before we even realise and I

want to savour the moment we become husband and wife.'

For two weeks Eleanor had barely been able to wait for Will's touch, each kiss and caress hinting more enticingly at what would await her. Now as she thought of what their wedding night would hold a flicker of apprehension creased her brow. Will had had women before—she was unsure how many and decided never to ask—what if he was disappointed with her? She drew away with a mumbled apology, a knot of anxiety in her stomach.

Will's eyes crinkled and the smile that sent Eleanor's stomach flying played about his lips. He bent his head and kissed her slowly, driving all anxiety from her mind, tipping the balance firmly in favour of anticipation.

'I don't want a quick, fumbled tumble from you before we go our separate ways. I am going to be your husband, Eleanor. We have our whole lives to discover each other.'

As he took her once more in his arms, his embrace both reassuring and alluring, Eleanor's heart glowed. Years stretched before them, full of possibilities.

'I imagine we both have things to learn about married life,' Will said, his voice thick with emotion. 'I've spent so many years trying to find somewhere I could settle and be content. Now I realise it isn't a place I was looking for. It's a person. It's you.'

Eleanor looked towards the house, soft grey walls in the setting sun. This time tomorrow she would have everything she wanted: her home and lands, and this man to share them with.

'What shall we do after tomorrow?' Will asked. 'Your father says we can stay here as long as we choose, and Lord Etherington says we are welcome to visit him.'

As Will wrapped her tightly in an embrace, arms easily circling her waist, Eleanor reached her arms around his neck and pulled him close. She knew exactly where they should go. Where they both belonged.

'We'll go back to Rowland's Mount,' she breathed as she leaned in to kiss him. 'Let's go *home*.'

\* \* \* \* \*

# MILLS & BOON®

## Why shop at millsandboon.co.uk?

Each year, thousands of romance readers find their perfect read at millsandboon.co.uk. That's because we're passionate about bringing you the very best romantic fiction. Here are some of the advantages of shopping at www.millsandboon.co.uk:

* **Get new books first**—you'll be able to buy your favourite books one month before they hit the shops

* **Get exclusive discounts**—you'll also be able to buy our specially created monthly collections, with up to 50% off the RRP

* **Find your favourite authors**—latest news, interviews  and new releases for all your favourite authors and series on our website, plus ideas for what to try next

* **Join in**—once you've bought your favourite books, don't forget to register with us to rate, review and join in the discussions

Visit **www.millsandboon.co.uk**
for all this and more today!